WARDEN

ELEMENTAL PALADINS: BOOK ONE

MONTANA ASH

This is an IndieMosh book
brought to you by MoshPit Publishing
an imprint of Mosher's Business Support Pty Ltd
PO BOX 147
Hazelbrook NSW 2779
www.indiemosh.com.au

Second edition
First published 2015 © Montana Ash
Cataloguing-in-Publication entry is available from the
National Library of Australia: http://catalogue.nla.gov.au/

Title: Warden
Author: Ash, Montana (1984)
ISBNS: 978-1-925353-79-2 (paperback)
         978-1-925353-80-8 (ebook – epub)
         978-1-925353-81-5 (ebook – mobi)

Cover design by Montana Ash, author, and Ally Mosher,
IndieMosh.
Stock photography from DollarPhotoClub.com

WARDEN

ELEMENTAL PALADINS: BOOK ONE

Dedication

To the man who gave me my writing genes ...

and

To my crash test dummies, thank you!

ONE

The scars were extensive and obviously hard won. Evidence of years of abuse at the hands of meaty fists, drunks and straight-up pricks most likely. After all, wasn't that always the way? Some of the lines were pale and flat and spoke of abuse long gone. Others were fresh and open still awaiting their endpoint from the healing process of time. She traced her fingers lightly over each dip and ridge but felt no pity at the number of silvery lines present. Instead, she found herself captivated by the evidence of such remarkable endurance. She had always found scars somewhat fascinating – a reflection of survival, resilience and courage – a testament to a purpose fulfilled. And although the pain of a fresh wound was always sharp, there was a comfort to be found in the healing.

The loud clang of a heavy bottomed glass hitting wood jolted her out of her inspection of the bar she was currently seated at. A thick palm also slapped the aged wood, leaving little doubt as to why the once rich cedar bar top was now riddled with all those charming scars. A garbled request for 'another' accompanied the hand-slap. He didn't appear to need 'another' of anything remotely resembling alcohol, she thought to herself, eyeballing the ridiculously inebriated older man. *Christ! It was barely four in the afternoon!* So yeah, okay, maybe that was a little hypocritical, given she had been seated at the same bar for a little over an hour herself. But it hadn't been the guarantee of bad booze and bad company that had lured her in. No, it had been necessity which had made her enter the very aptly named 'Dave's Dive' that day. She had been on the road nearly two full weeks now and she was utterly and completely exhausted. The relentless stalking from her enemies was catching up with her and she just needed somewhere she could sit and relax for a while. It was a fairly sad comment on her life that Dave's Dive was her salvation, but for some reason her foes always found it harder to detect her when she was in hell holes like this one. As gross as it sounded, she thought it had something to do with the smell. Cheap booze, sweaty men and stale cigarettes were apparently the perfect subterfuge.

She sighed miserably as she ate her last piece of chocolate. Okay, so maybe she didn't drink her feelings, but she was pretty darn good at eating them! The tiny brown squares of sugary goodness never failed to give her a boost no matter the time of day or night. In fact, vending machines had become her best friend over the years, sometimes her only friend. And if that wasn't the most depressing thought of the day, she didn't know what was! She wasn't normally such a gloomy person but she was finding it harder and harder to shake off the funk. She was just so tired. She couldn't even vent to anyone, let alone trust anyone to actually help her. That road had been tried and tested countless times in the past and always led swiftly straight to nowhere. Well, almost straight to nowhere, she acknowledged. There were always stops along the way at fun places like hospitals, funerals and mental institutions. No, she had learned the hard way that it was better for all concerned for her to remain a lone wolf.

She was more than capable of protecting herself anyway; she had trained mercilessly over the years to ensure it. She was also normally quite strong minded, finding relief and escape in her books. But she was just so … fucking … tired! And on top of that, her tremors were getting worse. She knew what would follow if she didn't get some down time and she couldn't afford that. She just wished someone would walk up to her and say, "Hi, I'm here to help you." But she was nothing if not a realist, so until that unicorn came along shooting rainbows and diamonds from its pristine white arse, she was doomed to content herself with such dens of marvel.

And what a marvel it was, she thought. In addition to old Drunky McDrunk next to her – who was now downing his fifth scotch in as many minutes – the bar currently accommodated a half a dozen other occupants. They were slouched in alarmingly similar poses and scattered around the rectangular room like half-dead insects. Every now and then one of them would twitch or startle awake, usually followed by the release of some grotesque noise or smell. They were all male. Small wonder she was single. For her own amusement, she speculated on which fine specimen of male wonder would break first and attempt to woo her with his magnetic charm. There were some things she could always count on.

"Getcha anythin' else?" Ah, he speaketh! She snickered. Those three words from the bar tender made a total of five words out of his mouth the entire time she had been there. When she had first stumbled in and placed her battered bag on the hard wood floor, the bartender had asked, 'Getcha anythin'?" At first, she could do no more than stare at the hairy monstrosity above the surprisingly clear blue eyes. It gave the term mono-brow a whole new meaning. She had to force herself to look away for she could swear the thing was actually moving! The large proprietor had lumbered behind the bar, polishing glassware that was already clean and wiping benches that already shone. Although his clientele were walking petri dishes, he obviously took pride in his establishment. She could respect that.

"No, thank you." A grunt acknowledged her reply.

She watched in bemusement as the owner pulled out an entire clean tray of glasses and proceeded to polish one with a clean, soft cloth. She didn't even bother to feign interest in the newest patron as they entered with a warm gust of wind, bringing in the fresh scents of the ocean. Oh, she loved that smell and couldn't resist raising her face to feel the welcoming caress of the breeze against her cheek. It whispered to her in comfort, gifting her relief from her pity party. She whispered a heartfelt thank you in return and dipped her head in gratitude.

Presently, an odd tingle shot through her body. It wasn't altogether unpleasant but it was disconcerting nonetheless. Aiming for subtle, she casually rotated on her stool in order to cast her eyes around the dimly lit space. She almost fell off the damn thing – so much for subtle! There was no way to disguise her reaction to the three men seated in the booth next to the door. Her jaw dropped and her eyes damn near popped out of her head. She dipped her chin to swipe it along her shoulder, praying there was no drool there. They were absolutely stunning in their masculinity; broad shoulders, muscled arms, strong fingers and chiselled jaws. What kind of magical pub had she stumbled into?

They made no move to come to the bar and were apparently talking quietly amongst themselves, but there was a stillness to them that wasn't entirely natural. They were all dressed much the same in cargos, boots and casual tees and she wondered if they all belonged to the same military unit or something. They were alert without seeming to be and were all seated so they had a clear line of sight to the exit. She had chosen her seat for that exact purpose also. She had only to raise her eyes and she could see the exit clearly in the well-polished mirror behind the bar. She couldn't really make out their individual hair colours under the dim, unnatural lights of the bar, but they all appeared dark. She loved dark hair. She was dying to see what colours their eyes were. Piercing blue? Deep brown? Intense green? She didn't really care if she was being honest with herself. She already had enough material stored in her slap 'n' tickle vault to keep her fingers happy for many a lonely night!

Obviously, she had been lost in her lust-induced haze for too long as one of the walking fantasies suddenly turned his head and locked his gaze on her. She couldn't hold back the gasp when those hazel eyes met her own. They were forceful and penetrating, apparently seeing all the way to her soul. The tingle from before now became a sizzle of awareness throughout her entire body. It should have been sexual, but somehow it wasn't. Instead, it was almost like a recognition. But she hadn't met this man before, had she? Surely she would have remembered. She found herself released from the strange pull when the inevitable occurred; a filthy hand landing on her shoulder.

Pushing the handsome trio from her thoughts for a moment, she eyed the brave soul who had undoubtedly strutted over in an attempt to get between her legs. Fuelled with his liquid courage he was predictably disgusting in a sweat stained singlet that had probably been white – three weeks ago. His hair was slicked to his bowl shaped head in a mess of grey and brown grease. Said hair continued over his shoulders and down his arms almost like a carpet, before ending abruptly at his knuckles. His belly protruded over his pants which were just as stained as the rest of him and she prayed it wasn't bodily fluids.

"Hey there, gorgeous."

She blinked. His voice! Now that voice of his far exceeded her expectations. It wasn't the gravelly result of years of nicotine abuse, rather a lilting feminine alto. It was utterly absurd coming from such a brute and she felt herself smiling for the first time in days. Unfortunately, the pelt on two legs mistook her smile for encouragement, smiling in return and displaying a missing front tooth, he leaned in close;

"They call me Bounce."

She blinked again. Bounce? Really? "Oh no! I'm really sorry!"

"What?" High level of confusion from the poor Bounce.

"I'm ... sorry." She repeated slowly, just to be helpful.

"Huh? Why are you sorry? That's my name!" *Epic* level of confusion from the poor Bounce.

"Ah, wow. My apologies. I thought you were telling me a sad story." She pasted on her best miserable puppy-dog look. The poor chap looked even more confused than before if that were possible and actually peered over the bar at the owner for aid. Mr Mono-brow kept right on shining as he stared back in pity. It was a few more seconds before; *Yep, there it is – light bulb!* She cheered silently.

"Why you little ..." He snarled as his hairy arms reached to grab her. She allowed herself a wasted second in order to roll her eyes over his predictability before expertly spinning out of his reach and side-stepping behind him. She had the furry idiot's right arm chicken-winged all the way to his shoulder blade before he could even grunt. Kicking a foot behind his knee, she forced him to lose his balance but caught him a mere inch before his nose made surface with the scarred bar.

"That could've been your face ..." she hiked him up straight and pushed him away, "... but I guess today's your birthday." Pleased with her witty repertoire – she liked to mix it up every now and then – she didn't count on the ape regaining his balance so quickly. He was surprisingly spry, latching onto her forearm and yanking her close enough she could smell the sour alcohol on his breath. A disturbance in the air warned her of movement by the door.

Perhaps the men were coming to her aid or perhaps they were coming to help hold her down. Either way, she had no intention of involving them or anyone else. She could take care of herself and pathetic menfolk like these were child's play in comparison to that which stalked her.

She opted to go with efficiency rather than pizzazz and punched him in the throat. She followed through with a generous kick to the balls and what do you know? Poor Bounce didn't bounce. The sound of gasping breaths were quickly replaced by a high-pitched animal whine as Bounce toppled heavily to the side, one hand at his throat and the other cupping his two favourite, but now abused, toys.

Shaking her head in resignation, she peeled a twenty out of her pocket and threw it on the bar. "Sorry about the mess." She tilted her head towards the now wheezing mass on the floor. A snort was the only response she received as she bent down to retrieve her pack. The beaten up bag held almost all of her earthly possessions and she slung it over her shoulder as she made her way to the door. As reprieves went, it had been a short but entertaining one.

Constantly aware of her surroundings, she registered the sound of several chairs scuffing the hard floor as they were pushed back from a table. She heard the thump of boots on worn wood even as she allowed the bar door to slam behind her. She would like to think it was just

7

coincidence and the handsome trio just happened to be leaving at the same time. But she doubted it. She wasn't that lucky.

TWO

She had almost made it to the densely populated bushland behind the pub when they caught up to her. When she had been forced to move on once again she had chosen this region because of its natural beauty. She had travelled all over the world in an attempt to outrun her pursuers. She had seen so much magnificence and wonder in the lands and the seas but nothing quite like the pristine coastline of Australia. The beaches were made up of soft golden sand you could actually walk bare foot on, and the oceans were filled with an array of majestic creatures. The surrounding bush was home to some of the most lethal critters on earth – as well as some of the cuddliest. It was all such a wonderful contradiction.

This particular stretch of the south coast had always been a favourite of hers. When she had awoken on the mean streets of Sydney as a teenager with no memory, no name and just the clothes on her back, she had known only one thing; that the concrete world of cars and noise was a suffocating weight. Using only instinct as a guide, she had fled and found herself about four hours south. With nothing but the ocean to her left and trees to her right, she had felt a sense of homecoming. To this day she couldn't figure out why. There had been nothing and no one she had recognised, but the environment had given her peace and that had been the most important thing at the time. It was also why she had decided to return now. She needed the security she had felt all those years ago. She hadn't ventured back this way in over twenty years because she didn't want to be responsible for the destruction that inevitably haunted her every step. But two weeks ago she had been in a quaint little village outside of Budapest when they had found her once again. The resulting fight had left the tiny township devastated, she was stretched so thin her hands wouldn't stop shaking for three days and she could barely function through the headache and the ensuing nausea. She needed rest. She craved solace ... and now she also wanted more chocolate. It appeared she was doomed to be disappointed though if the three men behind her were any indication.

She shrugged off her backpack and placed it on the ground at her feet so her movements wouldn't be hindered. She then turned and was met with a solid wall of testosterone. *My, oh my* ... they were even more pretty up close. The one with the hazel eyes sported a close-cropped do to his thick brown hair. It held a slight wave and she wondered if he kept it short deliberately in order to hide curls. Why men felt the need to do that she would never understand. Curls were sexy! The other two were rockin' the just-got-out-of-bed look with messy locks of blonde and auburn. The look in their eyes was just as intense as they peered down at her from irises of blue and green respectively. And a long way they had to look down too! She was somewhat vertically challenged, topping only five foot three in heels. Although it sucked at music concerts, it did make it easy to squeeze into tight places when she was on the run. The mountains in front of her all topped six feet easy which was actually a happy coincidence. She had always loved mountain climbing!

"Where are your paladins?"

"Huh?" *Great!* She rolled her eyes at herself. Apparently she now sounded like Bounce!

Hazel eyes narrowed at her as muscled arms crossed an impressive chest. "Your paladins! How could they allow you to go out on your own like this?"

"Firstly, my what? Paladins? And secondly, *allow?* Nobody *allows* me to do anything! I'm a grown-arse woman!" Clearly not the response they were expecting if the number of raised eyebrows was anything to go by. Even the deep frowns couldn't mar their manly splendour. It just made her want to rub the lines away and find out if their tanned skin was as warm as it looked.

"Which Order are you from? I don't recognise you." The designated speaker asked. The more he talked, the more confused she became. What the hell was he talking about? *Excellent question ninety nine!*

"What the hell are you talking about?" More with the frowning and the covert looks. "Really? Again with the silent communication? Whatever. Listen, it's been a long day already and as fun as this was ... I'm out." A tanned hand on hers halted her attempt to retrieve her bag. In addition to the solid warmth his hand provided she also felt a distinct zap, almost like a tiny electric shock. She could have sworn she felt the earth rumble minutely beneath her feet and she raised her startled eyes to meet the green ones of the so-far silent man with the reddish hair.

"We're not wrong here, Darius. She's definitely a Warden." He said.

"But what is a warden doing out here alone? Maybe she's gone off the reservation?" She had no clue what that meant, but the way blue eyes said it made her think it wasn't a good thing.

A rustle in the trees caused them all to glance to the left. She watched in rising trepidation as three sets of hands reached swiftly behind their backs. She swallowed hard; they were all armed which meant this shit was gettin' real. Confident in her butt-kicking abilities she might be, but stupid she was not. No way did she want to pit herself against these men. More rustling preceded a set of soft brown eyes and leathery wings from the top limbs of the Eucalypt tree. The fruit bat clutched half a pear in its tiny claws as it chewed determinedly. She felt more than saw the men around her relax but couldn't herself. It was a little late for the flying mammal to be out, and was that a chill on the breeze she could feel? The men seemed more interested in puzzling out the conundrum that was her than to notice such nuances but she had learned to listen when the world spoke – no matter how indirect. Fingers rudely snapping in front of her face redirected her focus.

"You really have no idea what we're talking about do you?"

She shook her head, "Nope, I really don't. And I really don't care either. I have enough crazy in my life. Trust me!" As if her own words had conjured them, the shadows beneath the trees started lengthening, reaching out with dark fingers to obscure the land. Clouds rushed overhead, blocking out the sun in a seemingly freak storm as the wind blew a gale. It was freaky all right, but it wasn't a storm.

It was them.

They were here.

She reached into her boot for her Joy. Her blade was the one thing she never left in her pack. It was with her always. She even took it into the shower and to bed at night. Joy had saved her life more times than she could count. She was readying herself with an explanation as to why she would be carrying an eight inch dagger in her knee-high boots but found herself blocked into a tight triangle of three broad backs instead. Were they protecting her? They couldn't be. There was no way they could possibly understand what was coming. Nobody else could see her stalkers. She had never been able to figure out why most people didn't see them, she just knew they didn't. Hence, her numerous trips to the aforementioned mental institutes. They always rolled in with an unnatural storm and people were always more fascinated by the abrupt display from Mother Nature than they were by the pale spectres hiding in their midst.

"Stay behind us." The order was bellowed over a vast shoulder, all his attention seemingly focused on the ivory figure slowly creeping forward.

She was incredulous, "You can see them?"

Mr Stoic gave one sharp nod of his head, "I can see them," he flicked a glance in her direction before barking the command once again, "Stay behind us."

Usually she didn't tolerate orders well, but given that this order involved a front row ticket to perhaps the best arse in history, she decided to heed the command. As the three men in front of her took up various practiced fighting positions, she tilted her head to the side and watched three sets of arse cheeks flex and clench. *Fuck yeah*, she'd stay behind them! And with that happy thought, the phantoms descended.

THREE

They were like a flock of morbid seagulls, circling and swooping on the men with their noxious claws, jaws stretched wide in an awful parody of a grin. They were silent, always so silent, in their lethality and for some reason that always creeped her out the most. The open gaping mouths combined with the determined lifeless eyes and the deadly precision of their attacks spoke of a purpose and a kind of horrific glee. Yet they never uttered a sound; no taunts, no laughter, no screams. They never responded when she tried to reason with them nor did they appear to feel pain when she kicked their butts! Well, almost never, she admitted to herself, but now certainly wasn't the time for those convoluted thoughts. No, these strange creatures that she had dubbed 'phantoms' because, hey, what else could they be? They stalked, attacked and vanished in distressing silence just as quickly as they appeared, with no rhyme or reason that she had ever been able to identify. She only knew they hunted her no matter how far she ran or how long she hid. Her whole life had been reduced to dodging, hiding and fighting. She had no time for friends or relationships. She had so needed this little slice of paradise from her youth, but it was clearly not meant to be. There would be no time for fun or time for work and she had desperately needed to work. In fact, that twenty she parted with back at the bar had been one of her last.

With no time to stop and write or draw, she hadn't been able to get a novel out in over a year and she knew even her most loyal of fans were beginning to give up on her. Not that it really mattered, she thought bitterly. She was too scared to access her savings account for the royalties anyway just in case the phantoms were somehow tracking her that way. She had no clue how that could be possible, it's not like they could stroll into a bank or anything, but she wasn't willing to take the risk. She had lost many a good friend over the years as well as many innocent strangers and her conscience was about to buckle under the guilt. In fact, she wasn't sure what she would do if any of these hunks were hurt because of her. Although, they did seem to have the situation well in hand, she admitted, refocusing all her attention where it should be. The strange men were obviously highly skilled as she had suspected and it seemed as if this wasn't their first rodeo with the phantoms either. She eyed them appraisingly and couldn't help but appreciate their technique. She knew just how much discipline it took to hone one's body into a weapon. And weapons they obviously were. They were like poetry in motion. The lethal grace with which they wielded their own strangely shaped blades was almost hypnotising. They were clearly a team of some sort going by the way they seemed to anticipate each other's actions. When one feinted to the left, one would strike from the right; one would defend low while the other attacked high. They were confident and assured of their abilities and clearly trusted each other. They fought back to back, and she noticed they were always careful to keep her solidly between two muscled rears at all times. That was at least until one of the grotesque creatures suddenly sniffed the air like a hound catching a scent and turned it's roiling black eyes her way.

She shuddered under the hungry gaze, knowing what would come next if it were to actually make contact with her. These things fought viciously and would battle to the death with a seemingly endless supply of stamina – but only after they were engaged first. They never delivered the first blow but a clash was always inevitable because she would never let them come in peace. As much as she loathed to partake in the nightmarish violence, the thought of what they would do to her otherwise was even more sickening.

Past experience had taught her to strike fast and to strike hard without mercy. Gripping the well-worn hilt of her perfectly balanced tanto sword she went for expediency over decency and let her shoulders and knees go lax as she executed a smooth roll, coming up behind the advancing spectre. She slashed quickly in two even lines aiming directly behind the knee caps. The phantom went down hard and although it made no sound, its mouth widened in a silent scream and its eyes glared mute accusations. She always found the whole experience deafening. Swallowing back bile, she swung efficiently again and severed the head with one blow. It should have been near impossible to cut through muscle and bone like that – especially for a woman of her height and stature – but as expected the pale head detached easily from the skeletal body. It then shattered into a shower of ash, forcing her to retreat hastily or risk becoming covered in the grisly soot. She had no idea why but they always turned into something different before being picked up by the wind and disappearing into the atmosphere. She could feel the shudder of the earth beneath her feet, the trembling from the desecration of the kill even as the last of the smoky particles floated away. They were joined by fragments of leaves, droplets of water, and even small insects and she knew the Buff Brigade had successfully dispatched the remainder of the phantoms. Not sure what to expect, she kept her grip on Joy tight and her muscles relaxed as she turned to face the music.

It appeared her worries were unnecessary. They weren't poised to pounce or attack. The three of them were, well *gawking,* with identical expressions of stunned disbelief. They looked like they had never seen a girl kick arse before! Typical macho men. Probably thought women spent all day picking out tampons or something! Although she was in a great position to rectify such misguided beliefs, perhaps now was the perfect time to amscray.

"Well, this has been *super* fun! But I need to be on my way now." Keeping her eyes on the stunned mullets, she retrieved her bag and maintained her grip on her blade. That seemed to snap them out of their dazed bemusement.

"You're coming with us." The decree was all drill sergeant and the tone brooked no argument. She hated it.

"Oh am I now? And why would I do that?" She asked sweetly, "No, let me guess. It's because you said it in that deep, serious baritone isn't it?" She fluttered her lashes. That finally brought out a genuine reaction as three sets of sensuous lips curved into grins of varying degrees. The one with the blondy-brown hair even barked out a quick laugh.

"I like you." He stated, then turned to his companions before stating again, "I like her."

"Yeah, well. Like her in the car. We need to get out of here. And you *are* coming with us."

She shook her head, "Ah, no thanks. Not really into the whole orgy thing." *Although I'm seriously tempted!*

"Look, we don't have time for this. More will be on their way." Looks like Mr Serious was back. Well, she didn't need him to tell her what she already knew.

"Yeah, no shit Sherlock. There's always more of them. They're like fucking cockroaches."

His eyes narrowed but it was the red head that spoke up this time, "Sounds like this is a common thing for you."

She snorted, "You could say that."

"Well, as you just saw it's not exactly new to us either. So why don't you let us help you out? Come with us and we'll talk. Seems like you could use some information." His sympathetic green eyes softened further as they looked down at her from his impressive height. "And some help."

She could tell the offer was genuine and she found herself having to swallow past the lump in her throat. Hadn't she just been wishing for someone to help her? Did she dare trust these men? Her body chose that moment to spasm ever so minutely and she knew the decision had been made for her. She couldn't continue on as she had been and these men obviously had answers. Maybe she could finally begin to understand. Praying she wasn't making the biggest mistake of her life, she relented.

FOUR

The atmosphere in the Dodge was extremely awkward, Darius thought as he kept a watchful eye on their unexpected guest. The air was thick with tension, confusion and distrust and it wasn't all stemming from the little warden either. Darius could sense the same whirlwind of emotions from his fellow comrades as well. It seemed they were all on the same page, and that page was *FUBAR* to put it kindly. He and the boys had been heading back to camp after a particularly maddening day at the Lodge when he had felt a slight disturbance in the air. It was nothing major and didn't have the taste of danger that usually accompanied trouble, but it was odd nonetheless. Because he had long ago learned to trust his instincts they had pulled into Dave's to investigate. At first, nothing seemed amiss but then the wind had greeted the solo female occupant at the bar like an old friend and he had begun to understand. Well, sort of understand, he amended silently. The woman was slight in frame and in stature – her feet hadn't even touched the bottom rungs of the bar stool she was perched on. She had dark hair, which he had mistaken as brown or even black, but when she had stepped into the fading light he had seen it was actually red. A deep, rich burgundy that fell in wild waves around her heart-shaped face. And those eyes! In all his years, Darius had never seen eyes like that before. If all that wasn't compelling enough, she was also pumping out Vitality in waves. It was a completely rooky and extremely dangerous thing to do. The distinct energy she had been emitting was like a beacon not only to paladins like himself but also to some truly wretched creatures. She was like a walking magnet and he had zero doubt that she was a warden. But where were her knights?

That seemed to be the question of the day. He hadn't felt any other paladins in the vicinity which should have been impossible. A warden was never without a paladin. The level of bizarre had increased exponentially as he watched in a kind of fascinated disbelief when the tiny warden crippled and decapitated their enemy. Darius had never seen anything like it from a warden in all his years. She had been confident and exacting in her skills, clearly having engaged in battle with the chades before. She knew just where to strike in order to dispatch her opponent with a smooth economy that would have half his brethren envious. She was clearly very well trained. The question was why. Why would a guardian of nature need, or want, to engage in any form of violence? It was absolutely unheard of. Wardens were passive, sacred beings and were protected at all times, at any cost. Hence, the existence of the paladins.

"It's okay. You're safe with us." Lark's voice was soft and friendly. He was obviously trying to put the odd little warden at ease. Apparently, it wasn't working for she gave a rather undignified snort of disbelief and clutched that damn sword of hers tighter.

"It's true. No one here would ever hurt you." He nodded towards the well-kept blade. "You don't need that." Her eyes never stopped their constant wandering, taking in the sites. He was positive she was cataloguing everything and committing it all to memory. She also didn't let up on her weapon as she replied sardonically;

"Like I haven't heard that before!" Those peculiar eyes of hers focused on each of them briefly before she muttered, "But somehow I almost believe you. Why do I believe you?"

"It's instinctual. The relationship between wardens and paladins is built into their DNA. You recognise us, just as we recognised you back at the bar." Darius explained.

She shook her head, sending all that thick red hair flying, "I don't know what you're talking about. I've never seen you before in my life. And what do you mean warden? I've never worked in a jail."

Axel raised his eyebrows in a classic 'what the fuck?' gesture. What the fuck indeed, Darius thought.

"How about we leave all the explanations for when we get back to camp?" Darius knew the others were there and he had a feeling they were going to need all of them to get to the bottom of this. He only wished he could predict how Ry was going to react. Despite his high paladin status, he really wasn't a fan of wardens in general.

"Camp?" She still sounded unsure.

Axel spoke up, "Yeah, camp. It's what we call our base – where we live and sleep when we're not needed at the Lodge."

She looked sceptical, "Um, camp? Base? Do you actually mean *home*? Because that's what it sounds like. You live and sleep at *home*."

Yes, it did sound a lot like home, but it wasn't really – not for any of them. It was a temporary place to stay where they could rest and relax and figure out what the hell they were going to do with their lives. They were lucky Ry was so generous.

Lark chuckled and answered in direct opposition to Darius's thoughts, "Yes. He means home." He winked. "But He-men like us aren't really big on flowery prose."

That made her smile even as her shoulders relaxed another degree. Thank heavens for Lark, Darius thought.

"I'm Lark by the way. This is Axel and our fearless driver here is Darius."

Darius groaned and slapped his own forehead internally where no one could see his stupidity. They had practically kidnapped this poor woman who was somehow ignorant of her own society and were driving her into the depths of the Australian bush ... and he hadn't even introduced himself. He was a moron. No wonder she was so nervous and still gripping that freaking short sword like a life line. Again, thank heavens for Lark!

"I wish I could say it was nice to meet you ..." she paused, "... but I don't know if it is." Her eyes lit up with mischief and her slightly rounded cheeks dimpled as she smiled. Had Darius been a weaker man, he'd be half in love with her by now. She spun to face the road, giving them her shoulder and back in the beginnings of trust, and stated simply;

"I'm Max."

FIVE

Max stood open-mouthed and gaping up at the 'camp'. Their 'camp' was a barn, Max thought, and not at all what she had been expecting. They had been driving for approximately thirty minutes, following the coastline south when Darius – as she had finally learned – had turned onto a well-used gravel road. At first Max thought that maybe they were taking her into the wilderness to use and abuse her in dirty and despicable ways. She was only half tempted to jump from the moving vehicle and make a run for it. The other half of her figured it wasn't such a bad way to go, so she had observed and memorised the journey and was confident she could retrace the route with her eyes closed if need be. She didn't exactly have a photographic memory but she was pretty darn observant and had a great sense of direction.

Although the road was gravel, it was obvious it was well maintained and used frequently. It was lined with tall native trees and short local shrubs that also appeared to be well conserved and it had suddenly clicked that it wasn't actually a road but a private driveway. The driveway continued straight for another couple of minutes before a gentle bend had revealed the most magnificent, the most beautiful stone and cedar barn she had ever seen. When they had said camp, Max had been expecting a couple of tents or maybe a shack with a fire pit or something. But this, Max thought, this by no means resembled any camp she had ever been to.

The barn stretched high into the sky for a full three stories with a curved roof arching gracefully against the horizon. She could make out the three distinct levels from the positioning of the domed windows that lined the east facing front of the home. It was clearly made from Australian red cedar given the rich reddish brown colour and the roughness of its texture. The logs had been kept in their natural state rather than polished and stained, displaying a genuine respect for the wood. From where she stood at the beginning of a forked stone path, she could make out the heavy brass knocker against the tall double doors. She allowed her eyes to follow the fork to the right and what do you know? Even the fricking shed was a thing of beauty. What she assumed was the garage, must have been two stories high itself and was fashioned from uneven stone and brick in various shades of grey. The sound of crashing waves in the distance was the perfect soundtrack to such architectural splendour. They must have been driving directly parallel to the coastline in order for them to be so close to the ocean, Max mused.

"Camp? Really?" She raised her eyebrows at the three men. She watched as Darius ran a critical eye over the building before turning back to her.

"Yeah. Camp. This is where we live. Come on, it's time to meet the others and get this all sorted out." He gestured for her to precede him down the path.

"Whoa, big fella. Others? What others?" Suddenly the impressive home no longer seemed quite so fairytale but more like a potential prison.

"Yes. We live here with a couple of other guys." Darius said. "But you don't need to worry. They're like us. No harm will come to you."

There he goes again with that baritone, no nonsense voice of his. She bet it usually worked wonders on the poor unsuspecting females of the world. Well, she wasn't unsuspecting, so although she would love to hear him whispering naughty words into her ear, she wasn't going to submit that easily. "Uh huh. Whatever you say ... stranger."

He released a huff of frustration and glanced toward his colleagues. Lark, the red head simply shook his head, while Axel appeared to be enjoying Darius's discomfort immensely if the grin was any indication. "Look ..." He turned to her and gripped his left forearm with his right hand, raising it over his heart, "I give you my solemn oath that you shall not be harmed in any way. You are an honoured guest at our camp."

"Dude! Are you really still going to stand there and call this place a camp?" She threw the retort back because a) she truly couldn't fathom anyone calling this place a camp, and b) she wanted to buy some more time. The weird gesture and the promise had tickled something inside her that she didn't understand. Back in the car when they had told her she was safe, she had believed them. She felt that same belief and trust now, she just didn't understand why.

They had said something about DNA and instincts. Max was all for instincts – they had saved her life more times than she could count. So should she trust them now? She could be wrong, stranger things had happened.

"Yes! It's a camp. That's what it is! But that is not the point. You –"

"Okay, okay. Chill. I kind of believe you." Max cut in. She was afraid the poor hunk was going to blow a blood vessel.

"Um, are we all just going to pretend we didn't hear her call Sir Darius here, 'Dude'?" Axel of the surfer-boy looks asked with a raised hand.

"Axel ..." Darius's voice held a note of dangerous warning that Axel was clearly unconcerned with. Lark managed to smother what she was certain was a laugh behind his hand and a hasty cough. "Enough of this foolishness. Max, please ..." He gestured once more.

Max finally nodded in agreement and switched Joy to her more dominant hand. She was yet to let go of her. She saw Darius eye the blade with caution and knew he was about to tell her she didn't need it.

"You can –"

"Keep a tight grip on my only weapon as I venture into a secluded mansion with a bunch of males big enough to snuff me when they sneeze?" Max cut in, "Thanks! I'll do that!"

Lark gave a low chuckle that had a pleasant tingle spreading through Max's stomach. Oh boy. And apparently there was more inside.

****

Max's reservations fled completely the moment she stepped inside. Those heavy double doors opened directly into a combined kitchen and dining room. Max stood frozen to the spot as she tried to take everything in. The northern wall was comprised entirely of stone from the hard wood floors to the two storey open ceilings. An arched recess was cut perfectly into the stone, housing a double burner gas stove top and oven that would have professional chefs drooling. A row of dark, glossy cabinets ran the length of the eastern wall below the row of windows looking out onto the backyard and the ocean in the distance. They were broken up only by the stainless steel dishwasher, toaster, kettle, and the deep double sinks positioned strategically for efficiency.

An island bench cleaved the room in two, resulting in a clear distinction between the kitchen and the dining area. The island was made up of the same rich gloss as the cabinets with the lower section showcasing the same uneven grey stones as the feature wall. Max looked up, up, up, marvelling at the high cathedral ceilings and moaning at the thick cedar beams that arched overhead, promising both strength and grace. She was officially in love for the first time in her life. This kitchen, this house, was everything she had ever dreamed a home would be. The contradictions of stone and wood combined with the arches and bold deep colours gave the room warmth as well as complexity and made it one big interesting mix. Max just knew this area was the epicentre of the house; it screamed 'lived in'. There were a couple of mugs sitting on the sink, papers and magazines strewn on the counter, muddy boots by the door, and were those ...? Yep, there was an assortment of guns and blades spotted across the massive dining table. Max found herself sighing lustily at the thick table top. It would easily seat sixteen people and looked like it had been pieced together lovingly from old recycled wood. She had to see more.

Turning to ask her saviours ... hosts ... captors or whatever they were, for a tour Max found herself under the same scrutiny she had likely been giving the room. Only now there were six pairs of eyes staring at her rather than the original three.

"Good God! They were right. There *are* more of them!" She exclaimed loudly in automatic reaction to the appearance of not one, but two more walking orgasms. A knowing feminine chuckle was the rejoinder from the only other human in the room that had a pair of breasts besides her. Max wondered if this was the woman's harem or something. If so, she was officially Max's new hero.

She was certainly beautiful enough to garner the loyalty of any man, Max thought, eyeing the woman critically as all females did – whether they admitted to it or not! She was absolutely stunning with long legs, a slender torso and high pert breasts. She had golden blonde hair that fell in a straight curtain past her shoulders to sit dutifully over those perky tits of hers. Max barely caught her bottom lip before it could lower in a pout. This chick was almost her polar opposite; she was tall and willowy where Max was short and curvy; she had straight light hair where Max had a frizzy mass of dark waves; and she had those perky apple tits! Max's own breasts were an extremely healthy handful. She'd never had any complaints but how she would love to be able to roam braless and free!

"Is this your harem? And do you accept new members?" Max figured it couldn't hurt to ask. The pale Amazon gave a throaty chuckle – almost as pleasant as the green-eyed cutie. Wow. She had never been so tempted to switch teams before, you only lived once after all and Max was all for living life to its fullest.

"No. This isn't my harem." She eye-balled the men thoughtfully, "But it's an intriguing idea. I'm Cali." She smiled warmly, her blue eyes twinkling.

Max smiled in return, recognising a kindred spirit immediately. "Max."

The other new hottie in the room dipped his head in greeting, "I'm Beyden. Welcome."

Max waited in anticipation for the remaining male to introduce himself as Darius spoke to him in hushed tones. He was the biggest male she had ever had the pleasure of ogling. Six foot four or five easy and packed with solid muscle, the guy must weigh a tonne! She couldn't quite make out his face as he was angled away from her, but his messy black hair had her fingers twitching with the need to smooth it out.

"We met Max at Dave's and ran into a bit of trouble so I thought it best to bring her here." Darius informed the room at large. The mountain masquerading as a man didn't seem inclined to share his name. *Typical.* Max thought, *the yummy ones are always the jerks.*

"Why don't we sit down?" Darius suggested, playing the courteous host.

"Ah, sure. But why is the Warden carrying a sword?" Newbie Beyden asked curiously.

Max gazed down at Joy lovingly, "Duh. It's my protection."

Beyden's expressive eyebrows rose disbelievingly. "Duh? Did you just say duh?" He turned to Darius, "Did she just say duh?"

Lark and Axel snickered as Darius gripped the bridge of his nose tiredly. She was beginning to understand these men a little, she realised. Lark seemed to be a genuinely nice and happy guy. Axel seemed nice enough too, but his sense of humour was clearly very wicked. Poor Darius seemed a little stuck up and a lot exasperated with the likes of her.

"Don't ask." Darius muttered, "She can keep the sword."

Max batted her lashes, "Why, that is just so kind of you good sir." Chuckles and shocked gasps met her sarcasm. She couldn't really help herself. Sarcasm was kind of her thing. Half the room appeared to appreciate it anyhow so she wasn't too concerned.

Darius. The name really suited him, she thought. He had an old world charm about him and his manner was almost courtly as he held her chair for her so she could take a seat at that magnificent dining table. Max finally allowed herself to give him a serious study as he lowered himself elegantly into the chair next to hers. Where most of the other prime specimens present all had a rough edginess to them, Darius seemed almost polished. Although he was dressed much like the others in dark cargo pants and a plain tee shirt he somehow made it look almost … sophisticated. He sat with his back ramrod straight, brown hair perfectly styled despite his earlier jaunt with the phantoms. His hazel eyes were serious but kind as they looked at her.

"What do you think you are?" His softly spoken question completely disarmed her.

She really had no idea how to answer that. She had a couple of theories about what made her tick but had never really come to any solid conclusions and every time she had dipped her toes into the 'trust pool' she had them bitten off. These strange, beautiful people in this strange, beautiful house acted like they had answers, but Max's faith in humanity was seriously thin. She had no intention of saying or doing anything else that may incriminate her in any way. It was all about the plausible deniability – *Law and Order* said so.

"I have no idea what you mean. I think the better question is what do *you* think I am?"

Max paid close attention to those now either hovering around the large table or seated at it, gauging reactions and judging intents. She prided herself on her judgement and so far she judged a third of them were confused, a third were intrigued, and the other third? Well, they were quite obviously suspicious; the woman and the one who looked like a serial killer. He stood still and silent, arms crossed tightly over a thick chest. His scowl was epic as he eyed her with complete disdain and Max was forced to suppress a shiver at the derision emanating her way. Lucky she didn't have self-confidence issues or she would have found herself melted into a puddle of insecurities on the floor. As it was, she had a rather healthy dose of self-esteem so was by no means cowed by the frigid stare. Out of the corner of her eye she noticed Darius raise his eyebrows; clearly a silent question. The almost imperceptible nod he received came from the scowling murderer across the room. Was he in charge or something? Maybe their boss or Commander if they were in fact a military team. She couldn't help scrunching up her nose at the thought of him holding a position of power – *Scary!*

"I don't need to think about it, Max. I know exactly what you are. You are by no means the first warden I have met. You are however, the first one I have met who seems to be completely ignorant of the fact."

Max frowned, there was that word again; warden. In all her years of research she had never come across that word. If Darius was telling the truth, wouldn't she have stumbled upon 'wardens' at some point? Google was pretty awesome after all. "What exactly is a 'warden'? And why do you think I'm one of them?"

Darius leaned forward and steepled his long fingers. Even his fingers were elegant! "You have an affinity with nature, yes?"

"Affinity?" She made the one word a question. No confirmations, no denials. *Just be cool!*

"There's no point playing dumb, sweetheart. We saw it at Dave's, *felt* it at Dave's. Besides ..." Axel smirked, "... it doesn't suit you."

Surprisingly, Max wasn't all that concerned about being caught out. She was more intrigued with the left handed compliment she had just received. He didn't think dumb suited her – what a sweetie pie! Tall, built and ridiculously handsome he exuded strength in every line of his body. He must have been a whole foot taller than her at six foot three with broad shoulders tapering to a narrow waist. His dirty blond hair was cut military short and combined with his blue eyes, he should have looked like the classic boy next door ... but he didn't. The heat in those baby blues elevated him from pretty to *pretty hot!* Add to that, he was likely a charmer with a silver tongue and Max was doomed. Womanisers didn't appeal to her; she wasn't interested in a guy who would stick his dick in anything! But she was a sucker for a charmer. Max decided to reward him with an honest answer;

"I think I know what you're referring to but I don't understand why. I've always had an attraction to nature and somehow, I think it has an attraction to me too." She wasn't really sure how to articulate herself, but a quick glance around the room revealed she didn't need to. They knew what she meant. Somehow, these people really did understand. A tiny ray of hope began to pierce through her cynicism. "Is it the same for you? Can you talk to the elements too?"

Darius shook his head, "No. It doesn't work that way for us. We're not like you."

"But I saw you! You fought the phantoms! You know what they are and apparently you know what I am! What do you mean you –" Max's steadily rising voice was cut off by an incredulous holler.

"Phantoms?" The woman, Cali, turned to Darius, "What the hell is she talking about? What phantoms?"

Max noticed Darius, Axel and Lark were struggling to suppress smiles. Were they laughing at her?

"I think that's what she calls the chades. I told you we got into a spot of bother that involved her."

"You didn't mention chades though!" Cali admonished.

Darius shrugged, "I mentioned it to Ry. Anyway, we're getting off topic." He focused on Max once again, "Yes, we can see those creatures. They are called chades by the way, not phantoms." His lips twitched once again. He *was* laughing at her! Max's jaw clenched tight. She hated being the butt of someone's joke.

"He's not making fun of you." The deep voice belonged to the one introduced as Beyden. He was as tall and as built as the rest of the Testosterone Taskforce with light brown wavy hair escaping from a loose tie and just touching his broad shoulders. He was seated directly across from her which afforded her the perfect position to peer dreamily into those magnificent eyes of his. She couldn't recall seeing eyes quite that shade before – not on a person anyway. Possibly on a lion or a tiger maybe given the amber glow of his irises. Perhaps that's why she felt almost immediately at ease with him – there was a kinship there. She couldn't count the number of times people had commented on her own unique eye colour.

"No one here would make fun of you like that." Beyden continued, "Darius just means that we are not wardens like you. We are paladins. We do each have empathy with one of the seven elements found in nature, but it is nothing like what yours must be."

"Seven elements?" Max was no closer to getting answers than when she walked in the door! They just kept throwing more words at her with the expectation that she knew what the hell they were talking about.

"In nature there are seven domains, or elements if you will: Earth, Air, Fire, Water, Beast, Death and of course, Life. The domains must remain stable, just as balance between the domains must be maintained. This balance ensures each domain doesn't become extinct, that each domain continues to survive and to thrive. Very simply put, the seven domains make the world go round."

"Okay." Max could kind of understand that. The fact that fire and water were elements wasn't exactly news and most of her research suggested a link to Mother Nature and her elements. It was also big on balance.

"So you paladins keep this balance?" Max tried not to take offense at the multiple snorts of derision.

"No, definitely not. Keeping the balance is above our pay grade. We're just here for the grunt work." Axel's low voice held no resentment even though the words held a hint and his teeth flashed white as he smiled her way. *Even his teeth were sexy!* Max thought.

"Grunt work? What do you mean?" Max forced herself to focus. She needed answers but there was just a little too much testosterone in the room for her to concentrate fully ... and probably just a little too much oestrogen pumping throughout her body, she admitted to herself.

Axel crossed his arms over his chest and leaned back against the dark cedar benchtop – his biceps flexed prettily. "We're the foot soldiers – at your service ma'am." He gave a flippant salute.

Max had known they were military from the first moment she laid eyes on them but it was good to get confirmation, "So you're soldiers. Is that why you call yourselves paladins? As in Charlemagne's Paladins? Like the Twelve Peers?"

"You know who Charlemagne is?" Darius asked, surprise evident in his voice.

Max shrugged nonchalantly, "I'm a history buff."

"And the Twelve Peers? I'm impressed."

"Well, you shouldn't be too impressed. My knowledge is rudimental at best. But I do know that the paladins were some of the first and most respected knights. They were the foremost warriors of their time renowned for their chivalry, honour and skills on the battle field. They form the basis of the romanticised knights in shining armour. Charlemagne was their liege." Max sighed as she stared into space, picturing rough-hewn warriors mounted on mighty steeds, riding fearlessly into battle to protect and serve. "The paladins were everything a man should be."

Max was startled out of her mini daydream by several snorts and one very loud laugh that came from Lark. His name certainly appeared to suit him for his laughter was infectious and the numerous fine lines surrounding his eyes hinted at years of smiles and laughter. He was the shortest of the group and also one of the leanest. Just on six foot, he had that whipcord wiry look to him much like professional swimmers had, rather than the bulk and the bulging mass of most of the others. But he was just as appealing to Max. What could she say – she was big on equality. His messy auburn hair flared gold under the unnatural light of the kitchen and his piercing green eyes were warm and friendly. Hard to believe he was also one of the fiercest fighters outside the bar when the phantoms had attacked. He had been the most agile and definitely the speediest, leaping and spinning calmly as he fought off the foul creatures.

"Aw darlin', you're gonna make me blush." Lark grinned.

Ookay. Cute and cut he may be but he was obviously delirious. Did they all truly think they were freaking knights?!

Darius must have read the look of disbelief on her face for he held up a hand, "Please, remain patient. I can understand how this may seem unusual to you but –"

"Unusual? Unusual? This all seems fucking bat shit crazy to me!" Max yanked at her hair in frustration, "And are you the king of understatement or what? *Come to my camp,*" She mimicked, "*this may seem unusual.*"

"Is she unstable?" Cali asked while appearing to reach behind her. Was she reaching for a weapon? Max tightened her grip on Joy.

Lark stood and placed an oddly comforting hand on her shoulder. "Easy Max. I don't think she's unstable Cali. I just think she's clueless."

Max pouted, "That's actually more of an insult to me. I'd rather be unstable than stupid."

Lark smiled and patted her head like she was a mischievous puppy, "Of course you would be."

"Max, we do call ourselves paladins. But we are essentially soldiers and guardians. It's our job to protect and serve wardens." Darius explained.

She nodded, feeling calmer and even happier with Lark's touch. "So you're soldiers and bodyguards. You fight those chade things and protect wardens. What do you mean when you say serve? Not literally like servants?"

Axel snorted, "Yeah, pretty much."

"No. Not at all." Darius glared at Axel. "We provide energy to wardens to ensure they don't use themselves up."

"Energy?"

"Yes. Energy. It takes a lot of energy to uphold a domain."

"It does?" Max wanted to roll her eyes at herself. She was like a freaking echo!

Cali stepped closer. "Yes, it does. But you would know more about that than we would. How have you been sustaining yourself all this time if you didn't have a paladin sharing their vitality with you anyway?"

Max was even more confused as she answered, "What do you mean sustaining myself? I eat, I drink, I sleep … that's it. I have no idea what sharing vitality even means."

"That's not possible. You must be absorbing vitality from somewhere. Paladins and wardens have a symbiotic relationship. Paladins are born with an excess of energy – what we call vitality. It's a by-product of our genes. It's what makes us knights, protectors, guardians of the wardens. You see, wardens use their vitality to maintain their domain but wardens cannot produce it or recharge it. That's where the paladins come in. We produce it in a continuous loop so the wardens feed from us, then they feed the world."

Max's head was spinning. The whole thing sounded completely nuts but at the same time it was the first time she had ever felt even a smidgeon of rightness. "So wardens are like vampires. Except instead of feeding off blood, they feed off energy?"

"What? No! Wardens are not vampires! They are the most revered people in our society. They are not morbidly imagined creatures of the night!" Darius shouted indignantly. He looked about ready to have a stroke. The one called Beyden on the other hand, was looking at Max thoughtfully.

"You know, she's kind of right. It is almost like a feeding."

"Be careful Beyden. What you're saying is close to blaspheme."

Max watched the exchange with great interest. Darius was obviously the serious one and his sense of duty seemed deeply ingrained but his defensiveness spoke of something more personal. Beyden and Lark appeared more open minded and easy going. She could picture them just going with the flow. She bet Axel was the rebel and he clearly had some kind of chip on his sexy shoulder, Cali had girl power going for her but she still seemed highly suspicious ... and the big guy? Well, Max had no freaking clue where he was concerned. He still hadn't spoken a word and she was yet to make out his features clearly as he was ranged in the shadows. Perhaps he was mute, that wouldn't be a bad thing. Big, built and silent, Max grinned, a perfect combination.

"What's with the evil smile? It's kind of freaking me out, what with the way you're fingering that pig sticker of yours." Axel didn't appear freaked out in the least. He was sinking those pearly whites of his into an apple, ankles crossed negligently. Even so, she wiped the grin off her face ... and stopped caressing the blade.

"What do you guys get out of this whole deal? It seems like you got the shit end of the stick. Wardens suck out your energy and then you have to babysit them and place their lives above your own? Sounds like you're getting gypped to me."

"It's not like that. It is our honour to serve. It is what we were born to do, our purpose. Just like your purpose is to monitor and preserve your domain. You must feel it? That deep sense of rightness whenever you communicate with your element?" Darius asked.

Max nodded in agreement. She did feel it. She had always felt deeply connected to nature and indeed every living thing. She didn't just crave it, she actually needed it. The longer she went without direct interaction with living things, the worse her tremors were and the worse her health became. Her mental health also suffered to a point where she would go on a major chocolate binge. It's a miracle she hadn't lapsed into a diabetic coma before.

"Darius is right. We're not *babysitters*. Historically, the term *knight* was synonymous with *servant* and *solider*. That is essentially what we paladins are. We are soldiers who serve." Although Beyden spoke softly, his voice resonated with a deep bass and a slight Spanish accent if she wasn't mistaken. Max could imagine what that deep Spanish tone would feel like whispered against her skin. She was a published novelist after all, which meant her imagination was very ... vivid. He also had a calmness about him that made her think he must be the mellow one of the gang. She already felt comfortable around him, which was very odd, given her trust issues. He somehow reminded her of a puppy – all eager and innocent. But there was a sharp intelligence in his amber eyes that told Max there was a wolf sleeping underneath his puppy façade.

"And it is wardens whom you serve." Max stated in response.

Beyden smiled, "Yes. Purpose gives us life. It gives us hope. We all need to fulfil our roles. Besides, because we keep producing vitality, we need an outlet for it. We can't expel it the way you wardens can. Without a warden to convert the energy into vitality, it's pretty much useless. It just circulates around our bodies."

"So where's your Warden?" She asked.

"That's enough." The two roughly spoken words startled Max so much she almost dropped her sword. The giant silent one had finally deigned to speak. Max noticed how everyone in the room tacitly acknowledged the man when he spoke. Her earlier assumption had been correct, the Hulk was some kind of boss or leader. His dark assessing eyes pinned her to her seat and Max felt goose bumps break out across her exposed skin.

"History lesson over. I think you've heard enough from us."

That voice! Like smooth molasses, deep and resonating but not a bass like Beyden's was. And to think she had pictured Axel's and Beyden's voice whispering sweet nothings. This guy made them sound like choking ducks! The tell-tale throb from her nether regions waned however, with his next words.

"Who the fuck are you really and why the fuck are you really here?"

SIX

Max stiffened and narrowed hard eyes at the Adonis. Just when she felt like she was beginning to get some solid answers, his harsh questions had her erecting her defences once again. She couldn't really blame him, she supposed. She didn't trust them any farther than she could throw them and by the sounds of it, it was extremely uncommon for someone to be a warden and not know about it. His obvious suspicions contradictorily made her less suspicious of them though; a person who asked questions was an intelligent person in her books. What really bothered her was the disrespectful tone he had used. Swearing she could handle – she knew she had a foul mouth of her own – but she couldn't tolerate bad manners.

"Excuse me?" She questioned coolly. When she felt offended she tended to get a little snotty.

"I want to know what game you're playing."

"I'm not really a sports fan. I don't play games." More snottiness. He hadn't even moved from his shadowy little corner. He could see her but she couldn't see him, giving him a distinct advantage. It was just plain rude!

The chuckle that rolled from the darkness was cutting and mocking, "Do you really expect us to believe you are a long lost warden? One of the most esteemed citizens of our society? That you have been bumbling around on your own out there in the big bad world with no knowledge of who and what you are?"

"So I'm lying am I?" Although she couldn't make out his eyes she somehow knew she was staring directly into them, "I can assure you, this is all news to me. You are the ones who found *me*, not the other way around."

"Yes. Very convenient."

"*Convenient?*" Max cringed internally when she heard the high pitch of her voice. She sounded like a shrew. How could this man blow all of her composure in less than five minutes? She gave herself an internal bitch slap and responded reasonably, "It was your fucking lemmings who dragged me back here! I didn't even want to come!"

"A convincing act I'm sure. It got you back here. But I'm not as gullible as them." He jabbed his thumb at the three men who had protected her from the phantoms even as he finally emerged from the corner, stepping fully into the light. "And I don't buy your whole innocent act."

"Ah, excuse me – gullible? I didn't exactly come in on the last wave Ryker! She's a fucking warden! We could sense her vitality clear across the room at the bar. And the chades were drawn to her like bees to honey!" Axel sounded angry but Max barely registered the words. She was too busy trying not to orgasm at the dining table.

Ryker! Finally a name to go with that body of his, Max thought as she shivered in delicious anticipation. The name certainly fit him. The guy looked like he belonged in a maximum security prison after all. He had a heavy five o'clock shadow, messy black hair almost touching his shoulders and bulging muscles displayed perfectly by his plain white tee shirt. He had a huge scar running from under his jaw all the way up the left side of his face and disappearing under his hair line. It was like someone had attempted to hack his face in half. But the imperfection by no means detracted from that fallen angel face. In fact, it made Max want to trace its jagged lines with her tongue – that was her thing for scars talking. She let her eyes roam south and, no – it couldn't be! Was that what she thought it was? *Please don't let it be*, she begged privately ... *Fuck, it was!* Her very own Achilles heel ... nipple rings! She could just detect the outlines of the metal under the white cotton where his nipples were situated. Lord have mercy, she was a sucker for a good nipple ring. Were they hoops or were they bars? She could work with either but she was a little partial to bars.

"Are you done staring?"

Max managed to refrain from jolting at the snarled words. Shit! She had obviously been staring at the inmate too long. He was glaring at her from across the room with those too-good-to-be-true deep brown eyes. They were the colour of her favourite chocolate ... dammit. He was like her own personal, life-size walking wet dream. She had to be cool.

"Not really." She answered, deadpan. "I was planning to take a picture. I hear they last longer."

****

The snickers were briskly smothered under Ryker's glare, he noted with grim satisfaction. Much to his consternation, Ryker had been appointed the unofficial leader of their ragtag little group of rejects. It wasn't a title or a responsibility he willingly accepted but it was something he was glad for given their current situation. He planned on getting to the bottom of the long lost warden ... and getting her the hell out of his kitchen. He had made a vow to himself over fifty years ago that he would never be drawn into another Order again. Paladins were duty bound and honour bound to serve the wardens of the world. But he'd be fucked if he would bind himself to another one – not ever again. It then followed, he was under no obligation to have one in his home. When Darius, Axel and Lark had strolled in, a half-size warden in between them, Ryker's immediate thought was to kick their collective arses! They knew the rules of the camp – no impromptu guests. Certainly not warden guests. Darius had stalled his objections when he started talking however; bar fights, chade attacks, short swords and decapitation. At first he had scoffed, there was no way a warden would ever take up arms in such a way. Besides, the woman was a freaking midget. What could she do really, besides kick potential assailants in the shins? But then he had looked at her, like really looked at her and he had known. She was going to be trouble. And wasn't it just his luck? He absolutely loved trouble!

She was short at around five foot three, with dark cerise hair and a body with curves in all the right places. She was pale with dark circles under her eyes, and although she was clean and tidy, her clothes were well worn. She clutched a short samurai sword in one hand and a battered back pack in the other and she was leaking energy all over the place like a sieve. She also seemed completely ignorant to that fact, which should have been impossible. Wardens were trained from the cradle how to control their vitality, just as paladins were trained how to protect. Even if by some miracle she truly didn't know who or what she was, there was no way she could have survived seeping vitality like that for any length of time. And with no paladin to replenish her? No. Fucking. Way. So he had side-lined himself and let the discussion ebb and flow around him.

He had watched the delighted wonder on her face as she had taken in the kitchen, the stark disbelief when Darius had told her she was a warden, the disgust when Cali had explained the energy exchange, and the barely contained fury from his blatant accusations. Her face hid nothing; all her thoughts and emotions were plain to see in those expressive eyes of hers. Although he was actually inclined to believe her original tale of ignorance in light of that animated face, he was also cautious by nature and he had never been a fan of coincidence or serendipity. The chances of his boys stumbling upon a stray warden were miniscule. So he was going to see what he could scare out of the female.

Despite what his stupid dick seemed to think, he was most definitely *not* happy to see her. The foolish thing had been hard as a rock ever since she stepped into the room. Everything about her seemed to rev his engines, from her voice, to her sarcasm and her wit. He appreciated a woman who could hold her own in a conversation. But what grabbed at his gut the most were those eyes of hers. He most definitely did *not* think her eyes were the most expressive, the most magical eyes he had ever seen. They were turquoise. There was no other colour that described them. They looked like the colour of the clearest of bays in the warmest of seas. He wondered if they would darken with desire during sex or perhaps lighten in the throes of ecstasy. *Stupid dick!*

"Perhaps it's you who would like to take a picture, hmmm?"

Ryker could hear the knowing smirk in her voice and it made his teeth grind. A pair of pretty eyes – and even prettier breasts – would not be enough to make him forget she was a warden with a very suspicious and questionable history. He crossed his arms over his chest and returned to the matter at hand, "Where are you from?"

Perfectly shaped eyebrows rose over mocking eyes, "Australia. I figured the accent would give me away. Yours is fairly close but not that of a native. Pommy?" She questioned.

He had actually been born in England but hadn't lived there for over fifty years. His accent only came out these days when he was very angry, very stressed ... or very aroused. At the moment he was all three so he supposed it made sense that she was able to pick it. She was very observant and astute, he realised. She was also quite adept at taking the focus away from herself.

"Where were you born?" He didn't believe in using twenty words when four were enough.

"Australia."

She grinned and his dick twitched from the clear challenge in her eyes. She would rue the day she chose to take him on. He stalked forward, power in each step, until he hovered over her much smaller frame. "You are an unbound warden with no Order in my territory. I am within my rights to report you to the Council and let them deal with you as they see fit. Believe me, they would not be so accommodating."

That was a total and utter lie of course. The Council was made up of a bunch of self-righteous, pretentious wankers and would no doubt be thrilled with the discovery of a new warden. Warden births were few and far between and after the massacre half a century ago the numbers had dwindled drastically. It was why the wardens were safeguarded so zealously now. The Council would celebrate her appearance and grant her all the trappings her station afforded. He could see the frowns on the faces of Darius, Lark and Beyden but they were too well trained to voice their discontent. Beyden and Lark were the softest of the bunch and although they were fierce soldiers he knew they would have been content to never fight a day in their lives. Darius's disapproval, Ryker knew, was due to him being a gentleman. A male just didn't treat a female like Ryker was. He wholeheartedly agreed with Darius really, but lying would serve a twin purpose. Firstly, it would reveal if she already had knowledge of the Council and she had in fact been lying to them. It should also induce her to be more cooperative if she felt threatened. Axel and Cali didn't seem too concerned, but then Cali was a practical woman and Axel was ... well, Axel was a bit of a dick. Ryker really liked him.

Max frowned, "There is so much I don't understand in that statement. Unbound warden? Order? Council?" She rubbed her forehead with a shaky hand and it was Ryker's turn to frown. Was she unwell? Beyden, ever the nurturer, must have noticed at the same time he did for he asked;

"Are you okay?"

The smile she threw his way, was strained and obviously fake, "I'm fine." She said, "Just really overwhelmed. It's been a long day and my head is spinning."

"I can imagine. Here, let me get you some water." He walked briskly to the fridge and filled a glass with the rain water always in supply.

"Thank you." Max clutched at the glass with two hands as she drank thirstily. In order to hide the fact that her hands were trembling? *Shit!* Ryker thought. She probably needed a vitality boost. Glancing around, he noted similar looks of realisation on the faces of his fellow paladins and knew the interrogation was over for now. He may be a jerk, but he was also a knight, and his very DNA demanded he provide for all wardens.

"You need energy." He stated.

Those turquoise eyes of hers still hinted at an inner strength of steel but the bright spark of defiance was much diminished when she raised them to meet his gaze.

"I need a good night's sleep and some time to wrap my head around all this Hogwarts business yawl are spouting."

"Hogwarts?"

"Yawl?" Lark and Axel questioned simultaneously.

She shook her head, sending that gorgeous mass of red hair flying messily around her arresting face, "Meh. Focus boys. Sleep first; Harry Potter education later. Can someone give me a lift to the closest motel, please?"

"No motel." His words brooked no argument. She wasn't going anywhere. Like it or not, she was now his responsibility until this whole mess was sorted out.

"Excuse me?"

She had reverted back to that ice princess, superior tone of hers. His dick jerked again. *Stupid dick!* "You heard me. No motel."

"So I *am* a prisoner? I fucking knew it! You're all a bunch of liars who have lured me out here so you can store my body parts in your freezer for future cannibalistic Sunday roasts."

"You're not a prisoner Max, but you truly are a warden. We haven't been lying to you and I don't believe you've been lying to us. Please, at least stay the night, eat a decent meal. In the morning we can discuss things in more detail." Darius responded far more reasonably than Ryker would have done.

"You really expect me to stay here? Dude, I just met you. I haven't stayed alive this long by being an idiot."

Ryker was so not arguing with the woman. "You're staying. End of story." Ah, there was that lovely spark of defiance he had been looking for earlier. Before she could send out another barb Lark jumped in.

"Max, you're safe here. Remember what we said in the car? No one here would ever hurt you. Trust your instincts."

She appeared to mull over Lark's earnest words carefully before responding, "One night." She held up a rather delicate finger. "And one night only."

"But don't you want answers? Don't you want to finally be safe? Wouldn't you like to not only understand your abilities, but also control them? We can do that for you. Or at least introduce you to others who can." Beyden assured her.

"I'll tell you what, because you have all been so kind as to disseminate your collective knowledge to me, I will return the favour."

"We're riveted." Ryker said blandly. The woman obviously had a stubborn streak a mile wide!

"Great!" She stated chirpily and held her empty right hand palm up. "Look at this hand here. Picture it loaded with all my wants and needs and deep, deep desires." She then raised her left hand, also palm up, "Now look at this hand, but this time picture it filled with a great big pile of gorilla shit. Now which one do you think I'm likely to get more of?" She moved her hands up and down as though she were balancing an invisible scale and continued, "Because past history dictates that I'm getting the primate turd. So thank you very much for your pep talk, but I think I'll pass. I will however, gratefully accept your kind offer of shelter for the night."

The silence in the room was resounding; Wardens just didn't speak like that. Nobody knew quite how to respond and to top it all off, the crazy woman was absolutely right.

"I like you." Axel stated, before addressing the room at large, "I like her."

So did Ryker. And that, he thought, was a mammoth problem.

SEVEN

Max turned the light off, plunging the pretty bathroom into darkness and simply rested her head against the cool tile. She had politely refused the offer of dinner, instead asking to be shown where she could sleep for the night. It was only seven or so in the evening but she hadn't been lying when she had said her head was spinning. She had been led up one flight of stairs onto a mezzanine level with numerous doors dotting the hall and overlooking what was likely the living room. The bedroom boasted a queen sized bed in the centre of the room, flanked by white-washed bedside draws with a matching tall boy dresser on the far wall. The room was decorated in navy blue and grey tones and was surprisingly homey with a conveniently attached ensuite where she now found herself. The throb in her temples pounded in direct counterpoint to her heartbeat and she sighed in relief at the blessed blackness and chill of the tiled room. She imagined the migraine was a combination of exhaustion, information overload, and confusion due to her latest predicament.

Guided only by the light filtering through the half closed bathroom door, she bent over the sink and let the cool water trickle through her fingers. Even that was a blessed relief. Cupping her hands with the intention of splashing the liquid over her face, she took stock of the shakiness of the digits. That didn't bode well and coupled with the migraine, Max knew a seizure was imminent and there would be no more staving it off. Although she detested being so vulnerable in a house full of strangers she at least now had a little privacy. If the seizures were to overtake her now she could be relatively recovered by morning and be in a better position to be on her way.

A full body spasm had her clutching at the porcelain sink in a vain attempt to steady herself. It was futile, for in the next instant her legs turned to jelly only to stiffen and jerk the moment she hit the hard floor. The next few minutes were a miserable exercise in fits and jerks and convulsions as her brain misfired in a series of waves. Max lay there alone, breathing hard and taking stock. She despised the seizures. They were a major weakness and she was constantly humiliated at being reduced to flopping around like a fish out of water every time she got too tired or too stressed or too angry.

She had been seventeen the first time she had succumbed to a seizure and she had been in a filthy alley in Sydney surrounded by the sleazy noises and seedy activities of the Cross. She had been absolutely terrified and had no clue what was happening. By chance, a good samaritan had come across her trembling body and instead of taking advantage of her vulnerable state, he had taken her to a local free clinic. After the usual probing questions and the obligatory call to child services they had run a series of tests and diagnosed her with epilepsy. They had explained it was a neurological condition caused by misfiring electrical impulses between her brain and her nerves – or neurons. The neurons would produce abrupt, uncontrolled spurts of electrical activity and a fit would ensue. They had prescribed her medication which she dutifully took to this day and had educated her on how to avoid the most common triggers.

Over the years Max had come to identify her triggers and unfortunately for her they were pretty unavoidable most of the time. It was a little hard to be stress free, avoid bright lights and harsh noises, and get adequate sleep when you were constantly on the run. She was able to manage the somewhat milder myoclonic seizures – they were brief shudders of her muscles and lasted only a second or two and they were pretty much a daily occurrence now anyway. Unfortunately, if she didn't listen to her body and acknowledge those early warning signs a more severe, and potentially very dangerous, tonic-clonic seizure would follow, as evidenced by her current position on the bathroom floor.

Max sat up gingerly giving her jaw a wiggle to release the residual stiffness. Her whole body was now one big tooth ache and she was thirsty as hell. At least she hadn't bitten her tongue ... but her bottom lip did feel a little swollen. Probing the offender, she groaned; *perfect!* She had bitten her lip and it was extremely unlikely it would go down by morning. Eyeing the deep bath tub Max almost whimpered from the desire to immerse herself in a vat of steamy hot water. Nothing would be more cathartic for her tense muscles. Unfortunately, if she had another episode she would likely drown herself. First item on the agenda in the morning would be bathing of some description but for now she would have to settle for some drugs and that big comfy-looking bed in the adjoining room. She only prayed her stupid brain would take this rare opportunity to actually sleep as opposed to the visions and nightmares that routinely plagued her.

EIGHT

After a restless but still a successful night sleep by her usual standards, Max basked for an indulgent thirty minutes under the hard spray of the shower. She then rummaged through her bag finding a semi-clean pair of faded jeans and a black tank that read 'Girls Rule'. Rubbing the towel over her wet hair and finger combing the now nearly black-looking damp locks, she considered herself done. She made her way down the spiral wooden staircase to her left rather than the straight stairs she had ascended the night before. Spiral stairs were cool. Her hosts had kept their word and no one had bothered her during the night but Max found herself nervous about her reception in the light of day. What did they expect from her? They had made it sound like there was a whole culture she was missing out on. Wardens and paladins and councils. And she still didn't understand the whole 'vitality' thing. Beyden had mentioned something about controlling her abilities and although she still didn't trust them fully, she was very interested to learn more.

Her powers had scared her on more than one occasion in the past. With no knowledge of where they came from or what they were precisely, the first few years after her 'awakening' had been a series of disasters in trial and error. She had hurt people on more than one occasion, destroyed property and damaged the landscape. After one particularly bad incident where she had almost drowned a wannabe mugger, she had come to realise her powers were closely linked with her emotions. Horrified at what she had nearly done she had spent the next few months in anger management, meditation and yoga classes. It was at the latter where she had met Daiki, a Japanese sensei who had taken her under his wing. After four months she had followed him to Japan and he had taught her how to defend herself and manage her emotions. Balance. It was all about balance. Where Daiki was actually a Kyoshi – an eighth dan black belt master – Max had now achieved the level of fourth dan black belt herself. In essence she could kick some major butt ... and also not cause rainstorms when she was sad anymore. Daiki had also been the one to present her with her sword. Lovingly named Joy after Charlemagne's sword *Joyuese*, the tanto knife was a type of Japanese short sword, single-edged. It was traditionally carried by the samurai as a last line of defence if their katana, or samurai sword, failed. Max found it a rather fitting weapon as she wielded it for that exact same purpose. She had the dagger on her possession as per usual but under the circumstances of being a good guest, had decided to keep it sheathed in her boot.

Making her way towards the wonderful aroma wafting through the home, Max found herself awed once again by the sheer magnificence of the structure. Not only was the architecture beautiful but so was the décor. Deep rich earthy colours of greens and blues and browns made up the majority of the furnishings and the walls were dotted with a mixture of abstract and realism artworks. It all somehow worked to give the huge open spaces a feeling of warmth and welcome. She followed her nose to the kitchen and determined the wonderful smell was emanating from the stove top where Cali was cooking thick, fluffy pancakes. Max felt her stomach rumble. She hadn't eaten since lunch time the day before. The other woman must have heard her yearning tummy for she turned and waved the spatula in greeting.

"Good morning."

If she could have a plate of those pancakes then it would be a very good morning indeed, Max thought. So she smiled, "Morning."

Cali motioned to the coffee machine. "Help yourself. The boys will be in soon. They're just finishing up their morning run."

Max didn't really like coffee but she didn't want to be rude so she thanked her and made a very weak, heavy on the milk and sugar, mug of the caffeinated beverage. Cali raised her eyebrows at the fourth teaspoon of sugar but didn't comment. "So you're in here cooking and doing the woman's work while the big manly men are outside working on their muscle mass?"

Cali chuckled and shook her head, "Not at all. We work on a roster system. Tuesday's I do breakfast. Besides, I've already had my workout in the weights room."

Max had noticed the other woman's incredible physique in what looked to be skin tight yoga shorts and a loose singlet top that had seen better days. Max sighed in envy. Her legs really were endless.

"Are you checking me out?"

Max raised her gaze and shrugged unapologetically, "Maybe." The bawdy laugh that followed had Max's own lips twitching. Cali clearly hadn't taken any offense. She finished with the last of the batter and placed the final pancakes under a covered plate. She picked up her own coffee and tilted her head towards the window behind the sinks.

"You want to check something out? Take a gander at that."

Max walked over and stood next to the blonde amazon. Her jaw unhinged. Outside were five half-naked, sweaty, panting Gods. All the men were dressed in either tracksuit pants or cotton shorts, running shoes ... and nothing else. Clearly they had been exerting themselves as their chests were pumping up and down in a frenzied rhythm, beads of moisture running over corrugated abs only to disappear beneath damp waistbands.

Then they started to stretch.

"Do they do this every day?" She asked absently.

"Yes. Every. Single. Day." Cali answered, eyes also glued to the erotic show.

"I bet you cook a lot of pancakes." They looked at each other then and burst into shared laughter. It felt good to laugh and relax. Max had almost forgotten what it was like.

Cali leaned against the sink companionably, "You know, sometimes they come inside like that. Just bypass the shower and sit right down at this table here, naked and sweaty."

Max held up her hands in a classic 'I surrender' gesture. "Please, enough! My heart can't take anymore." Cali continued to smile but began to eye her critically and Max had to stop herself from fidgeting under the knowing stare.

"Rough night?" She asked.

Max shrugged casually even though she felt anything but. She knew what Cali saw; too-pale cheeks under black-rimmed blood-shot eyes and a slightly swollen bottom lip. She had cringed when she saw her own reflection in the mirror earlier. The seizures often left her pale and listless for the first twenty-four hours or so. But she didn't exactly carry an arsenal of make-up with her, it just wasn't a priority, so there was nothing she could do to fix her appearance. Not wanting to invite further questions, Max replied offhandedly;

"First night in a new bed and all that." She was saved from additional interrogation by the slamming of a heavy door and a stampede of testosterone. Cali, bless her soul, had not been lying. The men descended *en masse*, no longer breathing hard but still shirtless and damp. Up close like this their bodies looked carved from stone with intriguing dips and valleys that had Max's fingers tingling with the need to touch. It also had her wishing she hadn't lost her sketch book when she fled from Budapest. They were such fodder for her graphic novels! She noted that a couple of them had faded tattoos gracing their left forearms, almost as if they had decided to get them removed or something. Max thought it very odd that they were all in the exact same position, although she couldn't make out the designs they all seemed to be patterns of some sort. She received a series of 'mornings' as if her presence was an everyday occurrence.

The next few minutes were a whirlwind of coffee-making, table-setting, and pancake-stacking. Max found herself seated at the table between Cali and Axel, her plate covered in bacon, maple syrup and pancakes and was horrified to find herself blinking back tears. She couldn't even recall the last time she had shared a home cooked meal with people who welcomed her.

"You look like shit."

Wait, what? Max looked up only to find Ryker staring directly at her. Was he talking to her? "Are you talking to me?"

He nodded and drank down half a bottle of water in one swallow, "Yes. You look like shit."

Max gasped in outrage. Although she didn't fancy herself as particularly pretty, she still had enough feminine pride to feel insulted down to her bones. Ignoring the stunned, amused and resigned faces around

the table she glared back. "Well you don't exactly look …"
She trailed off feebly as she took in his magnificent chest,
chiselled jaw and midnight hair. Damn the man – he was
absolutely perfect! Her stupid tongue wouldn't let her
form the lie so instead she went on the defensive. "How
do you know I look like shit? You only just met me! For
all you know, this is just my face!" She continued, "And
will you please put a shirt on? It's hardly hygienic. I'm
trying to eat here!"

Dark eyebrows arched over compelling brown eyes as
he smirked and completely ignored her, "What happened
to your lip?"

So arrogant! Max thought. She wanted to smack the
arrogance right off his face … and then kiss him all better.
What was it about this guy that pushed all her buttons?
She'd sooner die than admit that to him of course so she
answered sweetly;

"Last night when I went to bed, I thought of you as I
pleasured myself. I sank my teeth into my lip in order to
stifle my screams of ecstasy." She turned to Axel who was
grinning in appreciation, "I'm thoughtful like that."

Snickers and good-natured ribbing followed –
although Ryker didn't seem to appreciate her particular
brand of humour. Perhaps he had some sort of blunt
object shoved up his arse? Maybe she would ask him
about it one day. His narrowed gaze suggested that
perhaps today was not that day.

"You're so pale you're nearly translucent; the bags
under your eyes are so black they look like you've
rimmed them in boot polish; and your hands are shaking
so much you can barely hold your fork." He pointed out
emotionlessly. "You're running on fumes."

"Well, perhaps if you'd stop insulting me and let me
consume this wonderful breakfast, I could put something
in the tank."

Darius, ever the diplomat, jumped into the conversation, "He's not referring to your diet, although I'm sure you would benefit from a few good square meals. He means your vitality is low. You are worn thin Max."

Max frowned, "I still don't understand what you mean by vitality."

"It's the energy we paladins produce. To us, it's a by-product of everyday life – like carbon dioxide is the by-product of breathing. To wardens, it's the energy needed to upkeep your domain. It's taxing and you need to replenish it regularly." Beyden explained helpfully, munching on a pancake.

"And paladins do that by sharing this excess vitality that they produce naturally?" Max recited the information from the previous evening.

"Correct." Darius said, "You need to use us to recharge yourself." He held out a tanned arm, "I offer myself freely."

Max cringed back and held up a hand, "Please, no. You're going to make me lose my appetite."

"It's a natural thing Max." Lark assured her softly.

She snorted. "Maybe in your world. In my world people don't go around sucking out other people's life force."

"That's not ..." Darius began but Max cut him off.

"Please Darius, can you just drop it? I really appreciate all that you've done. But I need baby steps here. An overwhelmed Max does not a happy Max make. Besides," she continued, "I thought you said yesterday that I was pumping out this vitality in waves? How can I be doing that and yet not have enough at the same time?"

"You were – and still are – leaking vitality. It's practically seeping from your pores. Your element is probably excessively healthy everywhere you go but it is incredibly draining on you." Lark answered helpfully.

"I'm leaking?" She couldn't help scrutinising her body and patting down her arms. "How am I leaking?"

"It's because you have no control. You're fucking clueless!"

Ryker's harsh words were like a bucket of cold water. She pushed her half-eaten plate away, her appetite now completely gone. "Well this fucking clueless woman is no longer your fucking problem." She stood. "Thank you all again. I truly appreciate it but I think I'll take my leave now."

Lark rushed to stand. "You can't leave Max."

"No. You definitely can't leave." Darius intoned, frowning at Ryker in disapproval.

Max raised her chin, "Actually I can. You're not the boss of me and you said I wasn't a prisoner, so …"

Lark touched her arm in comfort even as assured her, "You're not a prisoner, Max."

"Absolutely not." Darius agreed. "You are, however, a warden and you need help, education, and training. You need to be introduced into our society. You need to be taught control, to learn your true potential. You need to form your own Order and bond yourself to your own paladins. It is your birthright."

"Well, I assume none of that is achievable in the next few minutes?" Max queried. "No? Well then, if you don't mind I think I'll go stretch my legs. Maybe leak some more nature-juice out of my eyeballs or something." And so saying, she marched from the room and out the back door where she took a deep breath and raised her face to the sky.

****

"You look like shit? Really Ryker? You look like shit? What were you thinking? Have you learned nothing living with me and Diana?" Cali asked furiously.

Ryker had to force himself not to fidget under Cali's frigid, feminine stare. Hell yes, living with the two female paladins had taught him a lot about how to deal with women. He knew never to ask if it was that time of the month, even if it was. He knew never to say their outfit looked 'fine', even if it did. And he definitely knew to never, ever tell them they looked like shit. Glancing around the room he noted the disapproving looks on every face and sighed tiredly. He was fairly ashamed of himself. He hated the look of hurt that had flashed over the warden's face and he certainly hadn't wanted to upset her to the point where she stopped eating. He had the feeling she could use all the decent meals she could get.

He had tossed and turned all night, plagued with thoughts and unwanted images of their strange guest. When she had asked to be shown to her room, Ryker wasn't sure she would even make it up the stairs, she had looked that unwell. He figured a decent night's sleep and a meal or two would do her wonders – and a vitality exchange of course, not that he planned on volunteering for the task. He wasn't that thrilled that some of the others had offered the evening before and again today, but he wasn't officially their Captain so they could do as they pleased. It wasn't that he wanted the warden to go without such fundamental energy but he just didn't want it going on in his home. This place was his sanctuary, his refuge, his place of peace and somehow, someway over the years it had become that for the other knights living there too. He intended to maintain his haven for himself and for his fellow soldiers for as long as humanly possible. Having any warden around was not conducive to peace in his opinion and he knew for a fact that this one female warden in particular was going to be a total nightmare.

Having said that, when he had walked in and seen Max standing in his kitchen still pale, still exhausted, and sporting a freshly bruised lip he had seen red. He had wanted to gather her up and kiss her lip. He wanted to feed her and hold her until she felt safe and fell asleep. He just plain wanted to make her all better ... and that just plain pissed him off. What was it about the female that managed to barge past his strongly erected barriers with no more than a single look from those incredible eyes of hers? He still knew nothing about her except for the obvious fact that she was a warden. That in and of itself should have had him running in the opposite direction. So instead of voicing his concern over her sick and vulnerable state, he had gone on the offensive and acted like a total prick so no one would suspect his true inclinations.

"Ryker! Are you listening to me?" Cali demanded.

He sighed again, "Yes, Cali. I'm listening. I'm sorry, okay?"

Cali snorted, "It's not me you need to apologise to. It's Max."

Not a chance in hell, Ryker thought to himself. He had a feeling she would like that a little too much. "I'm not apologising to the woman. It was the truth ... she does look terrible."

"She looks terrible because she is running on fumes both physically and emotionally if I'm reading her right. And has been for some time." Beyden chimed in, pushing his half-eaten plate to the side. Now Ryker knew he was in trouble, Beyden never left a meal unfinished. For a lean guy the man packed away food like it was going out of fashion. He was constantly munching on something from the time he rose in the morning until he crashed at night. Even then, Ryker often heard him up in the middle of the night raiding the refrigerator. Ryker had no idea where he put it all.

Despite being a bottomless pit, he was a good man to have at your back. Ryker had known him for over ten years now and he had been crashing at the camp for almost eight of them. He was soft spoken and humble and didn't often get involved in the politics of their world. But he was as observant as he was perceptive so when he chose to contribute, Ryker always listened – even if he didn't want to hear it.

"What makes you so sure it isn't all an elaborate act?"

Beyden's look was full of scorn. "That woman's face is an open book. I don't think she could lie to save her life. She may have dodged answering certain questions last night, but she never outright lied ... and you know it." The look Beyden gave him was reproachful, "You can read people better than anyone else in this room. So tell me; is she lying?"

Dammit! Beyden was absolutely correct, he was good at reading people. And not in the same quiet, attentive way Beyden was either. Ryker's domain was life itself. Although he couldn't see auras or manipulate a person's body to the extent of a warden, his element offered certain advantages when it came to interacting with his fellow humans. He was quite empathic and could pick up on the small bursts of energy produced by feelings, thoughts and emotions. Each one had a certain feel or taste to them and deceit was very distinct. It was bitter, always so bitter no matter how accomplished the liar was. Max had tasted like cinnamon.

He fucking loved cinnamon.

"She hasn't been untruthful yet." He admitted, responding to Beyden's direct question.

"Yet? Don't qualify it Ryker. We've hardly given her a chance to share her story. I don't know how or why but that woman is completely ignorant of her origins. She really does need our help." The man's amber eyes were earnest and Ryker always felt they were a direct reflection of his own domain; the beasts.

"But that is just my point. How is that even possible? How is she still alive if she didn't know about paladins? It doesn't add up."

"I agree." Axel was drinking milk straight from the carton again and Ryker waited for the inevitable explosion. Darius hated that particular nasty habit of the paladin of fire. He felt it was uncouth. Darius really was the gentleman of the group and had his work cut out for him in keeping them all honest. It appeared Darius wasn't rising to the bait today however, for he didn't even blink an eye. The little red head must have made quite the impression on his oldest friend as well.

"You agree?" Ryker addressed Axel, relieved to finally have one ally at the table.

Axel crushed the now empty carton with one hand, "Yep. I totally agree. But I don't care." He shrugged those heavy shoulders of his and threw a wicked look around the table, "I like her."

"You don't care because you like her?" Ryker was incredulous.

"Why are you surprised Ry?" Cali asked. "Did you see the breasts on the woman? I mean, jeez, talk about a handful."

"Cali!" Darius finally seemed fit to partake.

"What?" The female paladin was completely unrepentant. She turned to Axel, "Am I right?"

"Cali, my love. You are, as always, unequivocally correct."

Darius was still frowning, "When are you going to grow up?"

Axel rocked backwards precariously on his chair like the true rebel he was, "Now why would I want to go and do something like that?"

Ryker could feel a headache threatening and it wasn't even nine in the morning yet. Sometimes he felt like he was playing child care teacher and other times he thought maybe he was a zoo keeper. Ryker usually appreciated Axel's wry humour and dry wit. When he had moved in just three years ago he had brought a much needed levity to their little tribe of misfits. On this occasion however, Ryker was tempted to reach across the table and sucker punch the other paladin in the head. He shouldn't have been looking, let alone commenting on the chest area of any warden and the fact that Ryker himself had barely been able to drag his own eyes from Max's luscious breasts really was not the point.

"Enough. We need to sort this mess out. I want her questioned – properly this time. Then I want to contact the Local Warden Council and inform them we have a stray. They can get in touch with the International Domain Council and deal with her as they see fit."

"But Ry, don't you think we should see to her health first? She needs vitality." Lark stated.

"The Local Council will sort that out. It's their job after all. It's certainly not ours. Unless any of you have suddenly changed your mind about being in an Order overnight?" Silence met his question. "That's what I thought."

"I still think we should learn more about her first before we throw her to the wolves. Maybe just a couple of days for her to rest up, gain our trust. She seems skittish to me." Beyden sure was talkative today, Ryker thought. Not even twenty-four hours and the woman was already causing dissension in his ranks.

She definitely had to go.

Pushing his chair back, he stood to his impressive height of six foot four. "Look, we don't need some stray warden hanging around, bringing trouble to our doorstep. We've all had enough of it to last a lifetime!" Ryker gave them all one last stern look. "She goes. This is not up for debate."

NINE

Ryker hadn't even bothered with a shower before seeking the miniature warden out. He had pulled his long sleeve grey tee shirt back on though, more to conceal the faded coat of arms on his forearm than from any sense of modesty. It was his turn to ask the questions and he wasn't giving the woman any new ammunition to turn the tables. He was just about to follow her grand exit through the door off the kitchen when he caught sight of her through the windows behind the sink. She sure was stunning in a short, pixie kind of a way. She wouldn't be gracing any catwalks in Milan given the length of her legs but the whole package still worked for him. That hair of hers was now shining brightly in the early morning sun and Ryker could make out the red tones easily unlike the night before. She was slender but curvy in all the places a man wanted a woman to be curvy. Although her face was marred with lines of exhaustion and smudges of illness, it was still arresting. Some of that was due to those blue-green eyes of hers, but most of it was that crooked smile and the vibrancy she exuded. She certainly had a way about her.

Ryker frowned as he studied her face more closely. Was she beginning to look better? She didn't look quite so pale anymore and had some colour in her cheeks. The dark circles under her eyes appeared to lighten and the slight tremors he had seen in her hands were now practically undetectable. Even as he continued to watch her the answer seemed to unfold in front of him, although he didn't know if he could trust what he was seeing. She was walking around the garden at a leisurely pace touching a tree here and stroking a flower there. She bent down to pick up fallen leaves and gave a dandelion husk freedom by blowing it off a fingertip. She even picked up a spider and let it crawl over the back of her hand before returning it to its web. He could see her lips moving and although he couldn't make out the words he knew she was talking to the nature all around her.

She was actively communicating with her domain ... Amazing!

She appeared to be unwaveringly focused in her task and although her power was a thing of beauty to behold, it was also a danger. It was like she had no real concept of the power she was exuding or even what she was receiving in return. He had no doubt she was acting on pure instinct given the naiveté inherent in her actions. In the past, before the Great Massacre fifty years ago, such displays of power were quite common. But now wardens were more passive in their roles, preferring to act as conduits and guardians rather than catalysts. Ryker knew some of them still participated directly with their domains – some of them couldn't seem to help it, especially those very few powered by life itself. It was a little hard to ignore the whole world, after all. Still, he was pretty sure that what Max was doing was something altogether different.

"Stalking?"

Ryker jumped. He was so absorbed by the spectacle in front of him he had been completely unaware of his surroundings and Darius had managed to get the jump on him, "What?" He asked.

"You've been standing here staring out the window for ten minutes. I was just wondering if you had decided to stalk our new guest."

"Of course not! No." Ryker gestured with his chin in Max's direction. "What do you make of that?"

Darius frowned, "What am I looking at?"

"The warden!" Ryker gestured impatiently.

"She's playing with a ladybug. So what?" Darius answered before stilling and leaning closer to the window, "Wait a minute ... what *is* she doing?"

"Recharging."

There was a heartbeat of silence before Darius replied dubiously, "Recharging? Like vitality recharging?"

"Yep."

"That's not possible." Darius's response was swift.

"It shouldn't be possible. I've certainly never heard of it happening before, but that's absolutely what she's doing. She's asking the trees, the earth, even the insects, if she can borrow from them. When they give her permission, she takes just a tiny amount of their life force." He turned to Darius front on, "This is how she's survived on her own all this time without a paladin ... She's Life."

"She's Life? What do you mean?" Darius asked, but immediately answered his own question. "Her domain is Life?"

"Yes." Ryker answered simply. He knew Darius would understand the significance of this revelation.

"Are you sure? Ryker, there aren't many life wardens around and certainly not many females. Hell, I only know of a handful."

"There are twelve wardens connected to the domain of life scattered around the globe and only two of them are women." He should know. Being a paladin allied with life, he was constantly hounded by those wardens to join their Orders. Life paladins were not as rare as the wardens but it was pretty darn close and every warden wanted at least one paladin in their Order that mirrored their own domain. Ideally, they wanted more than one for when the vitality came from the same elemental source, the more powerful the warden became.

"Shit!" Darius swore harshly — well harshly for him anyway. Darius rarely cursed. "We have to report her to the IDC immediately."

The IDC was the International Domain Council and was the governing body of their people. It was comprised of seven Ambassadors, one warden from each of the seven domains of nature. They were all very old and all very powerful. They lived all over the world and congregated at the same location once a month to discuss business, uphold rules, pass judgements and address issues brought to their attention from paladin and warden citizens. The IDC acted as the judge and jury of their society; the Rangers were the executioners, but thankfully Ryker saw no need to include them. Ryker had met with the IDC numerous times in the past and although they were mostly fair they were also very inflexible and very out-dated in their thinking. Sometimes the old ways were not always the best ways in Ryker's humble opinion. But he was nothing more than a modest soldier, so what did he know? He did know that he wouldn't be informing them of Max's presence quite yet though.

"Not yet." He told Darius. "We don't report her yet."

Infinitely composed, Darius merely raised his eyebrows, "Any reason?"

"My gut."

Darius nodded. "That's good enough for me. I'll spread the word to the others." The friendly slap to his back forced him forward a step. Damn, that son of a bitch was strong!

"So, she was telling the truth after all, huh?" Cali voiced from behind.

Dammit! He hadn't heard her approach either! Ryker grunted and figured that was enough of a response. He should have known better. Bloody females!

"You going to apologise?" Cali asked.

Ryker merely raised his eyebrows at her to convey his feelings. The water paladin had been living with him for over fifteen years. She had been one of the first castoffs he had offered refuge to so talking wasn't really necessary anymore.

Cali snorted and shook her head, "Of course you're not. What was I thinking?" She leaned her hip against the sinks as she too watched the warden at work with narrowed, speculative ice-blue eyes. "Interesting." She remarked.

"Have you ever seen anything like this before?" He asked. Cali was originally from Sweden and had lived all over the globe before settling in Australia, perhaps she had come across something similar before.

"Not even remotely." She answered decisively.

"What about you?" He asked Darius when he felt him once more by his side. As well as being the oldest paladin in the house at over a thousand years old, Darius was also their resident scholar, although Lark was fairly close to having him beat in the book-reading department. The two always seemed to have a book in their hands whenever they weren't training or at the Lodge, but their tastes varied significantly. Where Darius was into the non-fiction and historic side of things, Lark enjoyed reading fiction in all its make believe glory. He read everything from crime to romance to sci-fi. He always said he had enough of the real world living in it every day so when he relaxed, he wanted to get as far away from reality as he could. Ryker couldn't really blame the man given his past.

Darius was staring at Max and appeared to be just as spellbound as himself and Cali. "No, never. And I haven't read about it either but you know so many of the *Warden Chronicles* were lost during the Great Massacre."

Ryker grunted; a great many things had been destroyed during the Great Massacre.

"It must have something to do with her domain. The fact that life is hers to see and hear and shape. Perhaps it is responding to the call of its master?" Cali suggested.

"Maybe." Ryker conceded, "But you know being a warden or a paladin of life doesn't literally give the keeper powers over life as the name implies. It's more of a spiritual and physical element – the mind and body."

"I know. But what other explanation is there?"

Ryker had no idea, he was completely stumped. Given that Life Wardens were such a minority, he didn't have much to do with them and didn't know any he felt comfortable enough to ask. But he did know someone who might be able to shed some light on the situation.

"Where's Diana?" He asked looking at Darius. The other knight looked startled by the abrupt shift in topic.

"How would I know? I don't keep tabs on the woman." He replied stiffly.

Yes, you do, Ryker thought to himself but knew better than to say so out loud. Instead he turned to Cali, "Do you know where she is at the moment?"

Cali nodded. "She's in New York working with the FBI on a serial murder case. You want me to call her?"

Ryker eyed the red head who was now sitting on the ground and running her fingers through the green grass; she smiled and laughed at something that apparently only she could hear. Yes, they definitely needed Diana here. Not only was she a seasoned warrior and associated to the domain of death, her previous liege had been a Warden of Life. If anyone would know the eccentricities of a Life Warden, it would be Diana. "Yeah. Call her. And tell her I want her back here ASAP."

"It will probably take a few days or more for her to get here. I didn't think you wanted the warden around for that long?"

"I've changed my mind ... she's not going anywhere."

TEN

Max had managed to steal about an hour of 'me time' before the Goliath sought her out. He was still in those black cotton shorts that displayed his strong calves but had covered his nipple-pierced chest with a long sleeved tee. It didn't really do much to calm her over active imagination, she already had enough material to keep her internal fires burning for years to come. Why did the man have to be so sexy? Well, at least until he opened his mouth anyway, then he turned into a total douche bag. Who tells a woman their face looks like shit? A man who's lookin' for a solid arse kickin', that's who! She had a feeling he was sorely in need of one and lucky for him, Max was the perfect person to deliver.

She had felt his eyes on her through the window almost like a physical caress and had to force herself not to squirm under his heated gaze. She had no idea how long he had been watching her before she actually noticed because she had been so absorbed getting acquainted with the life all around her. It was absolutely glorious here – so much natural beauty and so many critters! She had always loved just sitting and playing with the environment and she supposed now she knew why. She was like a steward of nature or something. She could talk to the trees and whisper to the oceans and joke with the animals. It was just something she could always do and she had taken it for granted that it was a normal thing until she had made the mistake of talking about it. Waking up with no memory had meant she didn't realise what was socially accepted as normal and what was just plain fucking weird! Turns out, most people couldn't bring a plant back to life by touching it, go figure! Which was probably why Max was feeling such a kinship with the people inside that house. To them, it was normal as well. Too bad tall, dark and handsome was also tall, dark and dumb!

"What are you doing?"

That was how he was going to start this conversation? Where was the apology? Max ignored him as she picked up a slater bug and watched it unfurl out of its protective ball. She loved watching the dozens of tiny little legs move under that grey body as it traversed the back of her hand. The little guy noticed how his legs tickled one particular area and he made sure to run back and forth over the same spot. Max chuckled at the cheeky little thing. She suspected most people would be very surprised to learn just how smart most living creatures were. Everything had its own unique personality. Insects had the best sense of humour for example, purposely dropping onto humans and clinging to their hair or clothes in order to achieve screams of terror or disgust. They were devilish little fiends, thriving on the chaos that they – a tiny little bug – could cause to the dominant species on the planet. They thought it was freaking hilarious!

"Max? I asked what you were doing."

Ryker's voice sounded closer to her this time and she realised he had taken a seat next to her on the grass, knees bent, arms resting across them. She moved her eyes to look at him, "I heard you. I'm not deaf. Like, take for instance back in the kitchen when I heard you tell me I looked like shit."

Max felt the petite spark of outrage from the little beetle still on her hand. Although she rarely communicated in actual words with animals she often felt impressions and emotions. She was very empathic. Mr Slater Bug then proceeded to generously give her a minute burst of energy, just as the spider and the leaves and the dandelion had when she had whined to them about the paladin's crass comment. They were all just so thoughtful and Max had thanked each and every one of them for their kindness. She also had a feeling that Ryker may experience a deluge of spiders in his bed tonight ... oops.

Ryker's massive shoulders moved up and down with the depth of his sigh, "I didn't mean it like it sounded. I was just ... concerned."

"If that's how you express your concern, then please stop concerning yourself with me." She responded.

"I wish that was an option, believe me. However, I fear it no longer is."

There was that slight British accent again, Max thought. It almost sounded like it came from snobby upper class England somewhere. But surely a man who looked like he had done hard time couldn't have had a stuffy upbringing, could he? Perhaps there was more to the man than meets the eye, Max pondered, perhaps he is a robot in disguise, she sang to herself and made herself laugh. She was so funny!

Ryker, not being a party to her *Transformers* analogy, peered at her critically. "Why are you laughing?"

"It's a joke. Don't worry, I'm sure you wouldn't get it." His frown dipped lower. Had she offended him by proposing he had no sense of humour? Men were so sensitive sometimes!

"Can you focus for a minute please and answer one question?"

Max rolled her eyes, "Fine." He turned and faced her front on and Max had to force her eyes away from the huge scar that formed a trench down one side of his face. She was itching to stroke it.

"You said you had no idea what vitality or recharging was until last night ..." he let the sentence trail off.

Max nodded, "That's correct."

He pointed to the beetle on her hand, "So what do you think you were doing just now?"

Max frowned, not understanding the question and cooed down at Bert. She decided that name suited him best. "I don't understand what you mean."

He was staring at her intensely as if gauging her sincerity. Let him look, she had nothing to hide. Well, okay, that wasn't exactly true. She actually had plenty to hide but not about this. He must have been satisfied with her innocence for his harsh features softened somewhat as he said;

"Max, you were recharging just now."

He seemed very genuine but he was wrong. "No I wasn't. I don't know how. This little guy, Bert, just sent out a flash of energy and I absorbed it, that's all. It's actually not that hard to make use of the free radicals in the air. I can't absorb much and it's nowhere near as efficient as eating and sleeping, but sometimes I use the spare energy produced by things around me to give me a little boost."

"Max, I can tell you really believe that but that is essentially what vitality is. It is energy in its purest form. I have never heard of a warden being able to renew their vitality through means other than a paladin before but I have no doubt that's what you were doing."

Max stilled, "What?" That couldn't be possible. She wasn't taking from these generous creatures and giving nothing back was she? "Am I hurting them? The bugs, the trees? Am I taking from their lives?" Max was absolutely horrified. She placed Bert back on the ground and scooted away from him.

"Easy. I don't think you're hurting them, you would have realised that by now. And the amount of their life force you're taking is so miniscule, it's probably of no consequence to them."

"Probably?" That wasn't good enough for Max. She had no idea what she had been doing all these years. It had been so natural to her, so instinctive, she hadn't questioned it. Yet another example of what she had taken for granted in her amnesiac state. She always gave back, couldn't seem to help herself, but the thought of doing the opposite left her feeling a little queasy. She felt a heavy weight on her arm and looked down to see Ryker's large hand.

"Easy now. It's fine. And uh, Bert seems fine too. See?"

He pointed to Mr Slater who was furiously moving his little legs in her direction in an attempt to comfort her no doubt. They were both being nice to her and that only made her feel worse. She felt the same strange soothing sensation with Ryker's touch as she had when Lark or Beyden touched her and she wanted to bask in it. Looking into his chocolate eyes, Max made her decision to cooperate more fully with the man. He had piss-poor interpersonal skills but perhaps his knowledge would make up for it.

"Will you teach me?" She asked. The man looked like he was making a not altogether palatable decision but he answered simply nonetheless.

"Yes."

ELEVEN

Max had dusted her butt off and allowed Ryker to lead her into the house where the others didn't even have the good manners to pretend they hadn't been eaves dropping. Beyden had suggested they adjourn to the living room and she was now comfortably sitting in a soft armchair surrounded by cushy pillows. It made her want to curl up and nap.

"What happened to your lip?" The blunt question was unexpected and made her jump. So much for the considerate, well-spoken man she had been conversing with outside. Maybe he was bipolar. Or maybe he had been pacifying her so she would drop her guards. She sniffed, *amateur!*

"What happened to your face?" The whole room froze and Ryker's brown eyes darkened almost to black. The serial killer had returned. She raised her eyebrows, "What? You're allowed to ask me personal, invasive questions but I'm not allowed to return the favour?"

He took one step in her direction before Darius blocked his path, "Not now Ry. We need to figure this situation out. Max, maybe you could try to be a little less combative ..."

"Me?" She poked herself in the chest. "He started it."

"So be the bigger person and end it." Beyden suggested, effectively cooling her jets. She nodded her head once and he smiled.

"Ryker thinks I'm recharging on my own." She may as well change the subject. She didn't want to discuss her health problems with anyone.

"We know. That's what we think too." Darius said.

"But I don't know how I'm doing it. It's not deliberate." She added hastily. It was imperative they believe her.

"It must have something to do with your domain. It's very important as well as being very powerful. It's actually the strongest element and I think you have somehow managed to adapt and evolve your abilities in order to survive without a paladin." Cali explained her theory.

Max frowned, "What do you think my domain is?"

The six knights looked around at each other as if having a silent conversation before Ryker finally piped up; "Life."

"Life?" Max repeated, ruminating on that for a few minutes. It kind of made sense, she could see and feel and hear so many things and was able to manipulate living beings. But somehow it just didn't seem quite right. "What makes you think that?"

"When we watched you earlier, you were actively communicating with your domain, with all the life outside." Darius answered.

"That doesn't really make sense. I was interacting with the animals and the trees. Why can't Earth or Beast be my element?" She asked.

"Beast Wardens can maintain the health and happiness of animals only. Their burden is to ensure species don't become extinct, to ensure the diversity of the animal kingdom remains and to ensure harmony is kept between the animals. They cannot speak to the earth or listen to the wind or create fire, for example." Beyden explained.

"So each domain is distinct?"

"Yes and no." Cali said. "You see, each element naturally overlaps with the others. The earth cannot be maintained without water for example. Air Wardens can control fog but so can Water Wardens given fog is made up of moisture. But each domain still remains unique with its own signature and its own peculiarities. Only a warden of each domain can see those signatures and hear those peculiarities. That's the intimate relationship we were telling you about last night. It is instinctive, something that is burned into a warden's DNA."

"So a Life Warden encompasses every domain?" Shit, Max thought, maybe she was totally badass!

"Not really. The element of life refers more specifically to humans rather than all things that are alive. It is an element of the body and the spirit. Life Wardens are very empathic. They can see auras, feel pain, and identify illness and weakness. They are renowned healers and are all about balance at their core. Their job is to absorb the pain of the people of the world and to give comfort in return. It is the heaviest burden of all the wardens, which is why they are regarded with such high esteem. It is also why they are the most powerful in their abilities." Ryker explained, looking serious.

"What about Bert?" She asked. "He's not human."

Darius frowned, "Who's Bert?"

Ryker's lips twitched in the beginnings of a smile. Boy, he would be even more lethal when he smiled, Max bet. "Bert is a slater bug. That's the overlap Cali was referring to. He's not human but he is alive and he does have an aura. As an empathic Life Warden you can't help but be drawn to him as well. But your influence on him would be nowhere near the calibre of what you could do with a human."

Max nodded, feeling conflicted. It made sense but once again she was struck with that feeling of unease, like she was missing something. But she *was* empathic, they certainly had that right. Looks like she was a Warden of Life. She let herself sink into the soft cushions once again. Finally having a name for what she was after all these years was very liberating. The next step would be to figure out a way to control her abilities so she didn't feel like warmed up shit all the time and to figure out a way to stop the phantoms from trying to suck out her soul. Maybe she could even get a decent night's sleep!

"So what does this all mean?" She asked the room at large, not really sure what to do now. They all seemed on board with her re-education, even Ryker, who had seemed the most suspicious the night before.

"It means you're about to be very popular." Axel enthused, "When the LWC learns who you are, they will be all over you like a rash and unbound paladins will be tripping over their feet to be in your Order."

"I assume the term 'Order' refers to a group of paladins and a warden?"

"Yes, an Order is a fellowship of paladins who have been bound to a liege – their warden. They are often as tight-knit as a family. They live together and work together." Darius continued.

"So if you're all an Order, where is your Warden?" Her question was met forcefully with negative shakes of the head and grumbled 'no's'. Axel set the record straight by saying;

"None of us have a warden. We're all rejects. That's why we're all here mooching off Ryker." He jabbed his thumb in the direction of their designated, but apparently, unofficial leader.

Cali swung the leg she had crossed over her knee, kicking bad boy Axel in the shin. "Speak for yourself, loser." She stuck out her tongue to show she was only joking. "We are trainers down at the Lodge. That's what we call our local recruitment centre. Someone has to teach the newbies."

"And the fact that nobody would have any of us in their precious Orders had absolutely nothing to do with it. What is it they say? 'Those that can't do, teach'." Axel clearly wasn't interested in letting them all off the hook. The words were sarcastic and tinged with resignation. Perhaps this was a common point of contention between them and others in their society.

Max didn't care what their reputations were. To her they were heroes, finding her, offering her information and shelter. And to top it all off, they were serious eye candy. She knew Ryker had said that he would teach her earlier that morning, so she figured she had until the end of the day to gather as much information as she could. Now that she knew she responded to all the people out there in the world, she could begin to reconcile why she was so sensitive to pain and fear. It also explained why she always had so many bad dreams – it was her job to heal people from their pain by feeling and taking it into herself. But by the sounds of it she was supposed to replace it with something better. She didn't know if she had been doing that. Maybe she needed a paladin or two to help her.

"So I have to make a mini family with some paladins. How do I do that?"

Lark perched on the arm of her chair, "Usually a warden has a visceral reaction to a paladin, an immediate connection. Their paladin's presence should comfort, their touch should soothe, and their vitality should replenish. A connection can be manufactured through the bonding process but those Orders are not as cohesive as those with a natural kinship."

Max thought back to when she had first seen Lark, Axel and Darius the day before. She had thought they felt familiar to her but she couldn't figure out why. She also felt like she could trust them and when any of them touched her, including Ryker, she felt a soothing warmth. Was that what they were referring to? If so, why didn't they feel the connection as well?

"Usually a warden will form a bond with paladins of their own element, although an Order cannot be made up exclusively of one domain; they must be balanced. But a warden can recharge more efficiently and draw more power from a paladin who shares the same element." Darius explained unaware of her internal dialogue.

"Paladins are allied, as you say, to their own element too then?"

"That's right."

"So what is your element?" She asked Darius.

He leaned forward and spread his hands out in front of him. "Why don't you tell me?"

Max frowned, "Is this a test?"

"No ... well not really. But if you are a Life Warden like we all suspect then you should be able to see our auras and therefore should be able to link us to our elements."

"See your auras?"

"Do you see colours radiating around people or animals or anything living really? Probably around their head or their heart?" The question came from Ryker.

Max frowned. She saw colours radiating *from* people almost like a shadow of themselves, full length and human in shape. The colourful doppelganger had threads escaping in hundreds of directions and hundreds of different hues tethering people to other people, places and things. She always assumed it was the connections people made, the energy left behind from their actions as they moved from place to place and formed different relationships. The spectrum of colours she could see far bypassed the normal band of colours that were present in the real world. It hadn't taken her long to figure out that each person had their own unique and identifying colours and that emotions and actions often dictated the variances in the shades she observed. She was pretty adept at reading them now but she didn't choose to see them all the time – they gave her a migraine and made her go cross-eyed! In fact, she had kept that switch firmly off since she had met the paladins, only peeking at them all once last night to ensure they weren't chainsaw wielding murderers. She could only assume that was what Ryker was calling auras so she nodded and answered guardedly;

"I can see colours."

"Do you know how to interpret them?" He asked.

Max shrugged, feeling inexplicably shy. "I guess."

"Why don't you tell us what you see?" Darius invited.

Max kept her eyes on her fidgeting hands in her lap. "Don't wanna."

"Why not? It doesn't hurt does it?" Cali asked.

"No. I just ... It just seems rude is all." A chorus of chuckles met her response and she glared at all of them. The only person to not find her comment amusing was Ryker oddly enough. He was watching her carefully and if she wasn't mistaken there was now a spark of respect in his eyes that hadn't been there before. It was almost like he understood where she was coming from. She hated to invade people's privacy. It just didn't seem fair that she could peek into a stranger's body and perhaps see their secrets. It was bad enough that she couldn't always turn off her empath abilities which meant she could feel their emotions. It was definitely rude.

"I know it seems invasive but Darius has given you his permission. Please, tell us your impression." Ryker bade.

Max looked at Darius carefully, which really wasn't a hardship, the man was gorgeous! His hazel eyes were kind and open and he was smiling. She slowly flipped her internal switch and watched as his colourful shadow emerged next to him, it was translucent and Max could see through it to the bookcase beyond but it also had enough form that she could make out its features. They were a mirror to the man himself. Strands of colours threaded their way around the room, connecting him to the other paladins and one very bright golden thread streaked out the window to disappear in the distance over the ocean. His particular shades of threads were mostly muted blues, greys and silver and moved softly in the air as if in a breeze.

"You're Air." She stated simply and with certainty.

The man grinned like a proud papa and Max couldn't help but notice how much younger and carefree he looked when his eyes lit up with enthusiasm like that. She had the feeling that he was too often the serious one.

"What about me?" Cali asked, her head tilted to the side so that her straight golden hair fell like a waterfall off to the side. Sighing, Max focused her eyes. The woman's strands were a mixture of cool tones – hues of baby blues darkening through to navy. Her shadow-self seemed to float and move as if under water, light and buoyant. The woman also had a swimmer's physique with long, lean toned limbs and her skin was tanned to an even summer glow.

"Water."

"Two for two." Cali smiled. 'Your domain is definitely life. Your connection is to people."

Lark jumped up and raised his hand, "Do me, do me!"

"That's what he said." Max was startled when she and Cali spoke at the exact same time. They grinned at each other and Max couldn't help but feel that sense of familiarity again. Odd. Very odd.

"What about me? Huh, Max?" Lark was practically bouncing on the balls of his feet, the man seemed to have a boundless supply of energy. And he was always happy. It sort of creeped her out because she thought perpetual happiness was just unnatural but he was too charming and nice to be creepy. Max peered into his green eyes for a moment and swore she could almost feel the floor undulate beneath her feet. He was all greens, browns and tans and his ghostly visage pulsed like a heartbeat. Like the heartbeat of the earth perhaps? He certainly came across as easy going and down to earth ... and he smelled good, like fresh green grass.

"Earth."

Lark clapped, "Now do Beyden."

"My pleasure." She purred at the broad shouldered man with the tawny eyes. He blushed and Max wanted to put him in her back pocket and keep him. His threads reached far and wide and were thinner than the others. They were yellow and orange and pink and made her think of a tequila sunrise. The impression she got from him was more noise than smell or sense. It was like she could see a constant hum of sound surrounding his double and it flickered quickly in and out like humming bird wings. His domain must be a busy one, she thought, lots of creatures big and small. He was associated with the beasts.

"Dr Dolittle." He laughed and Max was glad she hadn't offended the gentle giant.

Axel was ranged in the armchair across from her, seemingly bored with the game but he did raise his eyebrows in silent challenge. His grin was wicked and he blew her a kiss. Oh, he was so naughty, this one was. Max opened her senses once more and was immediately struck by a wall of heat. It wasn't scalding but was a little too warm to be comfortable for long. As expected he was red and orange and even black here and there. His form shifted and danced like a flame caught in a draught. No wonder he was so hot blooded, Max thought, he was fire.

She decided to blow a kiss back, "You're hot stuff!" Axel saluted her in appreciation. Now for the proverbial elephant in the room. Was Max supposed to ask Ryker if she could read him too or were they all just supposed to pretend he wasn't there? She was very surprised when he broke the awkward silence by saying gruffly;

"Go ahead."

She would have been lying if she said she wasn't curious so she opened herself up one last time … and was glad she was sitting down. He was absolutely beautiful. He was all light and bright – lilacs, purples and whites. The colours radiated out from him luminously in total disregard of any semblance to order. It was like they just couldn't be contained, like they were too joyous to be confined and they would do as they pleased. His doppelganger stood just as tall and just as straight as the man but where the flesh and blood version was stoic and cold, the translucent version felt festive and warm and it's energy practically leaped toward her in delight. You could have knocked her over with a feather. Not in a million years would she have associated the dour hard-arse with life itself, death maybe, but not life.

"Something wrong?" He looked smug, conceited and superior all at once. He loved that she was flabbergasted, well she wasn't going to give him the satisfaction.

"Life calls to you." She stated and shrugged negligently, "I'm not surprised, it really suits you. You're so warm and compassionate and mild mannered. From the moment I met you I thought 'now here is a man who visits nursing homes and cuddles new born babies'. I always trust my instincts."

This produced a round of ribbing and jibes from the peanut gallery, Ryker's trademark scowl still firmly in place. Max cast her eyes around the room once more. "Earth, air, fire, water, humans and animals. Where's Death? Still sleeping?" She asked jokingly.

"Diana isn't here at the moment. Although she's a trainer like us, she also has other duties so she comes and goes as she pleases." Beyden replied casually.

"Oh, I was only joking. There really is a paladin allied to death living here too?" She received numerous nods. "So you are all from different domains. Is that normal? Seems like a fairly big coincidence ..."

"It's not common, no. But we are not a normal group of paladins."

She opened her mouth to delve into that subject deeper only to be cut off by Darius as he continued, "I think that's enough for the moment. We don't want to overload you. Why don't you take a break, maybe eat some lunch and we can talk more later, hmm?"

"But I have so many more questions! And breakfast was like half an hour ago." Max pointed out.

"Yes. I also have so many more questions." Ryker eyed Darius austerely.

Darius paid him no heed and Max realised they must be very used to each other and had likely been friends for a long time. Darius persisted, "They can wait. We're not going anywhere and neither are you. Besides, breakfast was almost three hours ago."

Max's stomach chose that moment to growl as if siding with the brown haired soldier. She hadn't really eaten much given she had been too busy being insulted. Still, she wasn't that faint from hunger that she hadn't caught what Darius had said, "What do you mean I'm not going anywhere? I said one night. It's been one night. I'm grateful for the information and maybe you could introduce me to some others like me? But I really need to be moving on."

"Consider our minds changed. You will stay here as our guest." Ryker commanded. Before she could object, rather vocally, Ryker strode over until he stood in front of her. "You need to learn control. You need to learn to shield yourself from your natural enemies. And you need to learn how to renew your energy the way you were born to. We can help you ... if you let us."

Max really, really wanted to let them but she was still scared to stay in the one place for too long. On the other hand, they were knights so who better to protect her if the phantoms did find her? A few days, maybe even a week and she could rest and be fully rejuvenated, armed with all the knowledge she would need. Perhaps she could even access her bank accounts and buy some new clothes, some new supplies. She might even be able to get some writing and drawing in. It was all so tempting.

"Max? Remember those instincts?" Cali coaxed.

Max nodded and the room seemed to exhale in relief. "Do you have any chocolate?" She asked.

TWELVE

Ryker didn't bother wrapping a towel around himself after he finished his cold shower. He was trying to use negative reinforcement to teach his stupid dick not to respond every time Max was in his vicinity. The chilly water had the desired effect and he was now hunting up a clean pair of khakis to wear to the Lodge. He hadn't been there in three days due to their guest and he really needed to spend some time there today to catch up on things. He had put everyone on a rotation so at least two of them were here at the same time rather than all of them being at the Lodge.

The past two weeks had been a trial in patience and fortitude for Ryker. The warden was proving to be a fun, sexy, delightful addition to the camp and he knew he wasn't the only one who thought so. He had watched as the others grew more and more attached to the woman; she and Cali were practically inseparable, with Cali offering her clothes and scented lotions and all other kinds of girly crap that made a woman look and smell amazing. Max had been incredulous when Cali had first offered her the use of her wardrobe, *'I'll look like a kid playing dress ups!'* she had exclaimed. Ryker chuckled at the memory – she had been absolutely correct. The clothes of the tall knight had to be rolled and tied in order for the short warden to even walk successfully, but damn if she didn't pull the look off.

Lark was in geek-book-buddy heaven! Turned out Max was a published author of a popular graphic novel series. Something to do with demons and an angel assassin or something. She had asked about borrowing a computer to access her bank accounts, get in contact with her publisher and maybe order in some supplies so she could do some work. She had explained that she was a graphic novelist but hadn't been able to work for months thanks to the chades. Thankfully Darius had been the one to make the mistake of responding; *'you write comic books?'* Her light eyes had darkened in a death glare that should have flayed the skin from his bones, *'They are not comic books. They are graphic novels!'* Apparently there was a big difference.

Poor Darius had been properly chastised and had scrambled after her for the next hour, hoping to regain her good opinion. Ryker snorted thinking of Darius and Beyden. Both of the knights had poorly concealed crushes on the red head. They were utterly smitten by her kindness, humour and courage. Ryker couldn't blame them but it was a distraction he was hoping they would get over as soon as Max was no longer under the same roof.

Axel was just as infatuated, but where Beyden and Darius trailed after her like lost puppies, Axel was more overt in his attraction. He was constantly making comments and eyeing Max like she was his favourite chew toy. And Max was lapping it up, flirting and charming the fire paladin with her wit and charisma. If Ryker didn't like Axel so much he would have cut out his tongue and removed his eyes by now.

And as for himself, well, he was just managing to keep it together. His eyes tracked her movements whenever she was in the same room, the sound of her voice was like freaking music to his ears, and he popped wood every damn time he saw her ... or smelt her ... or thought about her. He was officially in a living hell and he was beginning to like it. Which was as crazy as it was dangerous. He couldn't come to care for and fail another warden again. He just wouldn't survive it. But it was almost fucking impossible to stay distant when her vulnerabilities kept showing just as much as her strengths. He was a knight after all and it was his nature to protect those weaker than him.

Take last night for example. The scream had woken him from a fitful sleep and had his heart pounding in alarm even as he took the extra seconds to pull on a pair of pants and grab one of his sickles. The sound had been feminine and filled with terror. Racing into the hall, he followed the high-pitch sound straight to Max's room and grabbed the door handle, keeping low in case danger lurked on the other side. But a quick sweep of the room had revealed no immediate threat other than Max thrashing violently in the middle of the bed. She was obviously in the throes of a nightmare. He had heard whimpers and restless movements the previous four nights as well but hadn't mentioned anything in the light of day. Her nightmares were her own business just as his own were his.

He had been startled shitless though when her eyes popped open and were no longer the strange turquoise he was beginning to grow accustomed to, but a swirl of colour; hues of reds and greens and blue, somehow opaque and translucent at the same time. They were absolutely extraordinary. He had never seen a warden's eyes change like that but somehow he knew they had been glowing with power. It was just one more eccentricity to add to the growing list of strangeness that was Max. But what really had his gut clenching in concern last night had been the stark terror and fear in those rainbow depths. He had approached the bed cautiously, speaking her name quietly, hoping to draw her out of the nightmare slowly. She had lashed out and slapped his hand away like a child would ... or a cornered animal. It had damn near broken his hardened heart. It had apparently done the trick though for she had swiftly dismissed him, but not before he saw her start to shake violently.

The woman needed to refuel her vitality in the worst way but she was being ridiculously and unaccountably stubborn about the whole thing. She was also not picking up the nuances of building a shield and controlling her powers as quickly as he believed she should. He wondered if she was stalling for some reason.

He was just walking past the window to grab his clothes when a flash of flesh from below caught his eye. Cali was dressed in her usual tight shorts and sports bra but it wasn't the sight of the willowy blonde that had him freezing in his tracks. No it was the shorter, curvier red head, dressed in tights and a belly-revealing singlet top. She was bending over, head flush with her knees, arms wrapped her legs with all that glorious hair brushing along the ground. So much for negative reinforcement, he thought as he glared accusingly at his once again rigid dick. The woman's arse was a thing of beauty, all round and firm, and his hands literally flexed with the need to touch. As if sensing his gaze, Max whipped herself upright, her turquoise gaze latching onto his form that was no doubt outlined perfectly in the early morning light. Hell, the window he was standing at was even arch-shaped, like he was posing for some cheesy romance novel or something. Panicking and acting purely in self-preservation rather than rational thought, he allowed his limbs to go loose and face-planted on the floor below the window.

For the next five minutes he could do no more than mewl like a kitten ... he had landed directly on his stiff cock.

****

Max stared up at the arched window, blinking over and over again, trying to get her eyes to recreate the image of a very naked and very erect Ryker. One second he was standing there in all his naked glory and the next second he had disappeared. Perhaps she had imagined it, after all, she had gotten practically zero sleep last night and one's brain tended to play tricks when one didn't get enough REM cycles. But surely this wasn't one of those times. There was no way she could have dreamed up a dick like that! Not even her imagination was that prolific!

"Max? What are you doing?" Cali asked her. She turned to the female knight and blurted;

"I just saw Ryker's meatcicle!"

Cali's azure eyes rounded comically and immediately darted to Ryker's bedroom window, "You saw what?"

"His meatcicle! I totally saw his meatcicle!" Cali offered a hand in the air and Max high-fived her in silence, both of them paying the appropriate respect to the auspicious moment. That was until she registered the wheezing sounds behind her. Turning, she saw Darius shaking his head frantically and seemingly having trouble breathing. She would have been concerned except Axel was laughing his fool head off. Beyden and Lark were both staring at Max wide eyed and in apparent shock.

Darius began to shake his head, muttering to himself, "No, no, no. She did not just say that. It does not mean what you think it means. The woman is not that crazy."

Axel slapped Darius on the back, "What exactly do you think it means?" He laughed before Darius even had a chance to reply.

Darius scowled at his fellow soldier before pointing an accusatory finger in Max's direction. "Don't you ever, *ever*, use that word again! Do you understand me? It is now banned from your vocabulary!"

Max pouted, "But it describes it perfectly, I mean, have you seen that thing? It —"

"Enough! La la la la la."

Max couldn't help giggling at seeing the prissy warrior plugging his ears and singing out loud to drown out her voice. She turned to Cali and said, "You know, I could have called it a meat missile."

"Aargh! Stop saying the word meat!" Darius yelled frantically.

Cali high-fived her again and Max sighed in satisfaction at the strange turn her life had taken. She was really beginning to like these guys. They were outside in the fresh air and Cali was going to take her through a series of exercises to help calm her mind and settle her powers so she could hopefully successfully form a shield. They had been working diligently with her for the last two weeks in order to help her understand how to shield herself so she wasn't seeping energy everywhere she went. Max really wanted to get it right. It meant the chades would no longer be drawn to her from far and wide. Apparently the chades were unavoidable and an accepted part of their society. They were the counterpoint to the wardens. Where a warden's instinct was to nurture and protect their domain, chades were fated to destroy. They were the balance the world demanded for their existence. Ostensibly, everything was about balance. Wardens needed vitality to survive and so did the chades. Unfortunately, chades couldn't recharge like wardens could, so they tried to suck the life out of the biggest batteries they could find; wardens. Which explained why Max had so much trouble with them over the years. She was like a walking halogen lamp to them. But hopefully she would soon be able to turn down her brightness.

Unluckily, she had little success so far which she found totally frustrating. She knew how to meditate – had been taught by the best. That was when she went through her whole angry phase. The paladins had spent the last couple of weeks lecturing her and tutoring her in all things warden related. Max had followed the paladins instructions to the letter and although she felt better than she had in a long time and she hadn't had a seizure in days, she was still experiencing nightmares and was apparently still mislaying energy. They all kept pestering her about replacing it by using their vitality but it still weirded her out. She felt comfortable with them, was soothed by their presence and trusted them so much that she no longer carried her tanto sword everywhere with her. But it still didn't sit right with her to use them in that way. They were unbound by choice so clearly they actively sought *not* to share with a warden. She didn't want them offering to her out of obligation. Also, it seemed too much like what the chades tried to do to her every time they saw her. How was it okay for her to take energy but not the chades? She didn't see a clear distinction and the moment she had suggested the same to the paladins, Max thought they were going to blow a gasket, especially Darius. So she hadn't broached the topic again.

Presently, Ryker came around the corner and walked briskly to them purposefully avoiding Max's eye. He had been so hot and cold to her over the last two weeks she was afraid of getting whiplash. She never knew if he was going to offend her or offer words of support. And now she had seen the man's very happy and very hard rod silhouetted through the window. She was finding it hard to look him in the eyes too but only because her eyes were glued to his crotch.

A throat clearing drew her attention, "I'm going to the Lodge. You all behave yourselves. And you," he jabbed a finger angrily in her direction, "try not to cause any more damage."

What had she done now? Before she could ask, he turned and stalked away. Was he limping slightly? Max wondered if he had hurt himself somehow.

"Why does he have so much repressed hostility?" She asked Cali. The men, having now limbered up in a very erotic show of stretching and lunging, were off on their morning jog.

"To be fair, it's not really repressed." Cali pointed out, seating herself on the ground.

"Very true." Max agreed.

"But it is his story to tell, not mine. I'm sorry." Cali did look sorry and Max could hardly fault her for not wanting to gossip about her friends. "Now clear your mind and picture a bubble around yourself. Then ..."

Max sighed and prepared herself for another day of lessons which she hoped wouldn't prove fruitless once again.

THIRTEEN

The morning had been semi-successful and Max felt as if she had a little more energy, as though she hadn't burnt off as much or lost as much as usual. Cali had proven to be a patient teacher and Max could easily picture her in a training role, schooling others. In fact, they were all rather patient with her; Darius had taken the role as historian, sharing his knowledge; Beyden had been teaching her to recognise when she was using her powers; Lark and Cali had been teaching her control and shielding; Axel was a constant humorous presence of support; and Ryker, well Ryker had been grunting at her and scowling in between dregs of information he dribbled out like crumbs. As welcome as she felt, it didn't escape her notice however, that the situation was temporary for all of them. Not once had they mentioned her staying and she had overheard a few conversations about Ryker speaking to the Council about her. Apparently though, they were waiting on the prodigal paladin to return as she may have some magical piece of information that could solve the puzzle that was Max.

Max could have told them not to bother ... she was unsolvable.

"We're going out back to get some training in. We may not be bound to wardens but we still need to stay in shape." Lark said presently, cleaning the table where they had been polishing their blades. Turned out the weapon of choice for a modern day knight was a sickle. How cool was that? Apparently the curved blade was the perfect weapon against the chades and they even had custom made holsters for them. Max thought they were wicked sweet and really wanted one for herself.

"You all look to be in pretty good shape to me." Max retorted, eyeing the earth paladin's rear end as he leaned forward. It was muscled and tight and filled out his cargo pants to perfection. "In fact, you're all insanely good looking. Is that something else that is branded into a knight's DNA?"

This produced a round of laughs and a couple of blushes from Darius and Beyden. They were just too cute! Max really wanted to dirty them up a little.

"I don't think so. That tends to be more of a warden thing. They're all attractive and talented and powerful. If they weren't so important, I'd hate them all." The female soldier said.

Axel nodded, "I agree. I've tasted my fair share off the warden menu. They are very tasty." He smacked his lips together.

Max knew she had been correct about him – he was a he-slut. Cali slapped him up the back of his head on her way past. The act was casual like it was an everyday occurrence and spoke volumes of the kind of relationship the paladins had. They were obviously as close as family and Max didn't really believe they were here on a temporary basis or out of some misguided belief that they were all rejects and needed to stick together.

"Can I join you?" She asked. It had been months since she had the opportunity to spar with others. She didn't want her skills to get rusty.

Axel shrugged, "Sure. Just try not to fall in love with me when you see my fine moves." He winked, those azure eyes of his twinkling. Max barely refrained from sighing at the flirt.

"I'll go get my other blades." Max said as she rose. She had her tanto sword on her as usual but she had a few other knives in her pack.

"Whoa there cowgirl. Why would you need blades?" Lark asked.

"Um, so I can practise with them ..." Max said slowly, Lark hadn't appeared dim witted before now.

"You're not practising. Not with knives, not with anything." Darius's voice was firm but Max was confused.

"What? You guys just said I could come!"

"Of course. Come out to watch. There is no way you will be participating." Darius explained.

Max stood and planted her hands on her hips, "And why not? I need to train Darius. Those phantoms or chades or whatever won't magically stop coming after me just because I have some scraps of information now."

Beyden rubbed her shoulder, "You don't need to train sweetie. You are a warden and therefore naturally passive. It is a great injustice that you have been forced to do battle in the past but those days are over forever now. You will meet your own paladins and if by chance the chades are still drawn to you, then it is your knights' honour to protect you."

Max glanced around the room to see similar expressions on the faces of the men. Looks like they were all on board Beyden's bullshit train. The only person apparently not riding was Cali, naturally!

"There is so much wrong with what you just said, *sweetie*, I don't know where to start." More frowns from the men except for Axel who was grinning as if in anticipation. "One: I don't have a passive bone in my body; Two: I have been doing battle my entire life, it's not a hobby or a choice; Three: I don't have paladins to wipe my arse for me and even if I do one day, I can assure you I've been folding my own toilet paper quite successfully for years now!"

The tips of Beyden's ears were red. "Jeez, Max. Paladins don't go around wiping … you know."

Was he for real? Could he really be that sweet? There was no way she could stay mad at him, not when those amber cat eyes of his were looking at her imploringly. She stroked his arm, "It's okay Bey. You can make it up to me by letting me kick your butt."

"Max, I know you're not the type of warden we're all used to and that fighting has been a common part of your world, but you're in our world now. You are a Life Warden. No more fighting."

Wow, Darius was using his Mr Stern voice. Too bad she didn't give a fuck. "I'll tell you what. If any one of you can beat me in hand to hand, I promise to never ask to train with you again and I will be a good little warden. I'll even learn how to knit. How about that?"

Silence. Nothing but silence. Seems the poor saps still weren't quite used to her. "Well? Axel? Lark? You guys have seen me in action before. Remember poor Bounce?" She asked.

Axel winced and grabbed his crotch. "I recall. And if that's the type of training you have in mind, you can rule me out."

Max held up her right hand, spreading her fingers so a vee formed between her two first fingers and her two last. "I promise to stay away from the goodies … scouts honour."

Mr Stern exhaled forcefully and shook his head. "That is not the scout pledge. That is the 'live long and prosper' sign from *Star Trek*."

"Well, well, well. What have we here? Sounds like Sir Darius is a closet Trekkie!" She teased.

"There's nothing closeted about it. He's out and proud." Axel revealed, "He has all six television series and all thirty seasons. That's seven hundred and twenty six episodes."

"Just when I thought you couldn't be any more perfect." She cooed and pinched Darius's high cheekbone. "Say you'll run away with me?" She batted her lashes.

"You can't charm me you little demon." He said smilingly as he tugged on her hair playfully.

"You can't charm me either and I haven't seen your mad skills yet, so I accept your challenge m'lady." Cali mock bowed in her direction.

Max whooped and fist-pumped the air. So did Axel. "All right! Girl on girl!" This earned him a slap to the back of the head as Ryker walked past but surprisingly he didn't can the idea. He had returned in a much better mood only minutes earlier. Must have worked out some of his tension on a poor unsuspecting recruit.

Five minutes later Max found herself outside next to the gym, on the dirt, facing off against four ancient knights. Her life was awesome!

FOURTEEN

Ryker had watched the proceedings with amusement initially. He knew Darius, Axel and Lark had said that the warden had killed a chade on her own and he had seen the way she handled that freaking sword of hers. She gripped it like an expert, caressed it like a lover and kept it on her person at all times like it was a limb. Only people who had extensive training and motivation treated their weapons like that. His own set of sickles were kept in a black velvet lined box for cripes sake! But as the paladins lined up one after the other to get their arses handed to them, sometimes two at a time, Ryker had stopped being amused. The woman was good. Fuck, she was beyond good. She would put half the paladins on active duty to shame and she had some moves that even he had never seen before. Nobody achieved that level of skill without a massive load of discipline and motivation. And the Goddess knew, fleeing from the chades was a major motivation.

The others had been amused, then shocked, then stunned, and then proud as they had sparred and lost to the short warden. They had all left a little in awe and a little dazed to go and clean up and get ready for dinner. It meant that Ryker now had the opportunity to observe the woman alone. She had stripped down to a sports bra and her leggings in order to make good on her deal of the hand to hand. She was dirty from being thrown and rolling on the ground and a fine sheen of sweat covered her exposed skin from her exertions. Even though her breasts were tightly restrained, there was no denying their fullness and her waist dipped in before her hips flared out in the timeless shape of the female form. She was the very epitome of a woman. He watched as she glanced down and swore colourfully before chewing off a fingernail that had obviously been broken from all the exercise.

She might have been a woman but she was by no means a lady.

It was all Ryker could do not jump her and mount her right there on the dirt. Her sleek muscles had stretched and bunched just as her arse and tits had flexed and bounced with every move she made. But that wasn't what turned him on the most, no, it was the look in her eyes. She had the look of a warrior; confident, lethal and charmed by the violence. He bet she would be the best screw of his life. And to top it all off? She had a massive tattoo covering the whole length of her back. He couldn't make out the design in its entirety but it looked to be some sort of comic book pattern in hues of greys, blacks and whites. There were specks of colours here and there, but again he wasn't close enough to figure out what they were.

Ryker loved tattoos.

"Are you going to stand there all day or are you going to take your turn?"

Shit! She was looking directly at him and talking. He was practically standing there with his dick in his hand and Max had managed to catch him off guard. It took him a moment for his big brain to compute what she had said. "I'm not sparring with you."

Her head cocked to the side, messy hair escaping the loose confines of her hair band. "Why not? The deal is still on the table. I did say if any of you paladins could beat me, I would back off. You could redeem the honour on behalf of your fellow knights."

"No dice." He said, deadpan.

Her cyan eyes sparkled with mischief and challenge. "Scared?"

Hell yes, he was scared! *Scared of fucking you into the ground*, he thought. Instead of saying that though he answered with an alternate truth, "No need for a re-match. Anyone who can fight that well deserves the title of Victor."

"Really?" She narrowed her eyes and drew the word out as if suspicious.

"Yes, really. You're a skilled fighter. It must have taken you hundreds of hours and many years of discipline to be this good. I have no doubt you are a worthy opponent for any soldier or any chade as I am sure has been the case."

She sauntered slowly toward him, sweat gleaming enticingly on her exposed abs. *Eyes up, soldier!* He commanded himself. When she was within touching distance she paused and eyed him from top to toes ... twice.

"Who are you and what have you done with the Inmate? The only time I hear you do more than grunt is when you're insulting me or being a prick in general." She said finally.

Although not thrilled with the nickname she had chosen for him and not exactly his intention, he was actually pleased with the perception she had formed of him. He did not want her getting comfortable here and he definitely did not want her discerning little butt noticing his inappropriate attraction to her. So instead of answering her, he merely grunted. Unfortunately, she found that to be amusing as a deep-set dimple flashed from one corner of her mouth. It wasn't present on both sides and Ryker found the asymmetry oddly alluring.

"So you're not going to spar with me?"

"No sparring."

"Because I'm hot shit and way awesome?"

Way awesome? "Your words. Not mine." Ryker answered, reverting to his stunted vocabulary.

"And it's not because I have a vagina?"

Ryker laughed – he actually laughed. He had no idea what the woman was going to say or do next but he found himself thoroughly enjoying her, despite the fact that she was a warden. The look of astonishment on Max's face said she was just as surprised by his amusement as he was. He answered her;

"No. It's not because you have a vagina. Cali and Diana, although you haven't met her, both have vaginas as well and they are two of the best paladins I have ever had the pleasure to work with."

"Cali made a few comments that made me think your whole warden/paladin society thing is a little misogynistic ..." Max let the sentence trail off inquiringly.

Ryker snorted rudely, "That's an understatement. Female paladins are few and far between. Those that are born are accepted in society but never really as warriors. They accumulate vitality the same as the males do so they still have a purpose in serving wardens but they are rarely recruited to be soldiers."

"Then why do you allow Cali – and Diana – to fight? Why do you have two female paladins in your Order?" She questioned.

Dammit. He should never have opened a dialogue with her. There would be no shutting her up now, he figured. But the most expedient way to get down to the bottom of the Max-Mystery would be to share information with her. Once she was lulled into feeling secure with them, he could then pry those secrets she had buried deep out of her in return. She had revealed very little personal information over the last two weeks. So he replied, "Firstly, we are not an Order. Secondly, because it doesn't matter to me. They sacrifice and serve just as well as any man. They uphold the paladin creed with every fibre of their being. I don't care what's between their legs."

She did that whole body once over again with those peepers of hers and he forced himself not to react physically to the visual caress. She then searched his gaze for a moment before scrunching her nose adorably. No, not adorably he amended. He didn't find anything *adorable*, not even baby bunny rabbits with flopsy ears. And wardens were absolutely, completely, unequivocally, very *un*-adorable.

"You surprise me. That doesn't happen often."

"Why?"

"I pegged you for being sexist ... like, super sexist."

"Why?" He repeated, curious despite himself. He was a firm believer in equality regardless of the situation. What the fuck did he care if someone was male or female, black or white, gay or straight? As long as they didn't piss him off, he could care less what they did.

"Well, you're very ... *Alpha*." Her gaze turned dark and her voice lowered about three octaves on the word 'alpha'. It took on a smoky, husky quality that had his dick straining the confines of his pants for freedom.

She was correct; he was exceedingly Alpha.

But being a leader and having a dominant personality did not preclude having a brain. It also seemed that the thought of him as such turned the feisty little warden on. He had been correct in his initial assumptions that her eyes would darken with desire. Now if only he could find out if they would lighten in ecstasy ...

"Can I touch your scar?"

"What?" Now that made his blood rush north again.

"Your scar. Can I touch it?"

It was on the tip of his tongue to tell her to fuck off. Here he was with his fantasies of a naked, rosy Max and she was bringing up the very obvious, very public symbol of his disgrace. The offending mark throbbed in remembered pain from the horror of the day fifty years ago when he had received it. He went from horny to livid in a millisecond. Berating himself for his stupidity for allowing a conversation to develop between them he scowled down at the woman, ready to blast her. He found himself stilling in astonishment when he saw her eyeing the disfigurement and licking her lips. The heat in her gaze was smouldering and he patted his shirt in case it had been burned off him. His initial assumption had been way off the mark. Scars clearly turned her on.

The female was feisty, curvy, sexy, tattooed, and ... kinky. She was absolutely fucking perfect!

One second they were both upright and the next thing he knew they were horizontal in the dirt. Her legs were wrapped around his hips and he had both hands filled with lush, soft flesh. He buried his face where neck met shoulder and inhaled deeply, taking in her natural coconut and cinnamon scent. He groaned in delight at the tropical smell and couldn't stop himself from nibbling a path up the tendons to the sensitive patch of flesh behind her right ear. Max shuddered and moaned tilting her head to the side, the sensual movement a subconscious show of submission. Ryker swirled his tongue in reward, tasting the saltiness on her skin from her earlier exertions. He rocked his hips, his hardness seeking out her softness and when Max undulated under him in response he had to grit his teeth to stop himself from blowing like a teenager.

Her body moved in fluid waves, her hips swaying in direct counterpoint to his causing an erotic friction even through the layers of their clothes. Squeezing the breasts he held firmly in his palms he delighted in the whimpering noises she made in the back of her throat. Her back arched, pressing those luscious mounds more firmly into his callused hands and her dark lashes fluttered, half obscuring her glittering eyes. He had been wrong; her eyes didn't change from dark to light. They came alive, sparkling and flashing, mimicking the fire in her body. Unable to think of anything other than assuaging the urgent need pounding through his body, his reached down to unzip his fly ... only to find himself on his back blinking up at the darkening sky.

What ... the ... fuck?

A low snarl alerted him to the fact that he and Max were no longer alone and he rolled quickly to avoid the heavy paladin boot trying to stomp him into the dirt. Flipping himself to his feet he used his forearm to block the spinning kick that would have likely taken his head off. Catching the offending foot, he gave a sharp twist with his hands forcing the attacker to twist his entire body or risk a dislocated ankle. The man landed in a crouch, not at all off balance or out of breath. But then, Ryker expected no less of the fire paladin, he was a fierce fighter because he hated to lose and his wrath flared just as hot as his element.

Max had obviously recovered from her own shock for she ran between them, arms outstretched. "Axel! What the hell are you doing?"

Axel never took his eyes off him, he was a true predator just like Ryker and his lips quirked despite himself. The fucker wouldn't go down easy.

"Get inside now, Max." Axel ordered.

"Excuse me?" Max's tone was incredulous as her eyes darted back and forth between the two of them.

"Please." The word was ground out between Axel's clenched teeth.

She looked to Ryker as if seeking assistance or maybe even expecting him to oppose Axel. Instead, he purposefully avoided her gaze. He knew why Axel was delivering this arse-kicking and it was well deserved. What had he been thinking?

Max huffed in disgust, "Men!"

He felt the warm swish of air as she brushed by him and caught the lingering smell of the coconut scent she left behind. Distracted, Axel swooped in fast and low and managed to get in a cheap shot to the kidney before he was able to defend himself. Roaring, he spun and kicked his fellow knight in the solar plexus but the bastard didn't go down. Blood boiling now with a combination of sexual angst and male ego, he went for brute strength and crash-tackled the paladin low and hard, slamming them both into the unforgiving ground. Axel was able to move as fluidly as fire in the breeze and he scissored his legs, reversing their positions with Axel now on top and a huge fist travelling directly for his head.

Instead of trying to avoid the impact, Ryker simply let himself go limp, hoping the blow and the resulting concussion would knock some sense into his messed up cerebral cortex. But the knock never arrived, Axel pulling his punch a hair breath from impact and Ryker silently applauded him for his control. He didn't think he would have been able to stop himself had the situation been reversed. Axel pushed himself back roughly, planting his arse on the ground. Ryker didn't bother to move and stayed on his back throwing an arm over his eyes – not that there was any way he could hide from the lecture sure to follow.

"Fuck me sideways man! I should kick your motherfucking hide across the motherfucking yard! She's a Warden, Ryker! She may not act like one and she may not speak like one, but she is. Her ignorance doesn't change her birthright. She's a warden," he repeated, "start treating her like one or I won't hold back next time. She's too good for the likes of you." The last part was snarled in derision and Ryker cringed as he felt the heat of the words.

The old adage, the truth hurts? So very right. How could he have forgotten his place for even a second? Not only was he not permitted to dally with a warden due to his paladin status but he was also a disgraced knight in their society with no warden, no Order and a faded Heraldry on his arm. He had no right whatsoever to even think about bedding Max, let alone touch her in any way.

"Ry?"

Ryker studiously ignored Axel, naively hoping the man would just consider his job of 'virtue defender' upheld and be on his way. But of course he hadn't finished paying his dues yet.

"Ry? Come on, man. Look at me."

He sighed and removed his arm as he sat upright. He thought he had successfully composed his features to his trademark blank façade but clearly he was wrong for Axel said;

"Aww, hell man ... you *like* her!"

Yeah, *so* not happening, he thought. "So do you." He slashed a hand through the air in irritation when Axel opened his mouth in denial. "Don't try to deny it."

"I wasn't going to. Yeah, I like her. We all do. But not the same way you do apparently." Axel stood up and brushed off his pants. "I know I tease and I flirt but I don't think of her that way. She's too ... sweet."

Ryker glared at the man in disbelief, "Sweet? That woman's mouth could burn the ears off a sailor!"

Axel shook his head and offered him a hand up. Ryker didn't hesitate as he gripped the strong arm and allowed himself to be wrenched to his feet. Now that his blood had started to cool he was infinitely grateful that the younger man had intervened and stopped what would have been a monumental mistake.

"I wasn't referring to her vocabulary, the Goddess knows that is very ... colourful. I was talking about her nature. Under that tough exterior there is an innocence there, a purity. The woman practically glows with it. Don't tell me you can't see it."

Oh, Ryker saw it. He also felt it, given his low grade empath abilities. It was one of the reasons he was so drawn to her. He wanted to bask in that warmth and that light, maybe selfishly hoping it would outshine the darkness in his own soul. And that was entirely unfair of him, he knew. It wasn't her job to heal his delicate wounded psyche. She had bigger fish to fry, like ensuring the world didn't go down the crapper.

"I mean shit, Ry. She's a fucking warden. What were you thinking?"

Apparently, Axel repeating that Max was a warden over and over again was supposed to make it sink into his thick skull. The problem was he hadn't been thinking, not with his upstairs brain anyway. It was a mistake he wouldn't make again. He rubbed his hands over his face roughly then turned to Axel.

"I wasn't thinking. Don't worry, it won't happen again. I give you my word." He locked gazes and offered his right hand. Just as Ryker had accepted the arm up, Axel didn't hesitate to grip the outstretched palm. Ryker gave a firm squeeze to seal the apology and offer thanks before adding just enough pressure to be uncomfortable. "But don't think I'll let you get away with another stunt like that. Kidney-whip me again and I'll lay you up for a week."

"Whatever you say, old man." Axel grinned with his trademark cheek before his dimples were replaced with a serious expression. "I didn't mean it like it sounded when I said she was too good for you. I –"

"Stop. I get it, don't worry." Ryker didn't want to hear the paladin apologising for hurting his fragile feelings. He also didn't want to see the pity in his clear blue eyes. But apparently he was determined to embarrass Ryker further for he continued on stubbornly;

"I just don't want to see either of you get hurt or the situation to get messy. This attraction can only lead one way; down a short road straight to nowhere." His sapphire eyes darkened and Ryker could discern a wealth of anger and pain in them. "Take it from someone who knows."

Before he could formulate a response, Axel spun on his heel and strode resolutely away from him in the opposite direction of the house towards the beach. His broad shoulders were stiff but he walked straight and tall. Feeling sorry for his friend and disgusted with himself, Ryker knew he should really listen to the expert here. And that was, unfortunately for them both, Axel.

FIFTEEN

Max was livid ... and confused ... and livid. She was also horny as hell! She was finally able to maul the object of her lust like she'd been dreaming about and Axel swoops in like some, well, knight! She couldn't believe the nerve of the man. Just who did he think he was? And to add insult to injury she didn't even get to watch as the two warriors fought each other. Oh boy, she wished she could have seen the two males grappling with each other in all their muscled glory. But no! She had been sent to her room like some teenager with a curfew. If they thought they could order her around and deprive her of a real honest to goodness male-induced orgasm, they had another thought coming!

Max stirred the pot of chilli furiously, taking out her frustrations on the minced meat. When she had entered the house the other four paladins had been in the kitchen figuring out the evening meal. They had been bickering like children and ordinarily Max would have found the novelty amusing and sweet, but not today. She had declared it was her night to cook and for everyone to get the hell out of her kitchen. She didn't often have a kitchen she could putter in but when she was able to she actually loved to cook. It was something people with a home always took for granted. Darius had been predictably horrified: *'wardens do not wait on paladins'*. But Max was in a mood and not to be trifled with: *'you say I'm some kind of a boss or leader with high status? Then do what I fucking say and vacate this area until I give you leave to return!'* She had snarled. Beyden – sweet, sweet, Beyden had then made the mistake of asking: *'Why are you mad? Did you get your period?'* The silent venomous look she threw his way had him scrambling out of the room, deserting his fellow soldiers on the battlefield. Darius's eyes had been wide in horror and Lark had held up his hands in surrender, neither coming to the defence of their comrade. They had then likewise scampered out of the room like the male rodents they were. Cali had offered the helpful advice that the saucepans were under the sink before also leaving.

She was now in multitasking heaven with a pot of churning chilli, bubbling beans and boiling rice on the stove top. She had flat bread rising in the oven and was mashing up avocado, squeezing lemons and crushing garlic for an amazing guacamole. The cheese had been grated, the chives added to the sour cream and the salsa was in the refrigerator next to the fabulous salad. She had even taken the liberty of opening a couple of bottles of wine to let them breathe. She knew Beyden was the wine connoisseur and figured they were likely his from his coveted collection but she also figured that he owed her for the period comment so hadn't batted an eyelash when she opened the expensive bottles. They were going to take away her man-toy, were they? Well, they would learn. Oh, they would *all* learn …

The back door slammed and Axel walked in. His face was flushed from the wind and his hair was mussed but other than that he didn't look like he had just gone a round with a legendary knight. He did look a little sheepish but he also looked resolute and not in the least apologetic. The man clearly thought he had every right to interfere and he had acted in her best interests. Underneath her sexual torment was a tiny spark of warmth that came from the feeling of someone caring enough about her to stand up for her – misguided though it may be. He was just trying to help, Max knew they all were. Even Ryker. She was at that point where she now believed everything they said and trusted that they knew what they were talking about in regards to paladins and wardens and domains. She wondered when they were going to do her the same courtesy of believing her when she said she knew herself and her thoughts and her feelings. It only seemed fair that they extend the same trust to her.

Before Axel could speak, she pointed her spoon at him. "Not a word. Go and wash up and tell the others that dinner will be ready in ten minutes."

"But –"

"What did I just say?" She snarled. Axel intelligently shut his trap and fled.

Not two minutes later, Ryker marched in. Max took one look at his pretty face and knew that Mr Hyde had returned. She had no doubt the original Ryker she had met two weeks ago who snarled at her, grunted at her, and insulted her with every other breath had made a comeback. Whatever Axel had said or done outside had caused the charming, articulate man to retreat and leave behind the only man in history to suffer from PMS. Max had been shocked to her core when Ryker had complimented her fighting skills and she had been pleasantly surprised when he had started to talk about the female paladins. She honestly didn't know he had it in him. She had him pegged for a chauvinistic, sexist, patriarch and would never have believed he was so liberal.

"Let me guess; what happened outside was a big mistake and won't happen again." She prompted drolly before he could open his yap and dig a deeper hole for himself.

"Yeah. That's pretty much the footnotes."

Max eyed him, "Why not?"

"Because I said so."

Max could only blink. "Are you taking the piss right now? *'Because I said so'?*" She continued quickly, "You know what? Suit yourself. It's not like I'm hard up for orgasms or anything. My fingers work just fine, I assure you." Ryker's scar flexed as his jaw clenched tight. He wasn't as unaffected as he wanted her to believe so she decided to tease the tiger, "Are you absolutely sure? Once we relieve all this sexual tension between us, our working relationship would probably improve."

"We don't have any sexual tension." The blunt reply was accompanied by a heavy scowl.

Max could feel her eyes practically bug out of her head at the man's nerve. "Oh, okay Pinocchio. Whatever you say." If he wanted to live in La La Land, who was she to burst his delusional little bubble? The paladin's balls could turn blue and drop off for all she cared. She continued to set the table, "Dinner's on in five."

His scowl darkened further, "Why are you organising dinner? Where are the others? You have no place waiting on us woman!"

Max spun and skewered his chest with a sharp finger. "Don't you 'woman' me! I'll do as I fucking-well please! Now go wash your hands!" She spun around, muttering about the fiasco that was the male species. What had the Goddess been thinking when she created them? Other than their pecs, or biceps, or dicks of course … So okay, fine. Maybe they weren't a total lost cause but they sure as shit aggrieved her.

SIXTEEN

So this is awkward, Max thought to herself. Everyone was seated stiffly as they watched her place the food on the table in silence like it physically pained them to have her waiting on them. It was completely ridiculous of course, it was the least she could do. She had been there two weeks now and cooking a meal was a small thing she could do to repay them all for their kindness. That morning she had offered to tidy the kitchen and maybe vacuum the house. She thought Darius was going into heart failure for a minute, so she had relented. But not tonight. It was their turn to be spoilt – even Axel and Ryker who were both on her Shit List.

"What's everyone waiting for? Dig in." She gestured to the food after taking her own seat.

Lark cleared his throat and bravely reached for the beef, "Thank you Max. It all looks wonderful but you really shouldn't have."

"Yes. I should. It's the least I can do for everything you've all done. You may not have noticed, but I'm a touch independent." This received several snorts and snickers and the tension relaxed. "I'm not used to being waited on or coddled. Dinner is a small way to say thank you. I appreciate you all very much for giving me your time and knowledge and experience. You're good eggs."

And cue the throat clearing. *So predictable,* Max thought. Seeing Beyden piling his plate only with salad, Max said, "Oh, hey Bey. You don't need to just eat salad. I made a great spicy bean dish just for you that I hope you'll love. I noticed you're a vegetarian. Probably because you're allied to the animals, huh?" She popped some bread into her mouth as she asked. When she didn't immediately receive a reply she glanced up. Beyden was staring at her in disbelief, his orangey eyes glowing with something she couldn't name.

"What is it?" She asked in concern.

"You made a dish just for me because you noticed I don't eat meat?" His deep voice was soft and more accented than usual.

"Of course." She didn't understand what the BFD was but apparently the others agreed with Beyden for they were all looking at her with something akin to … worship, if she wasn't mistaken. It was beginning to freak her out.

"Thank you, Warden." Beyden bowed his head before reaching for the beans.

"Ookay. You're welcome. It's just beans dude." She responded with a shrug. Maybe beans were some kind of sacred legume in their society or something?

Darius cleared his throat, "I know you said you grew up in the foster care system but do you remember anything of your parents?"

"No. Nothing." Max was surprised at the change in topic and certainly didn't want to encourage the line of thought. She didn't remember her parents because she didn't remember anything before she was sixteen years old … but she didn't want to tell Darius that. It was obvious she was already strange in their world, not quite fitting the usual pattern of a warden. There was no way she was going to add more fuel to that particular fire.

Darius continued, "I was just wondering if you knew what your real name was, that's all. It could help us figure out who your family is."

Max was intrigued despite herself. "What does my name have to do with anything?"

"A warden's name is a direct reflection of their domain. Their name is a portrayal of their natures and the world's needs. For example, my old liege was named Ariel and was keeper of air, Caspian is guardian to the domain of water, Fern – a warden of earth. There is no way your parents called you *Max*." The last was said with a derisive snort. She was immediately offended.

"And just what is wrong with the name Max? I'll have you know that I was so named after much thought and consideration." Even to her own ears she sounded cold and snotty. But it was the truth nonetheless. The fact that she had named herself was her business. At least Darius had the decency to look chagrined.

"Sorry, Max. I didn't mean it like that. I think Max is a great name. Really suits you."

Max kept her eyes narrowed on him, not willing to let him off the hook quite yet. Besides, their naming custom sounded way cliché. She bet there was a warden called Rain out there who was the guardian of water too. "What would I change my name to anyway? Cloud? Moon? Oh, I know ... Grass. I want to be Grass!" Max let out a rather undignified laugh-snort. The paladins didn't appear to share in her humour however judging by the frowns and eye rolls.

"Aurora."

Surprised and somewhat confused by Ryker's outburst, Max asked, "What?"

"Aurora. You know, like the Aurora Borealis? The Northern Lights? I saw it once. Like a floating rainbow; a coloured road of mist in the sky. Purples, pinks and blues swirling in the atmosphere. It was the most beautiful thing I've ever seen. Your eyes looked like that when you were having your nightmare."

Utter. Silence.

You could practically hear a pin drop as all eyes focused incredulously on their leader. Max could literally feel her mouth fall open as she stared at Ryker. Who'd a thunk the big lug could be so romantic and almost poetic even?! Max didn't really fancy herself as particularly romantic, but damn, you'd have to be dead inside not to feel a little swoon from that! And even more endearing? A red flush was rising steadily from beneath the collar of his shirt, highlighting those outrageous cheekbones, until even the tips of his ears were rosy. His eyes widened comically as he looked around the room frantically, brain apparently catching up with mouth.

"Fuck! I don't mean that you're beautiful – not that you're ugly or anything – I mean, you're pretty enough I guess ..."

Axel slapped Ryker's shoulder, "I'd stop while you're ahead if I were you dude!"

The dinner proved to be a loud, rowdy affair after that and Max relaxed and revelled in the camaraderie right up to the point where her brain decided to misfire and cause a small myoclonic seizure. Her hand jerked sporadically and spilled wine over the table top. Perfect! She still hadn't discussed her epilepsy with the paladins. It didn't seem like something any other warden suffered with.

"Max, you need vitality." The statement was swift and severe.

"Damn, Darius. You're like a freaking broken record! How many times do I have to say it? I'm not interested." Max bit off angrily.

"Why won't you accept what we offer so freely?" Lark asked, sounding genuinely puzzled.

Max sighed, suddenly feeling very tired. "Because it's not really offered freely ... you don't really mean it."

"What are you talking about? Of course I mean it Max. It is my duty." Lark said earnestly.

"That is exactly my point. You are offering out of some messed up sense of obligation. I have no desire to take anything from you that you're not happy to give." She forestalled all further lame platitudes by continuing, "Besides, I've managed all these years without it. A little longer won't hurt anything."

"We really need to figure that out by the way." Axel interjected, he looked at Ryker, "Maybe it's time to talk to the IDC."

Ryker seemed to think on that a moment, "Not yet. I would really like Diana's input first."

Max frowned. He seemed to hold the other female paladin's opinion in high esteem. She was taking longer to return than they had all expected. Cali had told her a lot about her friend and Max thought she sounded like a cool chick. Ryker obviously thought she was cool too because he was willing to put up with Max in his home and around his family even though he desired anything but, just so he could listen to Diana's thoughts. Max wondered if they were lovers. Maybe that was the real reason why Ryker was so pissed off by his attraction to her. Maybe he was a dirty, rotten cheater! The thought made Max's blood boil and before she knew it the glasses on the table were rattling. Looking around she saw that the wine and the water were actually bubbling. Was she doing that? She hadn't lost control of her powers like that since Japan.

"Max ... just relax okay. Remember what I said about breathing? Just concentrate on your breaths in and your breaths out." Lark's melodious voice was soothing but she paid no heed to the words. Her attention was fixed on the boiling liquids in front of her.

"Am I doing that?" She asked instead, seeking clarification.

"Yes. You are." Ryker responded as he stood slowly from his chair. "And you need to stop it."

Max curled her lips at his tone. She hated when he used that condescending tone on her. The wine glass in front of him cracked and split a second before it shattered, spilling its contents onto the table. The red wine looked like blood on the pale table cloth and Max felt her heart begin to beat faster in fear. She was losing control. People always got hurt when she lost control.

"Max! Max! Hey, listen to me okay." It was Cali. "You need to stop focusing on what you're doing. Stop focusing on how you're feeling. Just ignore everything but the sound of my voice, okay?"

Max focused and found herself calming when she felt five distinct hands placed on her. The only person not to touch her was Ryker – probably a wise decision at this point. About sixty seconds later, Max felt she was calm enough to speak.

"I don't understand how I'm able to do that. You all keep saying that wardens are passive, that their powers aren't active. How do I keep doing this?" She was still shaking and a headache was creeping up behind her eyes but her brain's need for answers overrode her body's need for rest.

"A warden's *purpose* is passive. Balance is the purpose. Balance is neutral. But your gifts and abilities are tangible so they can be used actively." Darius the ever-knowing answered her of course.

"And they can harm as well as heal. That's what you haven't told me these last few days." Max accused. They knew wardens had the ability to destroy as well as create and they hadn't told her. All this time she had thought there was something wrong with her. All those mistakes she had made with her abilities in the past; the fires, the floods, the explosions. She wasn't defective. Her powers weren't wrong. They were the same as all the other wardens.

"You've been lying to me."

"Don't get melodramatic. We haven't lied to you." The sensitive, caring response came from Ryker of course. Man, he was such a jackass! She couldn't believe she had wanted to climb him like her own personal jungle gym just an hour before.

"Oh, Really? And what would you call it?"

"He's right Max. We haven't lied, we just haven't discussed that part of your powers yet. We wanted you to learn some control, some discipline so you could better understand your domain before we touched on using them so actively." Darius reasoned. "You need to learn the basics before taking the advanced class."

Max eyed him, "You're hoping my logical, rational side will understand that. And it does. But my illogical, irrational side thinks that a lie by omission is still a lie."

"Max, you need to learn control. All wardens start out learning the basics like we have been teaching you; meditation, relaxation, breathing, shielding." Lark explained.

Max shook her head. "I trust that you really believe you have acted in my best interests. But you're forgetting something important." She made eye contact with each of them, adding weight to her words so they would actually listen and *hear* what she was saying. "I'm not like all other wardens. They start this training when they are children; I am not a child. They develop their powers over time as they learn; my powers are fully developed. They forge bonds with paladins and renew their vitality from infancy; I am an adult who has never exchanged vitality with a paladin." She paused and prayed they were listening, "I am not one of them. You need to stop treating me like I am."

The serious looks the paladins threw at each other told Max there was going to be no room for dessert. *Fuck it!* She had been looking forward to cosmopolitan ice cream all day!

SEVENTEEN

Ryker tossed and turned all night. The events from the previous night had left him restless and unable to sleep. Firstly, he had tried to dry hump Max into the next century and then he had watched as she had boiled the damn wine as easy as breathing. Even without the normal vitality boosts she was incredibly powerful. It made him wonder just how strong she would be when she finally had vitality from a paladin running through her veins. It worried him ... a lot. Max had asked many questions about the chades over the last weeks and they had told her everything she needed to know but there were some important things he had omitted. He really hoped he hadn't made a mistake by not telling her that chades were actually wardens who had succumbed to the allure of their own powers. If Max didn't get her abilities under control, she could very well be headed in the same direction. And a trip to the Rangers was *not* something any of them wanted. Those depressing thoughts had dictated his actions from earlier that morning and he was now attempting to justify those actions to his fellow knights.

"I think Max is right." He began. "I wanted to keep her here because I was worried about how different she was. I thought we should figure her out before informing the IDC of her presence in case there was something sinister going on. The last time something out of the ordinary happened that we couldn't explain, the Great Massacre was the result. But I don't think we're the right paladins for the job. We're not equipped to deal with a long lost adult warden. She needs other wardens. She needs experts armed with knowledge and experience."

"You want to get rid of her." Lark sounded accusatory.

"I made no secret that I didn't want a warden hanging around. You all know why, just as I know why all of you aren't bound to a warden of your own. Why all of you are without an Order." He looked around the table. "Have your circumstances changed? Are any of you wanting to join another Order?" Each and every one of the knights at the table had their own story to tell and their own reasons for why they were trainers rather than active paladins. Although he had gotten used to them all being around and offering his home as a kind of boarding house for misplaced soldiers had given him a sense of purpose, he would never begrudge any of them moving on. Paladins were born to serve, born to provide vitality, born to protect. He would rejoice if they decided to move on and fulfil their calling.

He didn't know whether to be relieved or saddened when he saw the resolute and resigned faces at the table. Everyone's demons were just too strong. It was a shame, he thought. If anyone could have convinced this scarred, traumatised bunch of warriors to step back into the light, it would probably have been Max.

"So you're going to call the Council? Which one?" Cali asked, looking him straight in the eye. She was the only one in the room not studying the table, or the floor, or the walls. It just proved his point about how strong women were.

"I've already called ... and I contacted both. I spoke to Garrett, the Life Ambassador on the IDC. He was shocked to say the least. He actually took some convincing before he believed me. He recommended that we take Max to the Lodge and introduce her to some wardens and other paladins in the short term. Lake from the Local Warden Council said the next local meeting is in three weeks and they will formally introduce her into society then and assign a mentor to her. In the meantime, we are to help her find a paladin or two willing to share their vitality regularly to help stabilise her powers and her health. Ideally, the LWC and the IDC want to have input into the paladins she binds to."

Darius's dark eyebrows lowered ominously, "They wish to dictate her Order?"

Beyden looked concerned, "But they can't do that. We all know what happens when the connection isn't based on a natural bond."

"They're not going to force her to bind with anyone. They can't. I think they're just hoping she will form an Order with suitably respectable paladins." At least Ryker assumed that's what they wanted. Max was the find of a lifetime and although Garrett was genuinely happy to learn of her existence for the sake of the world, he was also a politician. He couldn't help but be drawn into the intrigue and possibilities her presence in society would bring.

"She's a female Warden of Life. They're probably hoping she'll breed with a suitably appropriate warden and produce dozens of Life Warden babies!" Cali alleged, disgust lacing her tone heavily.

Ryker refused to let his mouth form the immediate denial Cali's words brought. Although a paladin and a warden could produce warden offspring, they also had equal chances of producing a paladin. Only two wardens together were guaranteed to produce a warden heir.

"Her fate is not our responsibility, it never was." Ryker stated assuredly. Now, he only had to believe it himself.

****

Breakfast was a relatively quiet affair with everyone apparently focused intently on their food. Max wondered what everyone was thinking about. She had gotten to know the six paladins fairly well and she now respected the hell out of them all – even Ryker. And she didn't care what he said, she knew these people meant more to him than some twisted sense of responsibility. The home he had created here was far more than some kind of pound for strays – it was a refuge to those in need.

Max took a deep breath and glanced around the table. She was in need of a refuge and found herself desperately wanting to stay, regardless of the unrequited lust she had for Scarface. She wasn't stupid, she knew her time here was running short. But surely there had to be some kind of fate in the works to bring her here? Six paladins – seven if you included the missing one – one from each domain, all congregated in the one place with no warden of their own. And here she was, a warden with no paladins. That had to mean something. She had spent the night flipping through books in the library, walking along the beach and working out in the gym, trying to instil herself with the courage needed to ask them if she could stay. As Lark stood and began to clear the dishes, Max dimly heard Ryker rounding up the troops for something. It was time for Max to gut up.

"Hey guys?" Everyone immediately ceased all movement and gave her their full attention. She loved that about them but right now it also freaked her the fuck out! "I was just wondering, maybe we don't need to find me other paladins. I mean, you guys aren't bonded to a warden. Maybe you could ..." Max trailed off noticing the uncomfortable tension that swept through the room like a storm. There was a lot of foot shuffling and avoidance of eye contact going on and Max felt her heart sink. She didn't need to finish her question to know what their answer would be.

They didn't want her.

"Just forget I said anything." Max muttered quickly, praying no one would see the tears gathering rapidly in her eyes. Why did she hurt this much?

"Wait, Max, please. It isn't you. We're all here and working at the training centre for a reason." Cali hurried over to her and placed a slender hand on her shoulder.

"We're damaged goods, Max." She heard Axel state bluntly from behind her.

Max risked turning around and facing the knights. She looked everyone in the eye pausing for the longest time on Ryker, "Not to me."

Nothing but silence. It was like they were all waiting for someone else to say something – anything – first. Talk about awkward. Ryker was the first to break the brittle stillness.

"I can't speak for anyone else in the room but I can speak for myself. I will never be bound to another warden again. I will never be bound in another Order again. I will never accept you as my liege. I'm ... sorry."

Max felt bile rise in her throat and it was all she could do to stop herself from barfing all over the hardwood floor. Ryker's words made her feel physically sick because she believed every single one of them. To his credit he actually did look truly sorry ... but he also looked resolved. She knew there would be no changing his mind. Whatever had happened in his past had well and truly ruined him. She knew she didn't need to hear the words from the other paladins. Ryker was their leader and Captain even though he didn't want to accept it. He had their loyalties and trust and they would never betray their saviour by placing that loyalty with another, even though she believed they had grown to genuinely care for her. Perhaps she was a masochist but she wanted to hear them all say it anyway.

"Darius?"

"I'm sorry Max. I can't." The air paladin replied, jaw clenched tight.

"Lark?"

The auburn haired soldier shook his head. "I know this sounds lame but it isn't you ... It's me. I can't be bound to a warden."

"Bey?"

"Jeez, Max. I really wish you hadn't asked. I don't want to hurt you." His amber eyes also had the suspicious sheen of tears. "No."

"Cali?"

"Max. You have no idea just how important you are. We've kept you secluded here these past weeks and we've tried to express just what a miracle you are but you don't really get it. Not yet. But the second we introduce you to society, you will realise how high in the totem pole you are ... and how low we are. You won't want to be associated with us. We're doing you a favour by turning you down. You *will* thank us for it one day." The blonde Scandinavian princess was so earnest but Max knew she was wrong. She wasn't about to argue though.

"Axel?" Max had saved him for last because he had oddly become one of her favourite people in the world over the weeks. There was just something about the irreverent bastard that Max really clicked with. He walked over and placed his hands on her cheeks and Max felt a tiny spark of hope ... until she saw the look in those crystal clear blue eyes of his. She imagined it was the look of benevolent pity he bestowed upon leagues of women after a hot night between the sheets when he crushed their dreams of a fairytale romance the morning after.

"Babe, if I was going to jump back on the wagon for anyone, it would be you. But that part of my life is over. I'm sorry."

Under the crushing weight of injury and disappointment Max knew they were wrong. Each and every one of them. She felt the connection, the rightness between them. But there wasn't a damn thing she could do about it. So it looked like it was time for her to suck it up.

"Okay. Let's go find me a paladin then. It's probably 'bout that time, don't you think?"

Cue awkward silence. *Ah,* Max thought, *they already have.* Instead of throwing a tantrum and crying like an adult-size human baby, she only nodded. She had told herself to gut up after all, but damn if it didn't hurt like a bitch.

EIGHTEEN

They had split into two cars, Max sitting shotgun with Ryker driving and Cali and Axel in the back seat. Darius, Lark and Beyden had taken the other Dodge and followed behind. The drive had been uncomfortable to say the least, each person caught in their own thoughts she supposed. All of the tension and uneasiness was forgotten however the second Max placed her sneaker-clad feet on the ground at their destination. The land had been damaged here and the resulting scars were still visible in the burnt and broken trees and the cracked, dry ground. Why hadn't the earth been healed? She thought this was supposed to be where the wardens met.

"This is the training base for the paladins? What you call the Lodge?" She asked.

"Yep. This is it." Axel replied, already striding forward. But Max didn't move.

"And where there are paladins, there are wardens, correct?"

"Yes. Of course. Not only is this where paladins receive their training but it is also where the wardens hold their council meetings. We explained this. Why?" Darius asked.

"Then how is it possible for the earth to be so scarred here? How can the wardens stand it?" She turned to them, "How can *you* all stand it?"

"A massive bush fire swept through this area a little under a year ago. The facility was completely burned to the ground. There were only a handful of paladins on site at the time and no wardens. They were able to use their connections with their domains enough to stop the fire spreading to the nearby towns, but not enough to save the base."

"That's not what I'm asking. Can't you feel it? Can't you hear it? The ground, the shrubs, the trees – they're still hurting. Why haven't the other wardens healed them? Especially the ones responsible for earth."

"It's not that simple, Max. Wardens and paladins are one of the best kept secrets in history. Most of the human race doesn't know we exist or what our purpose is. We have managed to live side by side with them since the dawn of time with few mishaps. If this land was suddenly, miraculously repaired what do you think people would do? It could expose the wardens."

Max did listen to Darius and although she could see his point, she still felt a deep unease at the thought of nature's so-called guardians trampling over the pain-filled land here, ignoring its cries, all for the sake of public image. Because earth was Lark's element she turned to him with silent accusing eyes.

He held up his hands almost in surrender. "I know Max. Believe me, I know. I feel it every time I come here but we have rules to follow."

"Sounds like a shitty excuse to me." Max preached.

Lark frowned, as if he didn't like being on the receiving end of her disapproval. "It's not an excuse. It's just the way it is."

"Whatever." Max wasn't exactly in the mood to be forgiving.

"See! This is exactly what we've been trying to tell you these past few days. You are completely ignorant. Not only do you have no idea how to control your own powers, you know nothing of our society. We are a society based on laws and regulations just like any other. It's a miracle you've managed to survive on your own all this time without exposing us all." Ryker ranted.

"My apologies for being an orphan!" Max's voice was heavy with sarcasm.

Ryker ran rough hands over his face and through his shaggy black locks. He looked to be grasping for patience. Well, that was fine with Max, she was too. He continued, "Let's just go inside. You can meet some other paladins and see about finding a willing paladin or two to help stabilise you in the short term. Maybe meet a few wardens if there are any around. Then when the next council meeting is on and we introduce you formally, the other wardens will help educate and mentor you."

Max gritted her teeth and forced herself not to retort. She spun on her heel and began to march up the paved walkway to the front of the building. It was large and rectangular in shape, made up entirely of corrugated iron if Max wasn't mistaken. Although the materials were by no means organic, the low sloping roofs and wrap around verandas ensured it didn't look out of place in its bush setting. The army-green colouring camouflaged perfectly with the surrounding landscape and made the whole thing seem like your average fishing or hunting shack – only three times the size. There were a series of smaller buildings dotted behind the main facility that looked to be old shipping containers. Those must be the training quarters, Max thought.

Walking up the few short steps to the main door, Max began to feel a little nervous. Inside were people just like her. Although she was relieved and happy to finally have some answers, she was also terrified of the changes it would bring. No more running. No more hiding. She could finally stay in the one place for more than a few months, maybe even make some friends. These were all good things – fantastic things actually. So why was she currently on the verge of hyperventilating on the doorstep to her future? Because it meant she now had so much more to lose. She now had people she could let down. What if she wasn't good enough? What if they didn't want her, just like the paladins behind her? *Shit*, Max thought, *I can't do this.*

Some of what she was thinking must have shown on her face for Beyden wrapped a comforting arm around her shoulders and gave her a hearty squeeze. "Hey, what's wrong? You look a little pale."

"I've changed my mind. I don't want to do this anymore." She said in a rush.

Beyden frowned, "What do you mean you've changed your mind? Max, this is a good thing. The people in there can help you."

Max was already shaking her head, "I think you've all helped me enough already. I have enough information to get by on my own now. There's no point in dragging a whole society into the mix."

"What the hell are you talking about?" Ryker demanded in his usual blunt fashion. "Get your arse inside. I haven't wasted the last two weeks of my life on you just so you can puss out now."

Before she even knew what she was doing, Max found herself out of Beyden's grip and in front of Ryker. The man was staring down at her in complete disdain again like she was nothing but shit beneath his shoe! *Bastard!* She thought, her fear completely forgotten in her rage. The big toe of her right foot connected solidly with the shin bone on Ryker's left leg. The curse he let out would have made even the most seasoned sailors blush and the pang in her toes told her the five little piggies would be sore for a while. But it was well worth it to see the big bad ancient knight hopping up and down on one leg and whining like a pansy.

"Who's the pussy now, huh?" She goaded.

"Why you little ..." The big brute made a grab for her but Darius was already holding him back.

"Easy now. Let's all just calm down. Ryker, you can't touch her you know that. And I'm sure Max is sorry. This whole situation is very overwhelming for her."

Max laughed loudly and insultingly, "Sorry? Me? Fuck no, I'm not sorry. Let him loose Darius. There's plenty more where that came from."

Darius exhaled roughly, "Really Max? Couldn't you just pretend to work with me here?"

Feeling a little bit sorry for him, after all, he was just trying to keep the peace, Max relented. "Fine. But he deserved it. You are such an insensitive jerk!" She snarled the latter toward Ryker.

Axel slapped her on the back, "He did deserve it. Good job mini ninja." He was red in the face and still chuckling. Taking a look around, she realised the others were all in similar states of amusement and she began to see the humour in the situation as well. She had responded like any child would in the playground when confronted with the school bully. She really shouldn't let her emotions get the better of her but Ryker just ... well, he pissed her off quicker than any other person she had ever met. And for some reason, his words had the power to hurt her more than any other person she had ever met too. Which was just insane, Max lectured herself.

"As entertaining as this is, we really should be getting inside." Cali said.

That brought Max quickly back to the matter at hand, the fact that she had indeed been 'pussing' out. "Are you all sure this is the best thing to do?" She asked, seeking reassurance.

"Of course Max. Why wouldn't it be? Why are you so worried?" Lark asked, looking concerned.

Max bit her lip and glanced around at the concerned faces surrounding her. Without meeting any eyes, she voiced her biggest fear, "What if they don't like me?"

Lots of shuffling feet and throat clearing met her question and Max rolled her eyes at herself. She sounded like a doofus! Shaking off her reservations and pretending like the past ten minutes never happened, Max moved forward and grabbed the door handle, "Just forget it. Let's get this done." And so saying, stepped inside.

****

To Max, the inside looked much like a mess hall she had seen at an army barracks with dozens of tables and chairs on one side of the room next to a serving station stacked with plates, glasses and cutlery. The other side was open plan with lounges, coffee tables, wall-mounted big screen televisions and pool tables. Various doorways looked to lead to offices or outside to the outer buildings. There were more than a dozen people milling around, with the amount of men outnumbering the women four to one. Her entrance garnered a few stares and halted conversations but beyond that not much interest. Max let out a relieved breath, no one was staring at her. The whole room seemed to take a collective breath however the moment Ryker and his crew stepped in. People didn't stop moving exactly but they all seemed to pause for a second or two before continuing on with their conversations or tasks. She noticed subtle nods of acknowledgment from some of the strangers and clear snubbing from others. Max found the whole dynamic very interesting. Maybe her paladins *were* bad arses! Not that they were *her* anything, Max amended, but if she was going into the lion's den then maybe it was a good thing she had these particular soldiers at her back.

"Well, welcome to the Lodge." Lark smiled, "As you can see, this is the main hall where everyone comes to eat and relax. There are main offices to the right where the wardens and paladins conduct business. The big room off to the centre there is the council meeting chambers. That's where the Council gather to discuss matters of importance, make rulings, that kind of thing. And the back door there leads to the half dozen or so recruit barracks and training facilities. It's quite a large set up." Lark pointed appropriately as he explained.

Max nodded and asked, "So you guys have an office here for when you train the newbies?"

Axel replied, "Yep. Last door over there on the right. But that's more Ryker's gig than any of us. He's in charge of the admin shit, we just get to knock heads together." Axel seemed inordinately pleased with that last fact.

"And how many young paladins live here that you train?"

"Anywhere from a dozen to thirty at a time. At the moment there are eighteen, which is fairly standard. This place is actually the largest facility in Australia. There's another one in Tasmania that houses about half that. The greenies come from all over the world and are only here on a rotational basis. They get trained all over by many seasoned paladins to ensure they're exposed to multiple skill sets and fully qualified before hopefully being bound to a warden and their own Order. As the Captain, Ryker has to sign off on every new recruit." Axel explained.

"And you guys are permanent trainers here instead of being in your own Orders?" Max asked. There was no way she could wrap her head around Ryker being a teacher. He just didn't have the patience or the social skills, she felt really sorry for the trainees here. And Ryker sitting in an office doing paperwork? That just boggled the mind. He was more suited to biting heads off chickens or making number plates.

"Someone has to train the new soldiers." Darius responded rather stiffly to Max's question.

"Besides, that whole Order thing is too restrictive. A man needs to be free to feel the wind in his hair!" Axel exclaimed with a wink. Max laughed at his antics, the man was never serious.

"That's dogs, man." Beyden nudged Axel with his shoulder, "Dogs like to feel the wind in their *fur*."

Axel narrowed his eyes, "Are you calling me a dog?"

Beyden held up his hands, all innocent-like, "Hey if the collar fits ..." He managed to duck the responding punch aimed his way. He laughed and grabbed Max's hand, "Come on squirt. Let me introduce you to a couple of friends of mine. Caspian is a Water Warden and his two paladins are brothers. They're really nice and not pretentious in the least. You'll like them."

Max let herself be dragged over to one of the lounges where a blond, slim young man of around twenty-one was seated watching a re-run of *MASH*. Next to him was a dark haired man almost twice his size, with another equally built guy on the bench seat opposite. All three were extremely good looking. All paladins had to genetically engineered to be hunks or something. It made her wonder if maybe Vin Diesel or Dwayne Johnson were paladins. They certainly fit the bill. Maybe they were in need of a lonely little warden to bind to? Max snickered to herself, that would be awesome!

"Max! Did you hear what I said?"

Max cringed, "Sorry. I was just thinking of something."

"Must have been something pretty good, judging by the gleam in your eyes." The cute blond said, drawing her attention. He looked much shorter than all the giants around her and had clear blue eyes that sparkled with life. Although he was amused, he wasn't laughing at her and Max felt herself relax further as she responded;

"Hmm. It was. The Diesel and The Rock. Pretty great thinking!"

Ryker frowned, "The what and the what?"

"If you don't understand, then you're too young to know." She shook her finger at a frowning Ryker.

The blond burst into laughter, obviously understanding her references. Beyden was right, Max thought, looks like she was going to like Caspian.

"Max, this is Caspian, guardian to that which sustains life. These are his two paladins; Lawson and Leo. Together they form the Order of Riparian." Beyden introduced formally.

Max responded in kind, dipping her head in a respectful nod and murmuring, "It's an honour to meet you."

Beyden grinned at her like a proud papa, "Caspian, this is Max ... she's new."

Caspian arched his fair eyebrows, "New to what?"

"New to the area." Ryker responded before anyone else could. They had all agreed not to advertise her 'stray' status until absolutely necessary.

"Whatever you say Ry." Caspian smiled but Max could tell he wasn't convinced. Seems cutie was also a smartie. And he must know the gang fairly well given he had just called Ryker 'Ry' with no adverse effects.

"Max is staying with us for a few days until she meets with the Local Warden Council. She is seeking out a new Order." Ryker continued.

"Really? Was your last one not to your liking?" Leo, the paladin seated on his own asked. "Good help is so hard to find these days." He winked.

Oh boy, another charmer! Max thought. "Nah, it wasn't them. It was me. I was too hot to handle." She winked back, getting her flirt on and damn if it didn't feel good.

He laughed along with his fellow paladin and liege, "Looks like you've got your hands full then folks." He said to the six paladins ranged around her. "You know we're just down the beach if you ever need extra help."

"Thanks." Ryker said dryly.

Beyden turned to Max and explained, "Riparian is only about ten minutes south of us, between the ocean and the river. They're our closest neighbours."

"Really? Then you must know the Buff Brigade pretty well then. This is excellent news!" She parked her butt on the arm of the lounge Caspian and Lawson were seated in and leaned close companionably, "You must tell me everything! For starters, have you ever seen this fabled stick Ryker has buried in his rectum? Does it ever come out or do you think it is lodged there permanently?"

Total silence reigned for all of a heartbeat before her newest three friends burst into laughter so hard, their faces soon turned red and they were gripping their heaving sides to contain themselves. Axel, Cali, Beyden and Lark were all sharing in the hilarity as well. The only one not smiling was the big man himself, although he didn't appear angry. In fact, Max could have sworn she saw amusement in his eyes. Perhaps the stick was removable after all.

Caspian wiped the tears from his eyes, "Oh, I like this one." He said to his soldiers before turning to Max, "I like you."

"That's my line." Axel joked.

Max couldn't be more pleased with how things were going. Seemed like there were a few good eggs in the whole warden basket and just because Ryker and his team didn't want her around permanently, didn't mean she couldn't find another good group of people who did. As the laughter died down, Max watched as Caspian went to pick up a glass of water only to accidently bump it off the table. The glass landed with a dull thud on the wooden floor as expected but to Max's astonishment the water did not. She watched in awe as it stopped a mere inch from the ground and formed a small ball of swirling waves as it hovered in the air. Lawson bent down and righted the glass before the wet mass somehow poured itself gracefully back into the glass. Caspian then casually picked it up and drank down the contents like nothing had ever happened.

"What the hell was that? That was so cool! Can you do it again?" Max asked eagerly.

Caspian appeared confused as he looked between herself and the others, "Um, I'm not sure why you're so impressed. Water is my element. It's kind of my thing."

"Well yeah, but that was –" Max broke off when she saw the look of warning Ryker was giving her. Right. She was supposed to be playing it cool. Sophisticated, knowledgeable, Warden Max wouldn't be phased by such childish tricks! Oh no, she saw this type of thing all the time, yes indeed! So she tried to cover her tracks although she hated to mislead such a nice guy. "It was just nice to see. Not all wardens use their powers so openly."

Caspian nodded, "That's true I guess … sad but true. I am somewhat more active with my domain than many of our brethren."

Max tilted her head, "You think wardens should be more active?"

Caspian sighed, "I think the Great Massacre has a lot to answer for."

The Great Massacre? She had heard that term thrown around but she hadn't really been satisfied with any of the answers. Maybe Caspian would be a little more forthcoming. She was just about to ask some more questions when a man with five others trailing behind him joined the party. He sauntered right up and sat himself down in the arm chair next to Max. The other five men remained standing, arms crossed over beefy chests behind him like guard dogs or something. Max found the whole thing a little rude and didn't think she was the only one if the amount of frowns was anything to go by. She then noticed that Caspian's face was suspiciously blank and he tried to sink further into the lounge as if trying to disappear. Leo stood up and flanked him on the other side. Bad blood perhaps?

The guy who planted himself in the only remaining chair leaned forward and extended a hand to Max. The smile on his face could only be described as oily as he introduced himself, "I understand we have a new warden visiting. I am surprised I didn't hear about your visit before now. My Grandmother is a member of the International Domain Council. I am Ignatius of the Order Vulcan."

Max eyed his hand warily. She really didn't want to shake it but good manners demanded it, "Hi, I'm Max." *Eww*, she thought. His hand was hot and sweaty and his grip was like a cooked noodle! You could always tell a lot about a person by their handshake and his weak grip spoke of a weak character to Max.

His smile dimmed somewhat at her curt response. "Just Max? Surely that is a nickname of a sort. What is your true name and Order?"

Darius responded before Max could formulate a half way decent one of her own, "Max is staying with us temporarily until her formal introduction to the Local Council. She comes seeking a new Order."

Ignatius raised his dark eyebrows and Max could swear they had been plucked as he said, "You're staying with *them*? Max, my dear, these paladins can barely call themselves knights. Although they are quite adept at beating newer paladins into submission, they are not very skilled at protection. If you are seeking a new Order, then you have clearly experienced failure in the past. If you don't want to repeat those mistakes, I suggest you make alternate living arrangements quickly. I can suggest some suitable replacements."

He smiled cockily and continued to fawn over her as if he were doing her a big favour instead of insulting the only people she knew and liked. There was no way she would trust one word out of this moron's mouth and she would sooner go back to living on the streets than take his advice for accommodation. She had a moment of fear though as she recalled the whole point of her coming here was to meet other wardens and paladins and find someone she could potentially bond with. That would of course mean she would need to stay somewhere else eventually but she just wasn't ready for it to be right now. And she definitely didn't want it to be with anyone like Sir Ignatius here. She cast a glance toward her group of paladins and was relieved to see the dark looks on their faces. Seemed Ignatius and his knights weren't popular.

"Thank you very much for your concern. I know they're hard on the eyes but I'm getting used to looking at them." The fake smile on the other warden's face didn't falter but Max could practically see the wheels turning in his head. What did she mean? Was she agreeing with him? Did she disagree? Was she insulting the paladins? Or was she complimenting them? *Sheesh, what a moron!* She was glad she had met Caspian first so she could use him as a standard for a warden instead of this guy. Caspian chose that moment to let out a small chuckle that unfortunately drew the attention of the new warden.

"I see you've been introduced to the resident fag. I must say Max, you need to start keeping better company. First the Rejects and now the only known arse-fucking poofter in our society. It's shameful."

Ignatius spouted his hateful words with a sneer and it was all Max could do not to reach over and bitch slap the mother fucker! Looking to her right, she saw Caspian hunch in on himself as if to make himself a smaller target. But it didn't matter how small the target was when the weapons used were words; they always hit home. Well, as luck would have it Max just happened to have an arsenal in her vocabulary. She leaned forward enthusiastically;

"Thank God! Finally someone who understands!" She exclaimed sincerely.

Ignatius's eyes lit with satisfaction and he smirked in the direction of said *'fag'* before leaning in even closer, "You don't say?"

Rage boiling internally, Max nodded her head eagerly, "Oh yes. I'm just like you are, you see," She began drawing small circles over the back of his damp hand, voice sweet as sugar. She felt Caspian shift uncomfortably in his seat as his paladins stood straight and ready but gave no signs of immediate action. Max could tell they wanted to jump to their charge's defence but they held themselves back. Those stupid politics Darius had warned her about, no doubt. Oily Ignatius of the Order Vulcan was looking smug and proud and ... well, oily at the added attention. This was almost too easy! She smiled seductively;

"I'm also a homophobic, ignorant, self-righteous, disgusting excuse for a human being – just like you!" She announced jubilantly. Max had the pleasure of seeing his smile replaced with a ferocious scowl before he yanked his hand away and jumped to his feet.

"You have no idea who I am! You just made the biggest mistake of your life." He threatened, bending down and invading her personal space once again. Max didn't even try to hide her cringe from the SOB's nasty breath.

"Somehow, I don't think so ..." she paused dramatically, pointedly ignoring the fact that nearly every person in the room was now focused on the action playing out in front of them "... Biatch!"

The lousy excuse for a warden actually raised a fist in warning before obviously thinking better given the amount of eyes trained on them. Instead, he lowered his hand and stalked from the room, all five of the still silent paladins following behind him like good little ducklings.

"Oh, don't go! This is the first intelligent conversation I've had in years! Don't you want to know what I think about the Chinese or women in the workplace?" Max kept shouting at the other warden's swiftly retreating back until he was out of sight. She turned to Caspian and his two paladins with a cheeky grin, "Guess not."

****

Ryker gritted his teeth in a supreme effort to not grab Max by the arms and shake some sense into her. She was trouble with a capital 'T'; a walking, talking incendiary device that could blow at any second! It didn't matter that Ignatius was a complete tool. In fact, Ryker daydreamed about punching him in his fat head every time they crossed paths. Ignatius was still a warden, and a very strong one at that. He had five paladins bonded to him, four of them sharing a link to the fire domain just like Ignatius. Max had just made a very powerful enemy. And to add icing to this already fucked up cake, watching her put that greasy jerk-off in his place had left him with a massive boner. He was so hard he was afraid the metal zipper of his jeans would leave permanent teeth marks on his cock!

Their little escapade the night before had left him even more volatile than usual. It was like no matter what he said to her, it was always the wrong thing. But she just turned him inside out and he had no clue why. Like take outside for instance, when Max had been about to enter the Lodge for the first time, she had hesitated and he had been taken aback by the fear in those blue-green eyes. So how had he dealt with his feelings of helplessness? Oh, that's right; he called her a pussy! His damn shin was still throbbing. The spunky little wench sure had a good kick on her. You'd think a bruised shin as well as a bruised ego would be enough to deflate his ... *interest*. But nooooo!

Stupid dick!

"She's ..."

Ryker jumped at the interruption from his inner diatribe, both hands reaching for his absent sickles out of habit. He felt naked without the twin blades and hated the fact that no weapons were permitted in the main hall of the Lodge. Having said that, it was Ryker who had actually instigated that little rule after one too many mishaps so he had no right to bitch. He had pointedly not asked Max if she was carrying that damn sword of hers in her boot. He didn't want to know. Forcing himself to relax, Ryker turned to the speaker. It was Kane, one of the famed triplet paladins currently unbound to a warden. Ryker didn't know him or his brothers well – they had arrived only one week earlier to complete their final round of training before graduating to full knight status. But they had a reputation as fierce fighters, in and out, of the bedroom. They were highly famous for their sexcapades in the paladin community all over the globe. Personally, Ryker didn't see the appeal. He decided to finish the half spoken statement;

"Insane? A menace? A walking disaster zone?"

Kane gave a small chuckle as he shook his head. His eyes roamed Max's profile appreciatively as he said, "I was going to say amazing."

Ryker felt the scar on his face pull tight as he scowled. He had the sudden urge to pluck out Kane's eyeballs with a rusty spoon. Because he wasn't exactly renowned for his garrulous ways, he simply grunted and continued to scowl in Max's general direction. She was now involved in an animated discussion with Cas, the other warden no longer pale or dejected. Even as he watched, Max placed a gentle hand on Cas's arm as she whispered something in his ear. He had to shake his head at her astuteness. She was essentially staking a claim on the young outcast, touching and sharing secrets, declaring him to be a confidant. She was proving to the rest of the room that she wasn't afraid or disgusted to be associated with him and he wasn't going to 'contaminate' her. It was exactly what the other paladins in the room needed to see. There were no other wardens present now that Ignatius had left and Max and Caspian were now the highest ranking people in the room, not that Max understood that.

Caspian laughed in response and Ryker couldn't help but notice the way the blond leaned into the touch of the older paladin next to him, nor the warm look Lawson sent Max in thanks. There was an intimacy between Cas and his paladin that couldn't be denied. Well, if you were going to buck a trend, you may as well do it right, Ryker thought. Not only was homosexuality forbidden amongst the upper cast but relationships between wardens and paladins was severely frowned upon. Oh, sexual relations where a warden used their paladin for the express purpose of a vitality exchange was entirely acceptable. But throw some feelings in there, some respect, some genuine affection and that was taboo. *Fucking hypocritical bastards!* Ryker thought in disgust.

Caspian was a relatively young warden and not a physically strong one, but he was one of the most courageous men Ryker had ever had the pleasure of meeting. He stood up for what he believed in and was true to himself and those he loved. Ryker respected the hell out of the guy. So when Leo had contacted him on his brother's behalf and told him they were having issues in their hometown in the US, Ryker had told them about the land for sale just down the road. The fact that it was Ryker's land and he hadn't intended to put it on the market at the time was his business. Ryker had trained Leo and his older brother Lawson here at the Lodge years ago and had been impressed with their fighting skills and good natures. It hadn't been a hardship to sell the land to Caspian. They were good neighbours.

"So, what's her story? I hear she's staying with you guys. You thinking of taking on another warden?"

Shit! Was Kane still there? Ryker moved his eyes in the direction of the other paladin but gave no other sign he had heard him. No way was he explaining himself to this young buck.

Entirely unfazed, Kane chuckled. "Alrighty then. I assume she's free game." He rubbed his hands together, "Excellent."

Now he did turn to Kane and pinned him with a hard stare. "She's not free game. You remember who you're talking about soldier. She is a warden of the highest cast and you will afford her the respect of her station. Am I understood?"

His stern voice brooked no reply other than the 'Yes, Sir' he received. That was more like it, Ryker thought.

"I think my ears are bleeding. Did you just lecture someone about respecting me?"

Ryker closed his eyes and groaned. The woman was so tiny she had managed to sneak up behind him. Naturally, her timing was perfect and she just had to hear his mini rant to Kane. How was he supposed to live with her after this?

****

"Are you going to introduce me?" Max asked Ryker. Although his eyes spoke volumes, his mouth did not. "I'll take that as a no. Hi, I'm Max." She smiled widely at the newest primo specimen in front of her as she held out her hand for him to shake.

"My name is Kane. It is a great pleasure to meet you, Max." Kane practically purred as he took her hand and skimmed his lips over the top gallantly. The way he said the word 'pleasure' had Max believing that he would indeed be a pleasure ... multiple pleasures in fact!

"Oh, my!" She twittered as she batted her lashes. Ordinarily, Max would think such flirtations were an insult to her feministic side but after the mass rejection of the paladins that morning, she was willing to go with the flow. She heard a low sound, oddly like a rumble or a growl and was just turning to place it when Kane's brilliant white smile widened and revealed a matching set of dimples. Now that was just plain wrong! That such a masculine, mountain of a man, so rugged and virile would have those boyish little dimples ... *sigh!* Looking around she noticed the band of merry misfits watching the exchange with varying degrees of amusement, shock, censure and approval. The approval, of course, coming from her fellow *chica* Cali.

Max tried to return her attention to Kane only to be distracted by that grumbling sound again. She pivoted and narrowed her eyes at Ryker. "Are you growling?"

"No!" Ryker growled.

Shrugging off the antisocial, perpetually premenstrual paladin, Max opened her mouth to ask Kane if he wanted to join her for a drink when her brain decided to have a seizure or something. Standing in front of her was not one, but three Kanes! They wore identical expressions of lust and had identical gleams in their eyes.

"I'm sorry," she apologised, "but I think I may have just had a stroke. You seem to have multiplied."

The three Kanes laughed in tandem. "No stroke." Kane the Second assured her. "There is absolutely nothing wrong with your fine self. I'm Kai, and this is our baby brother Kellan." Kai bowed graciously and indicated the remaining look alike to his left.

Kane the Third tilted his head and flashed his own set of killer dimples. "By baby, he means by two minutes. I promise you, there is nothing babyish about me."

Max held up hands. "Wait a minute. There are three of you?"

The three K's grinned devilishly whilst nodding their heads. Not one to believe in such luck immediately, after all, some hallucinations could be very vivid, Max turned to Cali for confirmation, "There are three of them?"

Cali widened her eyes comically and mouthed silently but distinctly, "There are three of them!" Her words held more power because of their silence and just like that, Max believed in Santa Claus again!

With nothing intelligent left to say, she simply twittered another, "Oh, my!" as she battered her lashes once again.

"You said that already!" The snarl from Ryker rudely interrupted Max's in-brain movie of herself in a sweaty triplet sandwich. She shoved him with her shoulder not even sparing him a glance as she spoke to the trio.

"Don't mind him. He has some kind of brain disorder that I haven't quite figured out yet."

The choking gasp from Ryker could be heard over the several loud snickers and chuckles. Max rolled her eyes, "See what I mean?"

Clenching his jaw, he rumbled, "Would you please try to contain yourself? It's embarrassing!"

"Who's embarrassed? I'm not embarrassed. You guys embarrassed?" She asked the triplets and received three vigorous head shakes. She turned to Caspian, "Yo, Cas. You embarrassed?"

"No ma'am," he replied swiftly, "you could very well live out a favourite fantasy of mine if you continue down this path."

Lawson gave him a playful swat to the rump, "Watch yourself, brat."

Max smiled, those two were so cute! She tucked her unruly hair behind her ears and stood a little straighter, causing her breasts to push against her tee shirt. Good posture was very important. It was times like these that she wished she had some nicer and newer clothes, maybe a little make-up or hair product. And wow, was she really standing here lamenting over her lack of feminine wiles? She had truly hit rock bottom but what was a girl supposed to think when she was a frumpy dwarf surrounded by a bunch of beautiful amazons? She was so out of her league, but if Ryker and the others didn't want her then she would damn well prove that somebody else did. The three hotties in front of her were a good place to start.

"How about I buy you boys a drink?"

The middle one, Kai, smiled. "Drinks are free here."

Max grinned back, "Even better."

A giant shadow seemed to suddenly block out all the light in the room. Max craned her head back, back, back, only to see a scowling Ryker directly behind her, his oversize head obstructing the above light. Max could tell by the look in those yummy eyes of his that he was going to ruin all her fun.

He flicked his eyes forward. "Go away now." Just three little words but it was enough to bring about a flurry of movement. Although Ryker insisted they weren't the most respected paladins in the room, it looked like they were the most feared for everyone scattered including the three pretties.

"That was not appropriate behaviour." He intoned.

Max spun around and poked a finger into his hard chest, "Are you kidding? Those three are my reward for being a lone wolf all these years! I totally deserve them! You can't have them!" Max yelled a little hysterically at seeing her new toys slip through her fingers.

Ryker rolled his eyes, completely unmoved. "You're being ridiculous. You can't keep them."

"Actually, she can. Isn't that the whole point of coming here today? So she could be introduced to unbound paladins and find those who would share their vitality?" Cali inquired.

"It's not going to be them." Ryker stated.

Cali placed her hand on a slim hip, "And why is that?"

"Cali ..." Ryker's low voice held a warning that she was pushing him past his limits.

"Ryker ..." Wow, Cali had a pretty impressive growl of her own.

"That's it. Show and tell is over. We're leaving." Ryker actually grabbed Max by the arm and began dragging her from the room. She managed to throw a 'nice to meet you' over her shoulder at Caspian before she found herself outside once again.

"Hey! Wait a minute Bullwinkle. You can't just drag me around like a piece of meat. I heard you lecturing the pretties about respect, how about you start showing some?" Max demanded, hands on hips. The others had followed them out and she noticed they were standing around her in various poses of displeasure. Looks like they were on her side for once.

"Ryker man, she's right. You can't be treating a warden that way, especially not in front of the other paladins. It undermines her authority." Beyden said.

Lark quickly followed up with; "And as a warden – a Life Warden nonetheless – her authority is absolute."

Max tried not to look smug. It was nice to have defenders. Ryker ran his hands through his hair in exasperation as he appeared to take on board the criticism. She had to give him that at least; he always listened to his fellow knights and weighed and measured their opinions before forming a conclusion of his own. She bet he would have made a formidable Captain.

"You're right. I apologise."

Max nearly fell over. "Was that an apology? I don't believe it." She turned to a stunned looking Darius, "Can we stop at a newsagent on the way back? I need to buy a lottery ticket."

"Yeah, yeah. Live it up while you can. I am sorry. I had no right to manhandle you but those three are not what I had in mind when I said you needed to bind yourself to your own paladins."

"Heck, Ryker. I didn't want to bind myself to Kane … I just wanted to sit on his face."

Could someone go into a catatonic state while standing up? Because that's what Ryker seemed to do. He was standing so still she wasn't even sure he was breathing, he was no longer blinking, and his face looked like it was carved from granite. Max glanced around at the other paladins and saw various looks of astonishment on their faces; Darius was blushing, Axel was grinning seductively as if he was picturing Max on *his* face, Beyden's amber eyes were wide in disbelief, Lark was laughing uproariously, and Cali was giving her a thumbs up sign. Clearly they weren't quite used to her yet. Too bad they didn't want to take the time to try, she thought, feeling dejected once again.

NINETEEN

She wanted to sit on his face? *She wanted to sit on his face?* Two hours later, Ryker was pacing the length of his room as his brain tried to compute Max's outrageous statement from earlier. He had been absolutely livid when he had heard her refer to the other paladin in such a way. He wanted to hunt the triplets down and mess up their pretty-boy faces so no female would ever be attracted to them again. After the green-eyed monster had calmed the fuck down, his one-eyed monster had decided to chime in with nothing but images of a naked, writhing Max. He wanted her to sit on *his* face.

After the tension-filled drive back to camp, everyone had separated to do their own thing. Ryker didn't know where Max had disappeared to, she had been studiously ignoring him the whole ride back, which was just as well for her. One more word out of that smart mouth of hers and he was liable to turn her over his knee and give her the spanking she so obviously needed. He groaned and pressed the palm of his hand against his straining erection – that imagery was so not helping. He had already undone the button on his jeans as a concession to his hardness and stripped off shirt and shoes in an attempt to cool his overheated skin. His lust had been on a slow simmer since she had first walked through the door sixteen days ago but he was now at boiling point. It was taking all of his iron-willed control not to seek out the woman and throw her over his shoulder, cave-man style. Maybe if he pounded his frustrations out on a punching bag, his body might deflate enough to allow him some sleep.

Although not the type of pounding his idiotic cock wanted, he decided to head down to the gym anyway, that was until he opened up his bedroom door and saw the object of his unanswered lust standing on the threshold. One look at the stubborn tilt to her chin and the flashing fire in those strange eyes of hers and all reason flew out the window.

"The only person you're going to be sitting on is me!" Okay, so that was totally *not* what he was intending to say but damned if he would take it back.

****

Max had been standing outside Ryker's door for over five minutes rehearsing the butt-chewing she intended to unleash on his unsuspecting arse. Who the hell did he think he was? He didn't want her but he didn't want anybody else to have her either? *So* not cool! Raising her fist to knock curtly, she almost swallowed her tongue when a half-naked Ryker opened the door. He was wearing a pair of unbuttoned jeans ... and nothing else save those two little silver bars through his tanned nipples.

"The only person you're going to be sitting on is me!"

Say what now? Had he just said ...? His hungry brown eyes were all the confirmation she needed. She had a split second to make her decision and considered her choice made when she stepped over the threshold and closed the door behind her. Apparently that was all Ryker needed as well as he began to stalk forward. Max swallowed hard as she took in his predatory grace. The man moved like a jungle cat, all muscle and sinew bunching and flexing in an erotic display of power. He was all muscle, not an ounce of fat on him and she found herself surprised at his leanness. She thought he might be bulky, but he was more smooth lines. She licked her lips in anticipation even as she felt a flutter of nerves in her belly. She had wanted to let the lion out of its cage and it seemed like she just got her wish. So what was one more stick on the fire?

"Really? You want me? Come and get me, big man." She taunted right before she turned and fled.

She made it one step.

One step, before she found herself sandwiched between two hard surfaces. The one at her front was hard and unyielding, cold and smooth against her palms. The one at her back was also hard, but dipped and yielded in the most interesting places. It was also hot. Very, very hot. Two large hands began a rough exploration of her legs and her back side and Max realised he was frisking her for weapons. She smiled as Ryker managed to find every last one of her blades and even her garrotte wire she kept in the waistband of her pants. The paladins had removed all their weapons before entering the training facility but she didn't go anywhere without her blades. All the weapons were carefully placed on the bedside table including her tanto sword. The last made her pause for a moment but Ryker was thoughtful and kept it in plain sight as if he knew how important it was to her.

She felt the breath rush from her lungs as she was swiftly spun around and Ryker's mouth wasted no time in swallowing her gasp of shock. Her mouth opened under the demand of his surprisingly soft lips and she welcomed his tongue as he swirled and plundered, mimicking what was to come. Moaning, she arched her back and hooked one leg around his hips, rubbing herself against the man like a cat in heat. He felt so good and all she could think was *more, more, more.* So she was a little bewildered when she felt Ryker pull back and do nothing but stare down at her with eyes darkened by desire. His strong, callused hands cupped her face as he leaned down once again and used his tongue to explore the inner cavern of her mouth, this time at a more leisurely pace as if he had all the time in the world. She growled in frustration at the change in tempo. Here she was about to self-combust and he wasn't even winded! Ryker obviously read her growl correctly for he said;

"Easy there. Let's slow it down."

Slow? Nuh uh. "Want fast. Want now." She demanded and cupped her hand over the sizeable bulge in his jeans. She had a second to think, *come to mumma,* before her hand was removed and chained with her other above her head by one very large, masculine fist.

"If we're going to do this, we're going to do it right." Ryker stated, nibbling a path along her collar bone before nuzzling her right breast through her shirt with the tip of his nose. The action was oddly affectionate and caused a pang of nerves to buzz through her system. Surely the man wasn't trying to get cuddly?

"Oh, we're doing this." She assured him confidently. She just had to get the predator back instead of this odd demonstrative version of the paladin.

Those russet eyes of his gazed at her in silence for a couple of seconds before a deliberate grin morphed his features into pure sin. He leaned in close and ran his mouth along the line of her neck this time causing her to break out in goose bumps, before whispering in her ear, "Then let's do it right."

She let out an undignified squeal as she was picked up and tossed unceremoniously onto the middle of the bed. She was then privileged enough to have a front row seat to the most erotic strip show of her life. It consisted of Ryker lowering his zipper carefully over his straining erection, hooking his thumbs under his waistband and sliding the denim over his legs. So okay, the man merely took off his jeans, but damned if it wasn't stimulating. He also went commando ... nummy! He prowled forward, the thick, long length of him bobbing up and down as she marvelled at his size. Was it even going to fit?

He straddled her torso as he began removing her clothing piece by piece beginning with her shirt and bra and ending with her jeans and underwear in one fell swoop. So much for taking his time, Max thought dizzily. When there was nothing between them but heat and lust she began an early exploration of those dips and valleys with her palms. Rough pebbles distracted her and she licked her lips in anticipation as she pulled back and eyed Ryker's piercings. Hers – all hers!

She placed her open mouth over the piece of metal running through Ryker's left nipple, outlining it teasingly with her tongue. The hard nub beaded perfectly and she gave it a hard tug with her teeth in reward. Ryker's growl vibrated in his thick chest and sent an answering shudder of desire straight to her clit. She moved to the other side and delivered the same treatment, tugging and pulling and licking until the constant rumble in Ryker's chest seemed more like a purr. Maybe he was a jungle cat after all.

Moving on, she smoothed her hands over broad shoulders and down strong flanks before finally coming to rest over two taut mounds of delicious buttness! She arched her back and rubbed her breasts against the ripped plains of his chest as she squeezed his firm cheeks ... hard. Ryker bared his teeth and hissed, jerking forward harshly and grinding his impressive erection against her clit. Max couldn't help herself, she cried out and anchored one leg over his hip as he began to rut against her in earnest, her pleasure ensuring a smooth glide. His cock provided a delicious friction along her sensitised folds and she knew she could orgasm from this alone. Before she was able to prove herself correct however, Ryker gripped her hips halting her frantic movements. He then proceeded to torture her to the point of insanity. He sucked on her stiff nipples, massaged her engorged breasts, teased her belly button with his tongue, and took her to the brink time and time again with lips, and teeth and tongue. Her nub was so ultrasensitive she was on the verge of begging when Ryker, aka the Sex God, reared up, hastily donning a condom and began to press forward slowly, stretching her exquisitely.

"So tight." He groaned through bared teeth.

Max gasped, "So big," and then proceeded to squeeze her internal muscles. Apparently that was all it took for the knights control to finally snap for he hooked his hands under her knees, pushing them back and spreading her wide, before pounding her into the mattress. So ... fucking ... good! Max was forced to brace her hands against the headboard to stop her head from smashing against the wooden frame. The position angled her hips slightly higher, allowing her to feel Ryker deeper with every stroke. It felt incredible.

Her orgasm, when it finally peaked, felt like a series of mini detonations cascading throughout her entire body and coalescing in her womb. A need she couldn't deny, and with such agonising pleasure roaring through her body, she didn't *want* to deny, revealed a hidden agenda in the very core of her being. With nothing but instinct guiding her she raised her right hand and placed her palm on Ryker's left forearm, directly over the faded tattoo there. The room seemed to explode around her much like her orgasm had with a series of small explosions sounding in the small space. The light bulb above their heads pulsed brilliantly before it imploded and rained a kaleidoscope of sparks and glass over the bed; the bedside lamp seemed to suffer a similar fate and it burst into a colourful rainbow of energy; the French doors burst outward as the wind shrieked into the room, also somehow bringing a rush of multi-coloured mist with it. Her confusion grew as she suddenly felt a rush of emotions that were not her own. She had grown used to her empath abilities over the years but this was something different, something ... *more*. It was completely overwhelming and her moans of pleasure now transformed into whimpers of fear.

"What the hell! What have you done? Do you have any idea what you've done?" The frantic words barely registered through the wind tunnel in her head.

TWENTY

So lost in his own suffocating pleasure, it took a few seconds for Ryker to register the chaos in the room. The moment he sunk his hard shaft into the giving, searing heat of Max's body, Ryker had been lost. He had set a furious pace, only dimly concerned that he was being too rough. But the erotic whimpers and moans leaving Max's throat attested to the fact that she had been right there with him. And when Max had orgasmed? Holy fuck! Ryker thought he might just have a heart attack right there. Her grip on him was so strong he could barely move and the rhythmic milking along his cock had his eyes rolling into the back of his head. His own peak was just as harsh and he released a long, low groan as he felt his pleasure jet from his body in a seemingly endless stream. Presently, a strange tingling heat seared his arm and Ryker glanced down to find Max's eyes opaque with brilliant colours. Her hand was wrapped around his sweaty forearm.

And just like that, his pleasure turned to dread.

"What the hell! What have you done? Do you have any idea what you've done?" He shouted as he practically flew from the bed. He was too busy being horrified to notice the fear and shock on Max's face. Ignoring the chaos in the room he looked down at his arm and almost staggered from what he saw. There, over his washed-out coat of arms was the beginnings of a new pattern, too pale to yet make out.

"Fuck!" He pulled sharply at his hair hard enough to feel the sting. This was a complete disaster! This is what he got for thinking with his dick. A fear-filled whimper returned his attention to the room. Max was in the centre of the bed, knees drawn up, rocking back and forth in an attempt to soothe herself from the self-induced mayhem she couldn't possibly comprehend. He approached the bed carefully, making no sudden movements as if she were a wild horse in need of currying.

"It's okay baby, everything is going to be okay. Easy now." His voice was ragged even to his own ears as he attempted to calm the warden ... and likely his new liege.

His liege! Fuck!

She looked up at him with wide, terrified turquoise eyes that were still a little glassy and she clutched at the sheet like a lifeline. The hand she reached out to him shook and those dazed eyes of hers began to take on the suspicious sheen of tears. "Wha ...? I ... I ... I don't understand. What is this? Why do I feel like this?"

Ryker accepted the offered hand and clasped it between his own to still its convulsive movements. He was now driven by a soul deep need to try to relieve her fears and make everything better. "It's okay. We both just got more than we bargained for, that's all."

"I don't understand." Max answered, a silent plea in her eyes that tore at Ryker's gut.

"I know you don't." And he did know. After all, he could feel it couldn't he? She was a mass of conflicting emotions from fear to confusion to pain and even anger. Seemed she didn't much like feeling out of control. Well, her and him both. The small hand in his own felt like the only anchor keeping him grounded right now. Just what the hell were they going to do?

He watched as Max's eyes focused on the shadowy imprint on his forearm. Seemingly as if unable to control herself, she raised her right hand and tentatively placed it over the outline. He couldn't help flinching as the connection between them flared to life once more and shared emotions, desires and needs churned like a live thing in their midst.

Max flung herself away from him and cringed against the headboard shaking her head. "What *is* that?"

"You just bonded us ... or at least tried to. The imprint isn't dark enough for a complete binding ... I hope."

"Bonded us? Wha? I ... I ... no idea ..."

Sighing, Ryker ran his hands over her shoulders and arms comfortingly and was relieved when the room began to stop its little light show. There was nothing he could do about the broken lamp and lightbulb at the moment but at least it didn't sound like they were in the midst of a storm anymore. Although he was absolutely horrified at the thought of being the warden's bonded paladin, he couldn't help but feel a little proud that his touch alone was enough to soothe her. It was his privilege and his right, his sole goal in life was now to ensure her wellbeing and safety.

And, hell no! Ryker shook his head vigorously, that was the bond talking, not the paladin. Jeez, the bond was potent, he thought. He had forgotten its intensity over the years. The binding of paladins was an ancient sacred custom and was a great honour, a great privilege ... and forged a soul-deep connection. It was always two-sided – a paladin had to be willing to be bound. So how the fuck had this happened? Ryker raged internally, he did *not* want to be bound to Max. He only hoped the connection Max had ignorantly forged had not been long enough to seal the bond into their souls. If that were to happen, he would be able to feel and even hear her in his mind in order for him to better serve as her personal knight. The pang he felt in his chest made a mockery of that last thought but he stubbornly ignored it. He never wanted to be bound into an Order again and even if by some miracle he were to change his mind, it sure as shit wouldn't be for some stray mini warden with no control, no clue and no real future in their society.

A small gasp had him raising his eyes and refocusing on Max. Her flat eyes held a dark knowledge and he knew she had heard or at least felt the last part of his internal monologue; she knew he had rejected her.

Pain that wasn't his own flared bright and sharp in his heart before the connection went black, as if it had never been there. He didn't know how but apparently he just got his wish – Max had managed to sever the binding in its infancy. Now he just had to tell his fool heart to be relieved rather than dismayed.

TWENTY-ONE

Max couldn't sleep. It wasn't because of the nightmares or seizures that usually plagued her either. No, it was the *intercourse* that was the cause of her most recent bout of insomnia. It had been the singular, most spectacular sex she ever had, and she was by no means a monk. Clearly Ryker had used his past time between the sheets to fine tune his technique. It was like he knew just where to touch and with just the right amount of pressure to keep her teetering on the edge of ecstasy. It had been maddening but had also resulted in the most intense orgasm of her life. The whole thing should have been nothing more than two consenting adults sharing a mutually satisfying romp between the sheets. But, no! Max had to go and ruin it, didn't she?

She sighed and grabbed the pillow from behind her head, placing it over her face. Maybe death by suffocation would put her – and the rest of the world – out of their shared misery. She was always fucking up where her powers were concerned. She had too much juice and not enough skill. All this power streaming through her veins and yet she was useless to wield it; she leaked energy all over the place and couldn't revive like a normal warden would. She was a complete failure when it came to being a warden, even after the weeks of tutelage by the paladins. And to top it all off she then went and almost bonded her and Ryker together. In her defence she didn't have any idea how she had done it but her ignorance was a weak, pathetic excuse this time. One couldn't go around messing with other people's souls. That was *so* not cool! She didn't want to be bound to the Sasquatch two doors down anyway! But fuck if it didn't cut her to the bone when she had felt Ryker's fear and disgust at the thought of being connected to her. Surely she wasn't that bad! She thought she would make a damn good liege actually and to finally have a family to call her own ... well, that would be a kind of magic she really couldn't afford to dwell on.

Giving up on the whole sleep deal, Max dragged the cover off the bed and made her way downstairs in her ratty tee shirt, bare feet, and Joy. She sighed as she eyed her Japanese short sword; she was back to carrying the thing around like a teddy bear again. Max found herself in the cavern-like kitchen digging through the cupboards like a rabid racoon. *Give me the precious!* Hissing in victory, she pulled out her bounty and retrieved a spoon from the cutlery draw. Wrapping the doona more firmly around her shoulders she went outside and walked the few metres to the edge of the sand. Opening the jar of Nutella, she dipped her spoon in and moaned when the delicious brown nectar of the gods hit her tongue. She would have to buy Cali another jar because this one was history!

She was about a quarter of the way through the jar when she felt a disturbance in the air. It was subtle and wasn't filled with danger but had her glancing around the dark beach for clues as to what was going on. Max drew in a startled breath when her eyes made out a shadowy figure heading her way. The subtle swaying movements from the hip region suggested female even as the form seemed to blend with the shadows, merging with them as if she was a part of the dark itself. Max gripped her sword under her covers even though she didn't feel threatened in any way. That was strange in and of itself but it hit her that this immediate feeling of security had only ever happened once before; with the paladins sleeping in the house behind her. This then, must be the missing paladin of death.

The woman strolled casually to her carrying an expensive looking large bag in one hand and flat, strappy shoes in the other. She was dressed in comfortable-looking linen pants, a silk blouse with a scooped neckline and a soft cardigan. She looked classy, *really* classy. Max continued her appraisal and noticed a lean waist, a decent sized rack and a face that could start a war. She was typically gorgeous with a pointy chin, high cheekbones and dark intense eyes. What sealed the deal for Max though was all that hair! It was dark and the corkscrew curls fell around her face and shoulders in complete disregard for gravity. Max's fingers twitched with the urge to pull on one. She looked like an elegant gypsy.

"You must be Diana." Max figured she should probably vocalise rather than continue to sit there staring.

The woman nodded, sending the springs on her head flying. "And you must be Max."

She shrugged. "Guilty as charged ... you're just as beautiful as the rest of them." She blurted and sounded grumpy even to her own ears.

Diana laughed and Max felt her own lips twitch. There was nothing feminine or subtle about that laugh, it was loud and robust and Max bet she even snorted sometimes. She was petty enough to be happy about that.

"Is that Nutella?" She pointed to the jar.

Max hugged her comfort food protectively to her chest for a moment before she loosened her hold and held it out to the other woman. "Yes. You want?"

Diana smiled, revealing one crooked tooth on the top row, "You don't mind if I join you?"

"You look a little too put together for beach-sitting and for someone who has just flown twenty four hours." She was still sulky ... and she really didn't want to share her chocolate.

Diana shrugged delicately, "I like to look 'put together'."

"Well, I'm not wearing any pants. So ..."

"Oh, now you're just trying to tease me." She winked and parked her no doubt perfect butt on the cool sand.

Max couldn't help laughing. Diana was obviously not the snob she looked like. She offered the jar and watched in fascination as the other woman forewent the spoon and dipped her finger in instead before passing it back. "So, you're here to fix me, huh?"

Diana's eyebrows raised in question, "Are you broken?"

"Apparently." Max tried not to sound bitter at the admission.

"She's not broken." The voice was soft and husky and seemed to blend with the sound of the lapping waves. Cali plonked herself down in the sand on the other side of her. "Are we having a slumber party?" She asked and leaned over to hug the other woman, "Hey girl. Did you get your sicko?"

"Nailed his butt to the wall!" Diana replied.

"Awesome!"

"I am so too broken. Damaged goods, on the fritz, useless, pitiful excuse for a warden." Max ranted pathetically to herself, shovelling Nutella into her mouth with every self-flagellation. "Things keep exploding and I

182

keep leaking and I go around branding people all the time ..." She trailed off when her mouth got too full.

"Wait, what? Branding?" Diana asked. "Who did you brand?"

"Myker ... mind of." Her mouth was filled with gooey goodness so she couldn't articulate very well but the new paladin seemed to understand all the same for her mouth dropped open in shock.

"You tried to bind him as your paladin? To imprint your souls?" Diana asked in shock.

Max swallowed and sniffed piously, "So *he* thinks. *I* think I was attempting to wrench off his arm so I could beat his stupid, insensitive, thoughtless butt to a bloody, pulpy mess." She shrugged, "But what would I know?"

Cali rubbed her back comfortingly, "You didn't succeed, and that's all that matters."

"Yeah but it's going to make for awkward dinner conversation; 'hey, remember that time I tried to meld our souls together and make you my indentured servant when we were orgasming?'" She snorted. "Real classy!"

"Orgasm? Why were there orgasms?" Diana was looking frantically between the two of them in an attempt to follow the conversation. Cali helpfully made a crude gesture with her hands that Max thought was scarily accurate. "Wait, wait, wait. You had *sex* with Ryker?" The dark-haired paladin's eyes were practically bugging out of her head and Max found herself once again considering the notion that she and Ryker were lovers.

"Yeah. That's when I supposedly tried to bind him –"

"Never mind that." Diana interrupted with an impatient slash of her hand, "You had sex with Ryker! Tell me everything!"

Max stilled and roved her eyes between the other two women. They were on their knees leaning forward intently and wore identical expressions of curious lust. Maybe Diana hadn't slept with Ryker after all, she was too eager for details. Max felt herself smile for the first time since the *intercourse*. Looks like it was girl talk time! "Let's just say I now know how they do it on the discovery channel." Max waggled her eyebrows suggestively and they all laughed.

"And his dick?" Cali asked boldly, "What's that like?"

Max licked her lips remembering the feeling of being stretched by Ryker's hard shaft. "His rig is massive! Long and thick and slightly curved so hits all the right places."

Diana shuddered delicately, "I knew it!"

"Too bad that mouth of his always ruins everything!" Max grumbled, spooning more of the hazelnut spread into her own mouth.

Diana's shoulders drooped almost comically, "You mean he's no good at the fun stuff? Nipples? Clit? I'm so disappointed in him!" She wailed.

Max sputtered and choked on her mouthful of Nutella. Diana was just as outrageous as Cali! And Cali was absolutely right – Max *did* really like the other female paladin. "That's not what I meant. He is most definitely a clit-man ... I was referring to his thoughtless, careless vocabulary."

"Really? Ryker's usually very articulate. Thoughtless and careless are not words I would use to describe him ... ever."

Cali snorted and stole the jar and spoon from Max, "You haven't had the privilege of seeing him when he's around our warden here. I think all of his blood settles in his giant rig Max just described and his brain finds it impossible to function at an adult level."

"Really? That's ... interesting." The paladin of death stated.

"Not the word I would have used. Anyway, I've royally fucked up the whole situation entirely beyond repair. The others here don't want to be my paladins and now I've essentially forced Ryker without his permission. It's unforgivable."

"Max ..." Cali started.

"No Cali, please don't. I'll be a grown up about the whole thing. It takes two to tango after all. But I think I've officially overstayed my welcome. I'm outta here tomorrow."

The two women glanced at each other intensely and some form of silent communication seemed to go on between them before the saucy gypsy grabbed the jar from the Scandinavian princess.

"Let's go back to Ryker's cock. Tell me, does he manscape?"

Max smiled, snuggled into her doona and let herself wallow in the freedom of feminine friendship. Just for one last night.

TWENTY-TWO

Ryker was absolutely furious ... with himself. His night had been filled with self-recriminations whilst hiding in his room with his tail between his legs. The look of devastation in Max's turquoise eyes when she had fled the room yesterday had seared him to the soul. For all her tough talk and hard-arse exterior he knew underneath it all there was a vulnerable, fragile spirit seeking acceptance and a home. Those few minutes of connection between them had given Ryker a glimpse into the soul of a brave, strong, selfless woman whose only desire was to find peace in a world that was a constant mayhem to her. He hadn't fully appreciated how difficult it was for her to learn to shield herself, to learn to recharge and to learn to accept help. She was so empathic, her mind was truly like a filter filled with thousands of tiny holes. She had no choice but to feel and no real choice but to secrete energy given she had no one to share the burden with. He had no doubt an Order of paladins would help stabilise her and plug those holes but he now feared he had done irreparable damage to that delicate spirit he had sensed. He had to find a way to make things right this morning.

Walking into the kitchen, he registered a blur of movement before he was slammed into the wall and pinned with a forearm across his neck. Axel leaned in close and spoke in a deadly voice;

"What the fuck have you done?"

Although he respected the hell out of the guy and even approved of his protectiveness, the challenge to his authority could not be tolerated. He was too much the Alpha to allow the blatant threat to continue. He had allowed the man one free shot at him previously – that was all he was going to get.

"Stand down, soldier." His voice was even, but brooked no room for argument; Axel would either back off or Ryker would make him. The room seemed to hold its breath as brown eyes stared into blue for several heartbeats before the pressure was removed from his throat and the other paladin took a slow step in retreat. He didn't lower his eyes however and Ryker couldn't help but be a little proud of the bold bastard.

"Where's Max?" He asked.

"She locked herself in her room yesterday and threatened us all with castration if we tried to get in." Beyden replied. He stared at him accusingly, "She didn't sound well Ryker."

"What the hell happened?" Lark demanded.

"Isn't it obvious? We all heard the cyclone going on in his room." Axel scoffed. "He fucked her."

Ryker growled and went toe to toe with the blond paladin, "Watch your mouth."

"Or what?

"Or I'll rip out your tongue."

Darius stood next to Axel. "Don't stand there and pretend to defend her honour now, Ryker. It's a little late for you to act like a gentleman. You don't go around sleeping with wardens unless they wish it for a vitality exchange. And please don't pretend that's what it was!"

"I didn't say it was!" Ryker defended. "We're both adults and we wanted each other. End of story. I am not discussing this with you."

"That's not good enough. You know Max doesn't know the rules. You took advantage of her." Beyden accused.

"It's forbidden for a reason, Ryker!" Lark added his two cents.

"You think I don't fucking know that?" He roared back.

Lark shook his head and his green eyes shone with pity. "Look we all know you two have chemistry. The air practically lights up whenever you're in the same room. But she's not for you, man."

"It won't happen again." He was firm on that.

"That's what you said last time!" Axel growled.

"Last time?" Darius asked.

Ryker ignored him. "This time is different."

"Because you've managed to hurt Max this time you mean?" Axel's blue eyes were flashing with banked fire and Ryker could feel the waves of anger wafting his way.

"No! Because she tried to bond us together, that's why!" Ryker yelled.

The collective shock in the room was palpable. "She's your liege now? You're in her Order?" Beyden's eyes were huge.

Ryker ran his hands roughly over his whiskers – he hadn't shaved in days, "No. She stopped the process before it was complete. There's no coat of arms but there was a shadow for a few minutes." He rubbed his arm remembering the feeling of Max being a part of him for those brief minutes.

"This is dangerous, Ry, very dangerous." Darius looked genuinely scared for him.

"I know. Believe me, I know. I'm going to make it right with her and then I'm finally going to stop thinking about myself and start thinking about Max. I *will* fix this." He vowed to his fellow knights and felt the tension dissipate. They all stepped back, even Axel.

"How's the 'brand' this morning?" Cali asked flippantly as she breezed into the room. She looked far too amused by the situation and it was obvious Max hadn't threatened her with castration if she knew what the hell they were discussing. *Typical females! Always sticking together!*

Ryker grunted as he rubbed at the now non-existent offending mark through his shirt. "It's faded, completely gone."

"Thank fuck!" The woman in question exclaimed loudly, walking into the room. "That would have been a catastrophe!"

Ryker frowned. She waltzed in looking fresh as a daisy and acting casual as if the past day had never happened. As if Ryker didn't now know what it was like to feel her move under him in the throes of ecstasy, to feel her clamp around him like a fist, to hear her cry out in passion. He inexplicably took extreme offense at her nonchalance and the evident relief in her voice, which Max must have noticed for she asked;

"What's wrong now?"

What's wrong now? Like he was some child trying her patience. Or worse, some simpering moron experiencing unrequited love. Which was insane, of course. He didn't want to be bonded to Max any more than she very obviously didn't want to be bonded to him. Then why was he feeling so hurt by her disregard? "What's wrong? You tried to force my soul into an eternity of slavery."

Max rolled her eyes, "You are so dramatic." She gave Lark a kiss on his cheek when he handed her a plate filled with bacon and eggs. The casual affection in the gesture had him frowning. Even after all the chaos her presence had caused, she was still burrowing her way into the hearts of his men. Not that he could blame them, she was a darn good burrower.

"I said I was sorry." She pointed out on her way to the table.

"Yeah, 'cause sorry fixes everything."

"It's a start. Sometimes words are just as important as actions." Diana sashayed into the room, clearly having arrived the previous evening. She looked typically rested and well-dressed despite what had likely been two previous days of constant travel.

He narrowed his eyes at the paladin of death. "Why do you look so good?" He accused, absolutely fed up with the fairer sex and their wily ways.

Diana smiled, "Aww, shucks boss. Thanks. I didn't know you noticed."

Ryker pinched the bridge of his nose. When he had met Diana, he had felt a certain kinship to the female paladin. They had both lost their Orders and were both astray in a world where they no longer had a function to serve. She had been the first of the misplaced paladins he had offered refuge to. He had always thought her beautiful and he had entertained the notion of a hot affair with her on and off over the years. It had never happened though as she insisted on calling him 'boss'. It made him feel like he would be taking advantage of a subordinate if he were to proposition her. In the end though, it was the right decision all round given the friendship they had managed to forge. Besides ... she was mouthy. So was Cali. And now that Max was here ... well, one female he could handle with ease. Two? Slightly more challenging. But three stubborn, sarcastic, strong, sexy women under his roof? He was in big trouble and so were the rest of the boys.

"Watch it Diana. He can be smooth when he wants to be. If you're not careful you could find yourself thrown on his bed and ravaged." Max told Diana calmly as if they were talking about the weather. She tilted her head curiously, "Or have you already experienced said ravishing? It didn't sound that way last night."

"Wait. Last night?"

"Yep. We had a slumber party on the beach." Cali smiled only to receive a woof whistle from Axel.

"And you didn't invite me?" He feigned a pout.

"Sorry." Diana shook those outrageous curls and despite Ryker's own situation he couldn't help but notice the way Darius's eyes tracked the motion. The man had it bad – filthy hypocrite. She continued, "It was for members of the Vagina Club only. We completed our sacred female bonding ritual."

"And what is that?" Beyden sounded intrigued.

Cali shrugged and buttered her raisin toast, "We discussed Ryker's sexual prowess."

Ryker choked on air as the rest of the men erupted into laughter. "You did not!"

Max leered and the three women shared a secret, evil smile that had his balls trying to crawl inside his body. "We did so too. We discussed you in minute, excruciating detail. I left nothing out." She assured him proudly.

She was telling the truth, Ryker knew she was. Dear God! How was he supposed to live with Cali and Diana now?

"Back to my earlier question; Cali? Diana? Ever romped with any of the boys?"

Diana laughed, "Nope. Can't say I have."

Max turned to Cali, "What about you?"

Did they not realise that Ryker was standing right there? And did Max have to sound so blasé about it? Couldn't she have sounded even a little bit jealous about the thought of him having sex with other beautiful women? She was a real blow to his ego.

Cali shook her head as she answered Max, "Not I. I don't go around fucking my friends."

Max nodded sagely, "It's a wise policy. I follow the same one." She turned pitying eyes on Axel, Bey, Darius and Lark. "Sorry boys, that means you'll never get to experience the sex machine that is Max."

"Well, damn!"

"What a shame."

"Now I have nothing to live for!"

"Say it isn't so!" Lark, Darius, Axel and Beyden responded.

"You slept with me." Ryker pointed out, refusing to be ignored. Was it too much to ask for a little awkwardness? Maybe a little tension?

Max's blue-green eyes swirled ominously with colour briefly before she responded coolly, "But you're not my friend ... are you?"

Ouch! Okay that one hurt and so did the looks of sympathy on the other paladin's faces. He was saved from trying to pick up his run away dignity from under the table when his mobile phone rang. Walking from the room he answered curtly and was promptly swearing two minutes later after listening to the speaker. He was about to get well and truly fucked again ... and not in the extraordinary way of the day before.

****

Max was super proud for holding herself together in front of the knights this morning. It hadn't been easy to get up and walk into a room filled with people she respected and who knew she had screwed their Captain's brains out the day before. Shit, Cali said she had even heard them! Thankfully everyone was acting normally and Max was able to relax somewhat as she ate her breakfast. It hadn't even been that awkward talking to

Ryker. Seeing him all big and pretty outlined by the rising sun hadn't helped her hormones any – she knew what he was packing now – but she was pleasantly surprised by how mature he was being. She was a firm believer that there was no issue unless you made one. Looks like neither of them were going to make an issue. She supposed they each already had enough of them without adding 'the morning after' drama into the mix.

But the dawning of a new day had brought with it the glaringly obvious matter of where to next. Max couldn't continue to stay here, it just wouldn't be right. And after her chocolate-filled bitch session with the girls the night before, she had come to the conclusion that she could not continue to disrupt their lives. She needed to find her place in this new society and sadly it wasn't going to be here with these wonderful people. She was going to ask them to take her back to the Lodge and this time she was going to be on her best behaviour. Before she could speak however Ryker stalked back in, his ever present scowl pulling his scar tight. An image of her licking that scar and Ryker's answering moan had Max licking her lips. Damn the man was potent.

"That was Magda from the Local Warden Council. They have *requested* that Max be presented to them." He threw the phone on the dining table where it skidded until coming to a stop under Lark's plate.

Lark raised his eyebrows, "We already knew that. The next meeting isn't for another three weeks, at the end of the month."

"It's been rescheduled – for today. Seems they've heard about Max's little display at the Lodge yesterday." Ryker said.

Max narrowed her eyes dangerously. "What display?"

"The incident involving Ignatius. His mother is a member of the Local Warden Council and his grandmother is on the International Council. He is a very powerful, very well respected warden." He looked at her sternly. "You made a mistake there."

"Did I just? Well, seems yesterday was the day for mistake-making." She stood up, placing her plate in the sink. She then sauntered slowly out of the room, pausing on the threshold, "But don't worry, I always learn from my mistakes. They won't happen again. I think it's a good thing they want to meet with me early."

"It's not a good thing when the six members have invited themselves to *my* camp."

That made Max pause. She knew Ryker's aversion to wardens and she also knew this 'camp' was his home. "I'm sorry. This is all completely unnecessary. Tell them I'll meet them at the Lodge or something."

Ryker snorted, "You still don't get it do you? I can't *tell* the wardens anything. They give orders, we follow. That is how it works." Max could feel a whole lot of rage and resentment funnelling from Ryker. She wanted to apologise again but knew it wouldn't be accepted so instead she just walked away. He had been doing that to her since the moment they met. It was her turn. Let the wardens come.

TWENTY-THREE

Come they did, and not four hours later. Max was peering out the library window, eyeing the newcomers with equal parts curiosity and trepidation. Lark had insisted they meet in the library as it was the largest room in the house and opened directly onto a small, perfect garden off to the side of the house. She also thought Lark knew this room would relax her the most. She smiled as she looked to the bookshelf on her left; her graphic novels were sitting pride of place on the middle shelf right next to her favourite crime fiction author, TJ Spade. Max had been tickled pink when she learned the earth paladin was a true fan and owned all of her works.

"Nervous?"

Max swivelled as all seven paladins walked in. Cripes, they were a compelling bunch all lined up like that. "Should I be?"

Axel shrugged, "You were last time."

"Yeah, well, kind of a lot has happened since then. Don't cha reckon?"

Beyden smiled, "You'll be fine."

"So who's coming again?" She asked. She should probably try and learn everyone's name.

"There are six wardens that make up the LWC. Magda, Fire Warden, is the superior; Slate, Earth Warden; Lake, Water Warden; Fawn, Beast Warden; Hades, Death Warden; and Ray is also a Fire Warden."

"No Life?"

"No. There are only a dozen left and they move from location to location on a rotational basis around the world, trying to maintain the balance as best they can." Lark explained.

Max frowned, "Twelve is not many for seven billion people."

"Well, there are thirteen now." Axel bumped her shoulder.

"Hazah! The world is saved!" Max mocked herself. She was saved from another 'you are uber important speech' by the slamming of several car doors. Looking out the window again Max counted over twenty people descending like ants, spreading out in different directions, about half of them making their way to the front door. Her stupefied look must have said it all for Ryker grunted;

"They have to bring their paladins with them of course. Now do you see why I don't want them in my home?" Apparently it was a rhetorical question for he spun and marched from the room before she could form an intelligent response.

"Don't worry about him. He'll get over it." Diana assured her, "Just brace yourself. Most wardens are very ... un-you."

Un-me? Whatever that meant, Max thought just as twelve people walked in. Half of them were in the same plain cargos and tees she had seen the others wearing and the other half were dressed in formal suits or dresses. Max spared a glance at her faded jeans, shoeless feet and Cali's tee shirt that she had tied at the waist. Perhaps she was a little underdressed.

"Thank you. We won't be requiring your assistance." The brown haired woman in front stated. It was clearly a dismissal and the woman was obviously used to being obeyed. Too bad for her the paladins in the room were not used to taking orders.

"She is entitled to a knight to serve her." Ryker was using his 'Captain' voice and Max felt herself melt a little.

"She has no knights. That is why we are all here in the middle of nowhere, after all." She bet this was Magda.

Squaring her shoulders, Max walked forward. "I'll be fine, thanks guys." She smiled and held out her right hand, "I'm Max."

The woman practically cringed at the offered palm before offering a brittle smile and a weak shake. "Magda, Fire Warden of the Order Blaze. It is very exciting to meet you and most intriguing to learn of your mysterious appearance."

She perched herself on the edge of a lounge chair daintily and gestured for the others to likewise sit. Max raised her eyebrows as the paladins were forced out of the library in their own home. No wonder Ryker was so unimpressed. Once the door was closed and the personal paladins arranged like sentries throughout the room, Magda spoke again, introducing the other wardens in turn. Max smiled politely and nodded.

"Have you recently lost weight?"

"I'm sorry?" As far as her first conversation with the famed wardens went, this one was unexpected.

"Your clothes, dear. They are far too big on you." Magda extrapolated.

"She must have recently shrunk too, because they are also too long." Slate, the earth warden, laughed at his own joke. It wasn't a pleasant laugh.

"I didn't have much with me when Darius and the boys found me." She explained, "Cali has been kind enough to lend me some of hers."

An older gentleman with hair greying at his temples leaned forward. "Yes. We heard about your tragic circumstances; no paladins, no wardens and no clue as to what you were. I'm sure your life has been horrendous." His name was Lake, Max recalled, and thought that he sounded entirely too gleeful for the sympathetic words.

"I've managed." She replied curtly. She wasn't giving the old vulture any gory details.

"Never mind, that is easily fixed. So is your hair." Magda waved away the water warden's fake concern.

"What's wrong with my hair?" Max fingered the dark red tresses. They were a little wild but Max kind of liked that about them.

Her laugh was condescending, "Oh, you are just too sweet. We're going to have to do something about your name too."

"My name? What do you mean?" Max was beginning to lose her composure. This woman was the queen of veiled insults and if she wasn't so fascinated by the odd, entitled woman she would have bitch-slapped her by now.

"Well, although I'm sure Max has served its purpose in your old life, it simply won't be acceptable now."

"It's my name. Not an old car. I can't just get a new one."

"Nonsense, my child. You must select a name more befitting of your station." Lake chimed in once again.

"My station? What station?" She asked.

"You are a Warden my dear. A Warden of Life – as well as a female. An extremely rare combination. Max is a decidedly *masculine* name and certainly not in line with our ethos."

Max glanced around the room to see four of the other wardens nodding enthusiastically. The only ones who seemed just as uncomfortable with the whole situation was the Beast Warden, the only other female in the room,

Fawn, and the other Fire Warden, Ray. Although, not outspoken they were both glaring at Magda and rolling their eyes. Perhaps the room at large wasn't a lost cause, Max thought, but so far these wardens were not a shining example of humanity. "Masculine or not, Max *is* my name and I am *not* changing it." She responded firmly.

"Perhaps Angel? Or something similar. We want her to create the right impression." Magda continued on as if Max hadn't even spoken.

Perhaps sensing Max's eminent detonation, Fawn spoke up; "Perhaps Max would like to learn a little about what it is we do."

Max smiled in thanks at the pretty blonde. "I would love to hear it from a warden's perspective. The paladins here have been wonderfully helpful but I have so many questions. I mean, what do you do every day?" At the various blank stares and furrowed brows, Max continued, "It's not like you just sit around, looking pretty and patting yourselves on your backs for being wardens ..." She finished with a snort. Her joke fell flat because obviously that is exactly what they probably did. *Oh boy!* Max was *so* going to love being an empty figure head!

Hades leaned forward, eyes intent. "I don't think you really understand what it is we do. What our purpose is ... you're very misguided, understandably so of course. We will guide you to your true purpose."

"Hades is correct. We must be circumspect. If we were to go around actively using our abilities extravagantly, people are going to notice." Magda said. "You have to understand Max – that would be a very bad thing. People as a whole are prejudiced, dangerous beings. They fear what they don't understand. And trust me, they wouldn't understand us."

"I get that a person is smart but people are dumb. I appreciate the need for secrecy. I just meant, what are our jobs?"

"Jobs?" Slate gasped in outrage, "We are Wardens. That is our jobs. Our very lives ensure that nature continues to exist! I know you aren't implying that what we do is unimportant?"

"No, I'm not implying that. I acknowledge that everyone here is born with tremendous responsibility and it is a heavy task to perform. But that doesn't mean it's all you have to be. I mean, with your affinity for animals Fawn can you imagine how much good you could do with lost and abused animals? Or your affinity with the earth Slate, you could create such beauty to the damaged lands here. Or –"

"Stop! Just stop! You have no idea what you're talking about! Working as a vet, a gardener?! We are not blue collar workers in need of ways to fill our days with mindless drivel! Now, you can be forgiven for your ignorance on this occasion given your obvious clueless background. But from this point forward, there will be no more talk of such nonsense. Wardens have a big enough burden to bear without adding in *manual labour*!"

Far from being cowed, Max was just getting started on her own soapbox, "I agree with you, it is a burden. But it is also a gift. A gift to share with the world. If you're not out there actually experiencing life and seeing the people and the animals and the world that you help maintain, then what's the point?"

"The wardens must be protected!" Lake yelled. "There are so few left and even fewer being born ..."

"Probably because you've secluded yourselves away like hermits!" Max yelled right back.

"Who are you to judge us? What have you been doing to help the 'people', hmm?" Lake patronised her.

"I've been on the run, moving from place to place for over twenty years. It's a little hard to set up shop somewhere when you've got chades breathing down your neck, trying to suck the life force out of you. But I help out when and where I can. I actually can't seem to prevent it. Surely you all must feel it too? It's like an itch or a burn just below the surface ... it's a compulsion. I could no more ignore the need to interact directly with my domain, than I could resist the urge to shit!"

There were lots of shocked gasps and rumblings and curses from the wardens and the surrounding paladins, but she was sure there was also a snicker or two as well. "Perhaps it is you who needs a re-education, hmm? Perhaps you have forgotten your purpose in your isolation." Max whipped out her very own snotty tone.

"*We* have forgotten nothing! We are Wardens – born and raised! Unlike yourself ... a stray warden bumbling in the dark! We took you in and offered our expertise and this is how you speak to us? With such disrespect? You are nothing but an insolent child!" Magda's voice was contemptuous.

Max looked around the room, seeing similar looks of contempt on almost all of the faces. Some, however, were looking at Magda with frowns or looking intently at the floor and she felt herself have another *lightbulb* moment. "Ah, I see. You haven't forgotten your purpose ... you just don't care."

"Why you little –"

Throwing out her left hand in a classic 'talk to the hand' action, Max interrupted Miss Magda, "Save it! I really don't think I can stomach any more of your self-righteous, entitled ramblings. Thank you all for your time this afternoon, but I wouldn't join your band of merry misguided morons if you paid me."

"Is there a problem?" Darius asked courteously from the doorway. Seems all the gasps of horror had alerted the occupants of the house.

"Yes, Sir Darius. There is a big problem. You have failed to teach your charge the proper etiquette required of her station. I am afraid we simply cannot be of assistance until her unruly behaviour is brought to heel." Magda replied piously.

Darius gave a low bow in Magda's direction. "She just doesn't understand, My Lady, Sirs. She has been so unaware of our world and her own nature. She requires time and patience."

"Excuse me. That is not true. And please don't apologise on my behalf Darius! There was no misunderstanding. These people are total hypocrites!" She addressed Magda once again, "And I am not some pup to be brought to heel."

"I knew it was a mistake to entrust such an important find with people such as yourselves." She said scornfully, glaring at the paladins and ignoring Max entirely. "You have obviously not succeeded in aiding this woman at all, feeding her misinformation and ensuring she is ill-equipped to deal with her situation in life."

Max couldn't believe what she was hearing. She was standing right there! And Magda was treating her people like third class citizens. Max hadn't really understood the prejudice the paladins had been alluding to the past week. She got it now and sympathised with the resentment Axel always had in his voice when he spoke of them as grunts and foot soldiers. Max opened her mouth to speak – forcefully – but was interrupted by Magda's prim voice.

"We will allow you these two past indiscretions given your newness to our society. But Max," Magda paused and locked her cold shark eyes on her, "I suggest you enlist in a better attitude ... and better companions."

She breezed out of the room, followed by her paladins and the remaining five members of the Local Council.

"What the fuck is her damage?" Max blurted out the moment the door slammed shut behind the last bonded knight. She wasn't expecting the heated silence and barely contained frustration in the room. Max felt her indignation wilt under the weight of the disappointed stares. *Okay,* Max thought, *what the fuck was* their *damage?*

TWENTY-FOUR

Ryker could feel the sizzle of change in the air. He knew things were going to explode and it was going to seal all of their fates. He only wished he knew how it was going to end. What's more, he wished he knew how he *wanted* it to end. If he was being honest he knew what his heart wanted but it had been so long since he had listened to that particular muscle that he couldn't bring himself to trust it. His mind still fought heroically for dominance so he once again found himself pissed off to the extreme with Max.

Her behaviour was just absolutely unacceptable. How was he supposed to get her to understand the full scale of the situation she was in? They had been trying for days and he felt like he was banging his head against the wall. She was the most stubborn person he had ever met. He glanced at her and found her oceanic eyes turbulent and – surprise – stubborn. He ignored the part of him that was turned on and led with the part that was angry.

"For once, couldn't you just try to behave? Couldn't you just try to act like a normal human being? Why do you feel the need to be so antagonistic all the time?" He demanded.

"I'm not antagonistic!" The little she-demon had the nerve to reply.

"Oh, please! How can you even say that with a straight face? In the two weeks that we've known you, you've managed to make an enemy of a powerful warden, embarrass yourself with the triplet spectacle, half bind us together for eternity, and now you've managed to insult some of the most important and powerful people in the world!"

"So I'm not perfect! Sue me!" She yelled back, actually looking quite stressed out to Ryker. Still, they needed to hash this out, so he rebutted;

"Not perfect? That's the biggest understatement of the year."

"I don't care, Ryker! Okay? I just don't care! I am so over this whole thing. I am over you and I am over the other paladins. I am definitely over the other wardens! They're wrong! They ... are ... wrong! Our job is not supposed to be passive – It's active!"

Max was getting less and less coherent and her voice was rising steadily. It was very unlike her, still, Ryker snorted and shook his head, "You really have a high opinion of yourself don't you? How can you possibly know if they're wrong or not? You didn't even know what you were until last week! You need to get over yourself, sister!"

"That's not true." Max voiced softly. She felt inexplicably hurt by Ryker's words. It was clear now he had a very low opinion of her and she hated it. She also hated that she hated it! What's more, it was really starting to piss her off that everyone believed she was some stupid little girl with no knowledge of the world. She was living in it wasn't she? She'd been living in it on her own, with no help and no family and no one to rely on ever since she could remember. She was willing to bet she knew more about the world than all of these paladins combined! How dare he stand there and patronise her!

Ryker raised his eyebrows in the arrogant way that made Max want to punch the smirk right off his pretty face, "What do you mean, that's not true? You had no clue what a warden was or a paladin or even a domain until you met us. And don't pretend you did. I may have thought you were hiding something in the beginning but monumental ignorance like yours is hard to fake."

Monumental ignorance? Now Max felt like crying. She never cried. She really didn't know how much more she could take from this man. She had been the bigger person these past couple of days since the whole *intercourse* thing. She had taken responsibility like a good little girl and sucked up her hurt feelings in order to keep the peace. But now ...

"You don't know anything about me."

"So enlighten us, oh sage one ..."

"Ryker ..." Darius's growl was a clear warning for him to back off. Ryker knew he should. Max was beginning to look pale, jaw clenched so tight it looked painful and the look in her eyes resembled hurt more than it did anger. Yes, Ryker knew he should back down but he just couldn't seem to stop himself. He had to make her understand the position they were all in and how dangerous her reckless actions were. She was a hazard to herself and all those around her at the moment with her ignorance and stubborn belief she was right all the time. She was going to get herself hurt ... or get his knights killed and that was something he wouldn't allow, not ever again. Not even for a vulnerable slip of a spitfire. So he pushed a little harder;

"Come on then. You know everything. Educate us."

"Ryker!" The growl belonged to Cali this time but he was resolute. Max had to be brought down to size, no matter if her delicate feelings got hurt.

"Stand down Cali. If you don't like how I lead then find someone else to follow." It was harsh, but Cali was his responsibility and he wasn't going to fail again. He searched the room only to find the rest of his fellow paladins in various states of unease and obvious objection. But none of them moved. Their loyalties were still clearly with him ... for now.

"Well? Go ahead ..." He issued the invitation to Max caustically. She raised her head slowly and stared directly into his eyes. Ryker barely suppressed a shiver. The look was somehow ancient; the knowledge in those turquoise depths, profound. He started to feel a little sick in his stomach.

"I may not have known *what* I was. But I assure you, I have always known *who* I was – who I *am!* Do you think I've been walking around all these years feeling the heartbeat of the earth under my feet, hearing the secrets of the world whispered on the wind, without realising I was something ... *other*? You think I can just walk past a homeless person on the street and not look into their eyes? Or see a stray cat and not feel its hunger? Do you really think I could ignore all of that? Just pretend to be blind, deaf, and dumb? I assure you, I have *always* known exactly who I was and what my purpose is and I'll be dammed if I'll let a room full of cowards tell me what my responsibilities are!

"You know, I don't sleep? Those nightmares you see me have every night? They're not really nightmares. It's the world. Every time I close my eyes I hear it – pounding out a rhythm of pain and fear and wrongness. Nature screams it's agony ... souls beg for mercy ... life cries in pain. The roar of injustice is a perpetual loop in my head. I can't turn it off, I can't turn it down. Life scrapes its tortured nails against my gut, peeling layers and leaving nothing but raw flesh in its wake. It's an acid in my veins, corrosive and scarring. It's all I hear and all I see; every day and every night. There is no escaping the world. No escaping life. So don't you dare stand there and accuse me of ignorance. After meeting the rest of your so-called wardens, I might just be the only one who knows exactly who I am!"

Max was so angry she swore she could feel the ground shaking beneath her feet. In fact, the chairs were beginning to rattle, the windows were trembling and the door burst open to allow for a gust of heated air to rush through the room like a locomotive. All of her calm, all of her logical thinking, all of the reasons why she was supposed to keep her powers in check no longer seemed important. She wanted to make them hurt the same way she hurt.

"Max! Max! Stop! Calm yourself. You don't really want to do this." Someone yelled.

She watched in fascination as birds landed in the open doorway and kangaroos lined up in the yard. She could hear the ocean pounding the sand and feel warmth spread from her centre and settle in her palms. "What I want is to be left alone unless you actually mean it when you say I'm important, that I'm your friend and you care what happens to me. I am more than a name. I am more than my past. And I will always be more than my future."

"We believe you." Diana kept her grey eyes zeroed on Max's. "We believe you Max and we're all sorry. You've been misunderstood and underestimated but we can see you now."

Max tilted her head and felt her hair dance around her face as if controlled by static electricity. "You see me?"

Diana, allied to the domain of loss and grief smiled and nodded and said the one thing Max yearned to hear; "We can see you."

Max released her powers on her next breath ... and felt her whole body go rigid as she fell hard to the floor, her stiff limbs jerked and shuddered and her neck arched into a painfully uncomfortable position.

"What the hell is wrong with her?" Ryker shouted, trying to hold her flailing limbs.

"She's having a seizure." That was Diana. Her calm voice was the complete opposite to Ryker's panicked one. "Don't touch her. You'll only do more harm, just make sure everything is out of her way. She should stop in a minute."

Max would have smiled if her jaw hadn't been clenched so tight. Diana seemed to know what she was talking about. Perhaps Ryker had been right all along to wait for the paladin of death to arrive. Max had no choice but to give herself up to the convulsions and was glad her eyes were closed so she couldn't see the look of horror and disgust on the knights faces. Hopefully she would pass out so she wouldn't have to deal with the aftermath. Two minutes later though she discovered her hopes were fruitless for her body stopped its jitterbug routine and she was left to face a whole room full of brittle silence.

"Max. Can you open your eyes?" Although Diana spoke softly, Max still hissed as her headache flared to life. She needed a dark quiet room, like yesterday.

"Max? Come on now. You're scaring everyone."

"Well we can't have that now, can we?" She jeered. "Wouldn't want to worry the poor paladins over little 'ole me." She cracked her eyes open and her worst fears were confirmed. All seven knights were crouched around her with varying expressions of concern, guilt and pity. It was the pity she couldn't handle. Going to push herself up, she swore colourfully as she realised her limbs were not going to cooperate. *Shit!* It was going to take her days to recover from this and all she wanted to do was get the hell out of dodge.

"I can make that happen faster for you if that's what you really want?"

The ambiguous words from Diana had her focusing on the curly haired gypsy. "Huh?" Oh, she was *so* articulate right now.

Diana's full lips quirked, "You were talking out loud. I can heal you almost instantaneously and then you can be on your way if that is your wish."

Max narrowed her eyes, or at least attempted to. Her muscles still weren't behaving themselves properly. "What's the catch Azrael?"

Diana laughed outright at that. "The Angel of Death, huh? I like it." She focused her soft grey eyes on Max once more, "The catch? You need to accept my vitality."

Before Max could voice her denial Ryker butted his big fat head in, "Good luck with that. We've been trying to get her to recharge for days. The woman is the stubbornest, most infuriating female on the planet!"

"Shut the fuck up Ryker!" Cali snarled before Max could snipe at him. She felt her jaw drop in sync with Ryker's. Had Cali just told the king of self-righteousness to shut the fuck up? He opened his mouth but couldn't get a word out before Diana started in on him too.

"Don't even!" Diana rumbled, sounding as equally as furious as Cali. "She has been here for over two weeks. There is no excuse good enough as to why a warden would be so low on energy that she is experiencing seizures. Wardens only do that when they are empty and practically dead!"

"She wouldn't let us!" Lark shouted.

"And we didn't know she was having seizures." Beyden said pitifully looking like he had been whipped.

"I don't want to hear it. She is a Warden and you are all paladins. Regardless of your histories your duty is first and foremost to see to the health of wardens. You should have forced the issue, found a way to get her to accept and understand. The lack is with you, not with Max." Diana reprimanded and Max fell in love with her in that moment. Not only was the dark haired beauty glorious in her indignation, she was also defending Max of her own free will, expecting nothing in return. The others had all been nice to her, but their allegiance was clearly with Ryker. Diana was acting in the best interest of Max alone.

"I accept. Tell me what I have to do." She stated simply. Max ignored all the shocked gasps around her and focused on Diana's smile.

"Look at my aura. See all the colours? Now concentrate on them, on pulling them towards you. The energy contorts to your will, see it, hear it, touch it." Max listened to the melody of Diana's voice and followed her instructions. She was surprised when the colours shimmering around Diana seemed to dance and flirt with her as they moved gracefully towards her. It was almost too easy.

"Gold." She said, probably making no sense to anyone, "Pretty."

Diana smiled, "I'm glad you think so. Now feel the gold as it goes into your body. Just let it in. That's it." Diana praised.

She had been worried it would feel hollow and cold like when the chades tried to drain her but it was nothing like that. It was warm and peace-filled and felt as natural as breathing. How had she gone her whole life without this? She felt freaking amazing!

"How do you feel?" Cali asked as she offered her hand.

Max accepted and smiled in thanks as she let herself get pulled to her feet. She stretched her back, shook out her limbs and cracked her neck. She felt like she could run a marathon! She didn't remember feeling this good – ever!

"I feel gooood. *Real gooood.*" She figured her smile was probably a little evil but shit, she felt like she could jump buildings with a single bound! She placed her hand on Diana's arm and bowed her head in thanks. "Thank you for your service." Diana acknowledged her silently with a dip of her head.

"Max ..."

Max finally raised her eyes and met those of the other paladins. They all felt guilty and sad and pissed off but the emotion that had Max dialling back her snark was hope. They were feeling hopeful. Of what Max had no clue and at the moment she didn't particularly care. She really did just want to get the hell out of there. "I'll get my things and I would really appreciate it if I could get that lift into town I was promised nearly three weeks ago."

"Max, please wait." Axel stepped forward.

"No more platitudes guys. I'm not your Warden. You are not my paladins. I'm a piss-poor excuse for a warden anyway. I'm going to leave so I don't fuck up your lives any more than they already are."

"Five minutes."

Despite herself, Max paused at the two roughly muttered words. *Be strong Max. He's an arsehole playing at a good guy. Not a good guy playing an arsehole.* She really couldn't survive another rejection from Ryker and his motley crew. And with all this lovely go-juice flowing in her veins, she was fairly tempted to smite his rock solid butt!

"Five minutes." He repeated.

TWENTY-FIVE

Max hadn't spoken a word but she had turned and walked out of the kitchen and straight down to the beach. She knew he followed because she could sense his presence as well as the air he displaced as he moved. She could also feel the way the sand shifted and absorbed his weight and hear how his pulse thundered in his carotid artery. Diana's gold energy sure was some potent shit! Max felt like a hyperactive chipmunk, she wanted to run and leap and dance and ... well, screw Ryker's brains out. She figured that would be an efficient way of relieving herself of some of the excess energy. But unless the man was here to grovel at her feet and beg for mercy, then she would have to find another outlet.

"Are you going to ask me to stay?" She asked bluntly.

Ryker grimaced, stretching his scar. She still had no idea how he had received the terrible injury. But that grimace said it all. Not interested in anything else he had to say she turned and headed back the way she had come.

"It hasn't been five minutes." He yelled after her.

She dropped her head to her chest and spun back around. "You have three minutes left."

He nodded and ran his hands through his unkempt hair in clear agitation. "It's not that I don't want you to stay Max. It's just …" He trailed off.

"You don't want another flawed reject around." Max filled in the blanks. "I get it, don't worry."

"That isn't it."

"Yes it is. I've heard a lot about you over the past few weeks. You were one of the most respected paladins in history, born from a long line of honourable men and women, bound to serve and protect some of the most significant humans in the history of the world. Then suddenly, you became nothing – worse than nothing – you lost your honour within a society based on it. You lost your purpose so you hid yourself away in this beautiful secluded home to lick your wounds. You gave up and surrounded yourself with people who were as equally flawed as you so you could never be hurt or disappointed again. You take the snide comments and ignore the whispers behind your back because you think you deserve it. You don't have enough guts to take on the responsibility of a warden again because you're too afraid of what might happen if you fail."

"Afraid? You think I'm afraid?" He stalked forward so he was nose to nose with her. "I'm not afraid, Max. I am bone-deep, piss my pants, makes me want to vomit, terrified!" His chest was rising and falling in rapid succession and Max could feel the fear pumping from him in waves. Despite herself she felt herself soften towards him as he continued;

"I failed! Don't you get it Max? I failed them all! My Warden, my knights … nature itself! I was their Captain, their leader and they trusted me to protect them. They're all dead Max. Every last one of them."

Max nodded her head, really beginning to understand him now, "And you're still alive."

He barked out a harsh laugh, "Yes. And I'm still alive."

Unable to help herself, Max placed her hand over his trembling arm. She didn't think he was even aware that he was shaking. But he was – shaking and trembling and pale beyond belief. "You have survivor's guilt." And likely a very healthy dose of PTSD, Max added silently.

"Survivor's guilt? Those two little words can't even come close to describing how I feel."

His body was turned to hers now, their fronts almost touching and she raised both arms to wrap around his neck, rubbing her thumbs back and forth just under his hair line. "Why don't you tell me then?" She held her breath, awaiting his response. This moment was it. The last chance either one of them were going to get.

****

Ryker stared into the abyss of Max's exotic eyes and felt himself falling even further under her spell. She was truly amazing, offering him comfort and an outlet for his steel-trapped emotions even after all the horrible things he had said and done since meeting her. And not ensuring to her health? Not forcing the vitality issue? Diana was right; he should be whipped. The feeling of her hands on his skin and the warm pressure of her body along his invited comfort, invited peace, and offered a safe haven for his thoughts and feelings. He wanted to bask in her forever. Dare he reveal his past to this incredible woman? A woman who had been born with great gifts and a higher purpose. A woman who had been alone her entire life with the hounds of hell snapping at her heels and yet still managed to be warm and giving and loving. A woman who experienced untold pain on a daily basis if this most recent episode was anything to go by. For the first time in decades Ryker felt thoroughly ashamed of himself. He had been feeling so sorry for himself for so long he had become blinded to the suffering of others. He had been assuaging his guilt by offering shelter to the others and offering his skills at the training lodge, contenting himself that his paladin status wasn't going to waste, that he was contributing to their society. In actual fact, he had been hiding out and Max was absolutely right; he had been surrounding himself with people he thought were just as damaged as he was. The joke was on him though, given that Darius, Axel, Beyden, Lark, Cali and Diana were some of the best people he had ever known. They were knights through and through and he was proud to be associated with them.

"Ryker?"

He glanced down to find Max's beseeching eyes once again studying his face. She was so beautiful. He had been around a lot of beautiful people in his time – Max was correct in thinking the paladins were blessed with good genes. But none other could compare to the tiny woman in front of him. Her hair was gleaming in the sunlight, throwing off rich flames of red and gold as it curled enticingly around her shoulders and breasts. Her face was flawlessly smooth, a rich cream canvas that was spread over rounded cheekbones before coming to a softly curved chin. She wasn't smiling but he could picture the one dimple on the left side of her face just above those plump, Cupid's bow lips of hers. They were naturally red and revealed even white teeth whenever she smiled – which was often. She had no hard angles on her anywhere, unlike many of the women warriors he had bedded over the years. Instead, she was soft and curvy from the top of her remarkable breasts to those flared hips of hers, ending in those smooth calves. That's not to say she didn't have her fair share of hard-won muscle. He felt the strength and resilience in her body each time they touched. He nearly groaned as his mind decided to give him a live action replay of their one time sleeping together. Now really wasn't the time.

He took a deep breath and bent down to rest his forehead against hers, "Are you sure you really want to know?"

Her answering smile made his pathetic heart skip a beat, "I'm sure."

Without thinking and doing what felt entirely natural, he placed a soft peck on her red lips and took her hand, "Let's sit down."

****

He started by telling her what it was like growing up in a loving home with one parent who loved him unconditionally and showered him with affection. His father had been an amazing man, a paladin of great honour descended from one of the highest ranking paladin casts in history. His domain had also been life and he was bound to one of the wardens on the International Council. When Ryker had been born, his father's warden had coincidently also been pregnant. She had then taken a secondment so to speak for the next twenty years in order to raise her own son. He had never met his mother, she was a warden and was apparently horrified when she had given birth to a healthy paladin son instead of a warden like herself. She had dumped Ryker on his father's doorstep and they had never seen her again.

Given he was now two hundred and five years old, he had grown up in the time before the Great Massacre. Back then in England, wardens were a lot more active in their roles and the role of paladins was a more extensive one than merely playing battery charger and bodyguard. Orders truly were like families, living and working together to ensure their domains were upheld, giving and taking vitality in equal measures. Ryker and Flint had practically been raised together and were like brothers. So when Ryker's father had been killed alongside his warden, Flame, when he was thirty-five, it was the most natural thing in the world to bind himself to her son. Flint had become his liege and Ryker had spent the next one hundred and thirty years of his life guarding an amazing man and heading up the Order of Ember, alongside five other paladins.

The Order had made their way to Australia at the request of the International Domain Council just one year before the bloodbath. Chades had always been a part of their society and were a constant threat to wardens but their numbers had been steadily increasing, their attacks becoming more vicious and no one had known why. Their numbers seemed to be highest in the southern continent and they were congregating along the coast line here. His first year here had been a blur of fighting and hunting and fruitless investigations. Nobody could figure out where the chades were coming from or how they were gaining their strength. But more and more wardens were converting or being drained. Then one day fifty years ago, when hundreds of wardens and paladins from all over the world had gathered to discuss the crisis, the chades attacked *en masse*.

The foul creatures had pounced like starving, rabid dogs, ripping and shredding everything in their paths with poison-tipped claws. The world had narrowed into one black storm, as the writhing mass of dark shapes cut through seasoned warriors as if they were nothing. Wardens had been sucked dry, their vitality drained in a heartbeat into the empty voids of what used to be human mouths before they had become abominations. The earth had groaned, the wind had cried, water had bubbled and fire had roared as the elements tried to answer the warden's call for aid.

During the pandemonium, he and his Order had fought back to back, always keeping Flint between them, but the noble idiot just had to play the hero and move from their protective circle. He was struck down in an instant. His Order had broken formation in pain and vengeance and began striking out at anything that moved. Ryker had watched in horror as one by one his paladins fell under the weight of the chades. Ryker took a nasty slice to his face and had believed it was enough to kill him at the time. It was certainly what he wanted given that Flint had died in his arms, blood foaming through his lips and eyes glazed with agony.

He had become a whirlwind of violence, unleashing his fury onto the chades, as one by one, they began to fall in turn. He didn't even realise when the massacre ended, but the silence had finally drawn his attention. When he tore his eyes from his fallen family and looked around, he thought his heart would stop on the spot. There was no way the wretched muscle could continue to beat when confronted with such gore. Hundreds of his brethren lay dead on the ground, stares fixed forever in sightless horror. The wizened husks of hundreds of wardens littered the blood soaked ground. And yet, there Ryker was, the sole beating heart in a field of silence.

By the time he had finished his tale, the sun had begun to set and the ocean was awash in reds, oranges and pinks. He was totally exhausted but in a good way, he acknowledged. Although he felt lighter and even relieved to finally purge himself of his past, he was terrified to face Max. He didn't think he would be able to bear the look of disgust and shame on her face when she came to the realisation that he was a disgrace to his DNA, his lineage and his name. A paladin did not outlive his warden. It was the highest dishonour in their society. Unable to look at her and unable to question her, he simply continued to sit in silence for another few minutes, the only sounds the occasional caw of a seagull and the advance and retreat of the waves on the sand.

"You know what I think?" Max's voice actually startled him and he turned to her more in reflex than anything else. But she continued on before he could form any sort of response, "I think you have served your warden, your paladins and your domain well. I think you have fought and bled and sacrificed for the Earth. I think the Great Mother seeks to reward those who serve faithfully, those who toil tirelessly for her cause."

Ryker was shocked to his marrow. Seemed his fear of seeing disgust on Max's face was senseless for she was responding formally, her words a soothing balm on his tattered soul. He wasn't sure where she had heard about the Great Mother, but she couldn't have given him a better compliment. He opened his mouth to respond, but for some reason only a croak came out. Shit, was he crying?

Max smiled gently in understanding and cupped his scarred cheek with soft hands, "I would grant your reward on the Mother's behalf."

Before he could formulate a response to that the warden raised herself up gracefully and straddled his lap, that pert bottom of hers nestling against his cock. She then raised both hands only to surround his face with her palms. Heat began to radiate from her skin and he felt a pleasant tingle spread throughout his body. His life flashed before his eyes, there was nothing else it could be. Wardens, paladins and chades he had met careened through his head at the speed of the light; he could hear screams as his Order was slaughtered all around him, feel the hot stickiness of his warden's blood on his hands as he died, and feel the coldness seeping into his soul as he disgraced his knighthood. Perhaps she was killing him, he thought, perhaps that was her great reward. But almost immediately, the pain and terror and rage was replaced with a feeling of hope and healing and warmth. There was compassion and forgiveness and Ryker knew he was somehow touching an entity of great power and compassion. Was this the Great Mother? The creator of them all? Was Max somehow acting as a conduit in order to offer the priceless reward of healing and forgiveness?

He found himself ensnared in Max's gaze as he allowed her to touch that cold, dark place inside of him. Once again, her eyes became like living opals, flashing fire with blues and greens and pinks against an almost white canvas. The warmth from her palm travelled from his ruined cheek and spread throughout his body. He couldn't quite contain his small shudder as it streaked over his dick, resulting in a semi he hoped she wouldn't notice – talk about inappropriate. Max's lips twitched and her eyes sparked almost teasingly one last time before fading back to their normal shade. Dropping her hands, she took a deep breath and inspected his face before announcing ambiguously;

"Damn, I'm good!" She then proceeded to go sheet white and face plant straight into his arms.

TWENTY-SIX

Max woke to a live heavy metal concert inside her skull, complete with drums, bass and pyrotechnics. She moaned, placing her hands over her ears in an attempt to stop her brain from leaking out of them. What had she done last night to warrant such a nasty hangover? She couldn't quite recall which meant she must have gotten stuck into the tequila again. Tequila was the devil's work and she had made a pact with all that was holy never to touch the poison water again after the whole donkey-and-the-train incident! Clearly she had relapsed big time.

"Devil's work?"

"Poison water?"

"Donkey-and-the-train incident?" The questions came from all around her, each sounding more incredulous than the last.

"Hush! Hush, spawn-of-diablo-water-voices! Be gone!" Max muttered, not even bothering to open her eyes to the loud-mouthed hangover intruders. How did they even know what she was thinking? Obviously they were also a part of the tequila conspiracy.

"Ah, yeah. We're not a part of any devil water conspiracy, Max. You're talking out loud ... again."

Now that amused voice did sound vaguely familiar. Where had she heard that voice before? Because thinking hurt too much, Max decided to bravely open her eyes in order to figure out this strange post-tequila puzzle. Immediately regretting the action, she squealed in insult as the light in the room attempted to fry her optic nerves.

"Ye Gods! My eyes! My eyes! It burns us!" She yelled dramatically and quickly covered them with her hands. Unfortunately, that now left her poor innocent ears unprotected and completely vulnerable to whatever sadist was in the room with her as he lent down and said loudly;

"Max, would you snap out of it?! You're acting like a delinquent!"

"Ye Gods! My ears! My ears! It burns us!" She screamed this time, only to hear a series of muffled laughs and one huge sigh.

"She's obviously going to be fine."

Obviously going to be fine? What did that sadistic jerk know? Satan had used his terrible powers and lured her with the bad water again and – Max cut off her somewhat insane inner ramblings as the events of the last few hours came rushing back to her. She had tapped into her seemingly endless pool of vitality and used it to right the wrong dealt to Ryker when he had lost his family. It wasn't fair that he had to look into his mirror every day and see nothing but dishonour. It had been so long since she had used her powers to such an extreme that she had forgotten the consequences though. Especially as she had also used them not long before when she had her little tantrum. It was just too much energy expenditure with not enough intake.

"Has she passed out again? She's not moving anymore." Max was now able to identify the sadist's voice. It belonged to Darius. Figuring she couldn't stay laying on her back with her hands over her eyes forever, she decided to bite the bullet and try the whole seeing thing again. She was laying on the lounge in the living room and there were six giants looming over her. She sighed. They were all so pretty.

Axel started to laugh hysterically which Max found to be a little inappropriate given the circumstances. "What are you laughing at Chuckles?"

"You're still talking out loud. You said we were pretty. Well, sadly I am no longer the pretty boy of the gang." He chuckled. "Ryker gets that title now."

Max scrunched up her nose, "Huh?" She pushed herself up and bit back a groan as every muscle protested. "Did I have another seizure?"

"No. You just passed out. You probably used up the one dose of vitality from Diana. You need another hit." Cali explained, settling next to her. "Go ahead."

This time Max didn't even hesitate, she tugged on the blue threads and felt a lovely coolness seep into her bones, soothing and relaxing. This whole vitality thing was sweet! A movement to her right drew her attention and she almost passed out again. Now she knew what Axel had been referring to. Ryker stood in front of her, tall and strong ... and whole. His fallen angel face was unmarred, his tan skin smooth and scar free. Although a part of her mourned the loss of the sexy scar, another part of her rejoiced that he no longer had to look in the mirror every day and be reminded of the worst day of his life.

"How did you do it?" Ryker asked, awe lacing his voice as he touched his face.

Max shrugged, feeling uncomfortable from the gratitude wafting her way. She didn't really understand where the words or the urge to heal Ryker had come from. She just knew she had felt an urgent burning need to relieve the paladin's grief and had followed her gut. It wasn't the first time she had felt another ... presence and not the first time she had healed like that but knowing she was already an oddball, she went with a simpler answer;

"Life heals."

"She's right. As a Life Warden, she has dominion over the human body." Diana said. "I saw Verity use his powers to heal countless times over the centuries."

Max frowned, "Centuries? What do you mean centuries?" She turned to Darius – the walking encyclopaedia. "What does she mean centuries?"

"Ah, well. Wardens can practically live forever because they are continually regenerating with vitality. And a paladin's lifespan matches that of their warden if they are bound to them. I'm over a thousand years old."

Max laughed, looked around the room and laughed again. *No way.* "No way! I don't believe what your shovelling there Darius, no matter how convincing you sound when you use your Raden voice."

"My Raden voice?"

"Yeah. When you get all serious, your voice gets lower like this." She dropped her voice a few octaves in a piss-poor imitation of him. "You sound like Raden from *Mortal Combat*."

Those that understood her pop culture reference laughed – Cali, Diana, and Lark – but Darius just looked worried. "Don't worry, it's totally hot." She winked and watched him blush.

"How old are you?" Ryker asked, still touching his right cheek like he couldn't believe the scar was gone. She bet he would spend the night preening in front of the mirror, not that she could blame him.

"I'm forty ... something."

"Forty-something? How do you explain your young appearance?" Darius taunted.

Max smirked, "Clean living."

Lark leaned over and unexpectedly, inexplicably kissed her on the cheek. "Come on lovely. Let's get some food into you."

"Food?" Max perked right up and happily followed the tight butts into the kitchen.

Once they were seated and munching on oven-cooked pizza, Ryker spoke up, "I think it's time you tell us a little bit more about yourself, don't you?"

She paused, ham pizza half way to her mouth, "Why?"

Ryker focused his chocolate eyes on her. "You helped me in ways I don't think I fully understand yet. I think it's time we did the same for you. Besides, I just spilled my guts. Time to reciprocate, huh?"

Of course he had to ruin it with that mouth of his. "So this is quid, pro, quo?"

"Not at all. Don't get prickly on us."

She was *not* prickly!

"We want to help you Max. Information is knowledge. You're an author, you must believe that doctrine." Lark said, appealing to her logic and ego. The man knew her well.

She took an overly large bite out of her pizza in order to buy some time. She knew they were right. But could she trust them, like really trust them?

"You can trust us." Ryker assured her as if reading her thoughts.

She sighed, "What do you want to know?"

"Where are you from?"

"Where have you been living?"

"When did your seizures start?"

"Who taught you to fight?"

The questions came fast and furious and Max realised how desperately curious they all were. Clearly they had been masking their need to question her. In order to ensure she could create a shield? Control her powers?

Give her information? She started to feel a little guilty for her earlier harsh thoughts. They really had been providing for her since she arrived. Taking a deep breath she began where any good story did; at the beginning.

"I don't know who my parents are or where I'm from. My first memory is waking up in a park in Sydney about twenty-five years ago. I was fifteen, maybe sixteen and I was wearing plain black clothing. I didn't have any shoes or money or any identification. I didn't know my name or where I was. I wandered around aimlessly for days, watching and listening and trying to understand the world around me. I could talk but it took me a long time to figure out what everything meant. I was just one of hundreds of nameless, faceless people roaming the streets. Some people were kind – gave me food and showed me to shelters. Some people were not – preying on the vulnerable. I felt sick most of the time, tired and weak with constant headaches and muscle twitches. I noticed that I always felt better when I was out in the open, so I stayed in the parks as much as I could. By the time a police officer was able to round me up and send me to child services for the first time, I had found my first friend. He was a ragged little mongrel stray.

"He was skinny, ugly and cranky but he would follow me everywhere and was eternally loyal. When the police took me away they took him away too. I couldn't read or write but I could copy so when they asked me my name I copied down the only three letters that I knew ... M.A.X. They were the letters on my little friend's collar." Pausing in her story, she dared to look around the room. Naturally, she had the undivided attention of its occupants. Their expressions were rapt but also held a common theme of disbelief and pity. The disbelief she could handle, the pity? Not so much, so she forged ahead;

"I was in and out of group and foster homes and moved from school to school only to eventually find myself back on the streets a couple of years later. I managed to go to a local TAFE to get my high school certificate but I was too restless, was too sick and had too much barely restrained energy to stay in one place too long. I began to realise I could do things other people couldn't, like feel their emotions and understand animals. Nobody believed me of course and my powers were so unpredictable I could never prove it. It was the lack of control that had me learning meditation and martial arts from my sensei, Daiki in Japan. I'm a fourth dan black belt amongst other things. Turns out I needed it, for creatures of nightmares began dogging my every step twenty years ago and attempting to suck out my very soul it seemed. I've managed to write and draw a bit over the years, enough to keep me from starving and a roof over my head but I haven't been able to stay in the one place for more than a couple of months at a time. I've never met anyone else like me before and never seen another paladin before you guys either." Max finished her tale in a quiet voice, "I thought I was all alone."

The stillness in the room was stifling and Max couldn't bring herself to make eye contact. Did they believe her? Did they think there was something wrong with her? Did they think she was lying? She felt her pulse speed up and her breath began to puff out in pants. She was going to have a panic attack, going to hyperventilate right there in the kitchen!

"You named yourself after your dog?"

Max whipped her head around to Axel, only to find him balancing his chair on its two back legs like he didn't have a care in the world. He was smiling and his blue eyes held their usual cocky mirth, "You know Indiana Jones did the same thing right?"

Max felt the breath leave her body in a rush as she laughed a little hysterically, "I didn't know that at the time. I didn't even know it spelt *Max*." The unnatural stillness had dissipated thanks to Axel and the others took it as permission to ask questions.

"You don't remember anything? As in nothing?" Darius asked gently but intently.

She shook her head. "Not a thing. I've tried hypnosis and regression therapy but it's like there's nothing to remember, like I wasn't *there* until I woke up in that park."

"But that's not possible. It's not like you were born a teenager." Darius refuted.

"I know how it sounds but I'm telling you, it's like I didn't exist until then." Max swallowed hard. "There is something very wrong with me."

"There's not a damn thing wrong with you! You are perfect in every way!" The heart-melting comment was yelled very enthusiastically by Ryker and punctuated by his fist slamming hard on the table top. Max was startled to say the least. That was the third time he had spontaneously stated words of praise and poetry. She eyed him suspiciously;

"Oookay. Whatever you say. Anyway, that's me pretty much in a nut shell. I'll understand if you want me gone immediately."

"Why would we want you gone?" Lark, the perpetual Mr Happy of the group was scowling ferociously. Max had no idea why he seemed so mad.

"I just thought maybe, now that you know I named myself after a mongrel dog and am even more flawed —"

"You're going to make me very angry if you continue that sentence." Lark growled in a fair imitation of Ryker.

She was confused by his vehemence but hated to upset him so she simply shrugged, "Fine ... Is there any chocolate?" She asked imploringly.

Cali chuckled, "You've decimated the entire stash. I think you have a cocoa problem."

"I'll go get some." Lark jumped up before she could do what any self-respecting addict would do; *deny, deny, deny*.

"What? No! Lark, I don't want you making a special trip just to fuel my sugar craving!"

But the earth paladin was having none of it, "I insist. It's my turn to do the groceries anyway. Be back soon." He bent down and squeezed her hard and long before striding from the room with purpose.

Max grimaced sheepishly, "I feel bad."

"Don't feel bad. We need to shop anyway. If you want chocolate, then chocolate you shall have." Darius stated firmly before also standing and hugging her half to death.

That seemed to be the theme of the moment for she received squeezes and pats and rubs from all of the paladins, save Ryker. He was back to his usual scowl and had a faraway look on his face. Figuring they could all do with some alone time, Max left them to it and headed outside for some fresh air. Confessions were hard work and she needed the light.

****

As usual the beauty of her surroundings took her breath away. The horizon was afire with a spectacular sunset, the waves caressing the sand in a gentle rhythm and the garden awash in blooms and critters. She was terrified of the discussion she assumed was going on inside the house but she also felt liberated from sharing her past with the paladins. She wondered if this was how Ryker felt after he shared his burden-filled past with her. If so, she hoped it was as cathartic for him as it was for her. A butterfly fluttered past her face and she smiled as she held out a finger. The Blue Ulysses landed with a whisper on her outstretched digit. Max was surprised to see the Ulysses this far south and couldn't help cooing over the electric blue wings.

"Do you think they would still have such striking beauty if their lives weren't so elusive?" For once Ryker's voice didn't startle her. She knew he would be the one to seek her out first and was both pleased and nervous about his initiative. She watched as his strong finger sighed over the vulnerable azure wings and answered his question decisively;

"Yes, of course they would. Time doesn't dictate loveliness." She didn't really understand why he would burst into an unrestrained, full belly laugh. It startled her so much she accidently jerked her hand, forcing the butterfly to flap its wings madly for purchase before settling back down. Holy cow but the man was gorgeous when he smiled like that!

"How did I know you would say that?" Ryker shook his head, still chuckling quietly, "Not a philosophical bone in your body, huh?"

"I don't know if that's an insult or not." Max frowned.

"It's not. I'm on your side. I've always thought so too." Ryker was still smiling and shit, Max wished he would stop before she melted into a puddle at his feet. Stepping forward he held out his finger and the gorgeous butterfly merrily flapped its wings once, twice, to land gracefully on the outstretched invitation. He studied it carefully for a moment before turning those deep pools of chocolate to Max and scanning her face with equal intensity.

"Having said that, I do believe that it is their fragility which gives them their great beauty. That clear vulnerability beneath all that fleeting strength and purpose. They are one of nature's most exquisite sad endings."

Max was just as mesmerised by the soft crooning tones as much as the romantic words. He was leaning closer with every syllable and was now just a breath away – lips to lips. Almost against her own will, Max found herself inching forward ... but no, she wouldn't make the same mistake twice. She was not going to allow herself to be charmed by Ryker's considerable ... charms. Despite their earlier conversations and the fact that they seemed to have bridged the chasm between them, she wasn't going to stay. She couldn't afford to. She knew the others meant it when they said they would help her and also keep her secrets. She was hopeful but not optimistic and she also knew that no matter the outcome, she would be moving on. Yep, it was time to put on her big girl panties. Unfortunately, her panties could have nothing to do with Ryker but she could do him the courtesy of being honest.

"Look Ryker, I think you've been right all along. I was playing with fire, flirting with you and taunting you and I was wrong to do that. I had no idea what I was getting myself into. My ignorance and pig-headedness almost trapped us in a situation for the rest of our lives that would have been a disaster."

"Max ..."

"No, let me finish please. You see, I can survive anything that doesn't kill me. And trust me, I have survived things that would make even you knights falter. But I couldn't survive you Ryker. I know I couldn't. I think you are the one thing in this world that could ruin me. So please don't do this. Leave me be. I'm sorry if I've been unfair to you, if I've led you on. But I just ... I just wouldn't survive you Ryker." And thus saying, Max walked away.

TWENTY-SEVEN

Yeah, fuck that shit! Ryker thought, grinning from ear to ear. Max no doubt believed every word she just said but it was just too bad for her that Ryker's heart had undergone a changing of the guard recently. He had been steadily and systematically falling in love with the red head since the moment she stepped into his kitchen, caressing her sword. The healing she had given him had done more than remove his scar, it had lifted the dark veil obscuring his heart. The stains he felt on his soul from failing his liege and his Order had now been cleansed and he felt like he could begin to make steps. And he had decided that Max was his next big step. He may be slow on the uptake, but he wasn't stupid. Max was pure perfection and he didn't plan to let anyone stand in his way – not even the woman herself.

Releasing Mr Blue, he headed inside in search of Lark and the promised chocolate stash. Hearing sounds from the paladin's room, he yelled, "Lark? Is that you?"

"Yeah. I'm back." His voice sounded muffled somehow.

"Good. Because I need you to do me a solid. I – what the fuck?!" Ryker let loose with a string of curses as he took in the bruises darkening his friends face. Lark grimaced as he lowered himself to the bed hinting at further injuries. "Chades?" Ryker spat out.

"Not exactly." Lark's voice was a little raspy. Had he been choked?

"Then what exactly did happen? Who did this?" Ryker demanded, feeling a sinking sensation in the pit of his stomach.

"Forget it Ry, it was just a misunderstanding at Lonnie's." He assured him, naming the bar down the block from the closest store. It was a common hang out spot for paladins and wardens alike. "It's no big deal."

Ryker grabbed his chin gently and moved Lark's head this way and that. Someone had pummelled the paladin so that his right eye was practically swollen shut, both his bottom and top lips were split and bleeding, and there was a ring of blue around his neck. "Who did this?" He commanded again.

The knight's trademark green eyes were bloodshot but hard with stubborn pride as they met Ryker's in silent communication. Ryker swore bitterly and paced away in agitation. He could guess what had transpired and it was going to break Max's heart, as well as Lark's face. "I'll kill him." He vowed.

"You'll do no such thing." Lark's voice was uncharacteristically stern, "It will only cause more problems. We let this one go."

"Like hell we do! I will —"

"I *said*, we let this one go." Lark wasn't asking and Ryker knew he had to abide by his wishes.

"Fine. But one day soon there's going to be a reckoning." He promised.

Lark's eyes glittered with challenge, "And I hope I'm there to see it. But in the meantime ... what did you need me for?"

Ryker released an agitated breath and did as Lark bid; he let it go ... for now. "I want to give Max the chocolate."

"Why?" Did Lark have to sound so suspicious?

"To buy her affections of course." He answered honestly.

"Why would you want to buy her affections?"

"I'm wooing her."

Lark winced when he jumped in shock. "You're *wooing* her?"

Ryker nodded decisively, "Yep. I've decided to pull my head out of my arse and be smart for once in my life. That woman is the single most miraculous creature on the planet. I'm keeping her."

"You want to keep her?"

Ryker frowned and looked more closely at his fellow paladin. He sounded like a freaking echo! Ryker was concerned maybe he had a concussion or something more worrying. "Yes. I want to keep her."

"But she's a Warden."

"Don't care."

"But you're a paladin."

"Don't care."

"But she would have to bind you as her liege – something you swore you would never allow."

"Don't care."

Lark's smile was slow in coming and a little warped given his split lips but it was filled with appreciation nonetheless. "About fucking time! I am so very glad. You deserve her and she deserves you. You're two of the best people I've ever met."

Ryker cleared his throat, feeling suddenly shy. "Thanks man."

Lark seemed to find his discomfort amusing because he risked a bigger grin and a bigger cut when his smile widened. "What does Max have to say about all this?"

"She pretty much told me to fuck off."

"Oh." Lark's shoulders slumped.

'But you know what?" Ryker asked.

"What?"

He grinned. "Don't care."

****

"Ryker's acting weird!" Max exclaimed as she threw herself into the soft chair in the library where the others were congregated. They were all there with the exception of Lark, the Chocolate God, and Ryker, the Butterfly Whisperer.

"I'm afraid you'll have to be more specific." Cali stated, casually flipping through a magazine.

"He's being all ... *nice.*" Max sneered.

Diana rolled her eyes, "He is nice, Max. That's what I was trying to tell you the other night. He's been disillusioned and he's been hurt but underneath all that, he's actually a really good man."

Axel snorted, "Ryker's a prick! He's pig-headed, opinionated, sarcastic and violent."

Cali's face crumpled adorably, "Aww, Axel has a wittle crush!"

Axel grinned and made no attempt to correct her, "What can I say? I like 'em nasty!" His grin dimmed somewhat as he turned to face Max, "He's also the most honourable, most decent, most fair guy I've ever met."

Max huffed, "Well he hasn't been very decent or fair to me."

"That's because he's been in a state of constant arousal since he met you. A chronic stiffy is bound to make any man a little cranky."

"Cali!" Darius admonished.

The blonde finally deigned to look up from her magazine, "What?"

Darius narrowed his eyes at her innocent act and decided to add his two cents, "Max, your mojo didn't just heal his body. The real Ryker is finally re-emerging and I cannot thank you enough for what you did."

Max squirmed uncomfortably, "Whatever. It was no biggie. I think I prefer the jerk to the poet." She muttered.

"The poet?" Diana asked.

"He called a butterfly 'nature's most beautiful sad ending'."

Diana fanned herself, "Pardon me while my knees go weak!"

"Right?!" She jabbed her finger in the air aggressively. "It's very disconcerting."

"He's wooing you." Beyden said, sagely.

Max felt her neck crack as she whipped her head in his direction, "He's what?"

"Wooing you." Bey repeated helpfully.

"He's trying to get back in my pants?" She asked. "Because I gotta say ... I'm kinda easy. He really needn't go to such trouble, I'm pretty much a sure thing."

Axel snorted again and she narrowed her eyes on him. It wasn't a supportive sound but more like a 'ya don't say' kind of a sound. Bey saved his fellow knight from a sound tongue-lashing by saying; "Sounds like he wants more than in your pants sweetie."

She felt her eyes widen in panic and shook her head vigorously, "Well he can't have that ... more ... whatever!"

"Would it be so bad if he wanted something more permanent? Now that you've removed that giant stick from his butt, he's probably thinking of the future for the first time in decades." Cali pointed out.

Beyden nodded, "Uh huh. And it looks like he wants his future to include you."

"Well, that's just too damn bad for him! He can't just decide he wants me when it's convenient for him." She pushed her nose in the air and continued snottily, "My life won't be dictated by the whims of one man."

"Ah, bring on the feminist." Axel sure was digging himself a nice little hole, Max thought, scowling at the handsome trickster.

"Ignore the idiot in the room Max." Darius advised, "And focus on one important fact."

"And what's that?"

"I think, for the first time in a long time, you can start thinking about your future too."

Max swallowed convulsively and had to look away from all the shiny hope in the room. It was practically seeping from the paladin's pores and their colourful little doppelgangers were all sparkly and pretty and shit. *Nope, nope, nope.* Max thought. *Not gonna happen.*

"He's had his chance." She said out loud.

"You only give people one chance?" Darius queried. "Seems a bit harsh."

"Two." She held up two fingers. "I give people *two* chances. Ryker's already used up both of his." She made sure her eyes were strict yet gentle at the same time as she cast them around the room. "You guys are only at one."

"Shit, Ry! That stuff stings!" Lark's deep accented voice mixed with Ryker's rougher tones as it floated from the kitchen. Max clapped her hands and stood. "Lark, did you get my chocolate?" She yelled as she followed the sounds into the kitchen, thankful for the timely interruption. She frowned when she realised Ryker and Lark were at the sink with an open first aid kit. Rushing forward, she was brought up short when Lark turned around and she got a gander at his face.

"Oh my God, Lark! What happened to your face?" She rushed over, placing her hands carefully on his poor abused face. She could hear the others rushing in behind her and the multiple gasps of shock.

"Chades?" Darius immediately questioned.

"Nah. Nothing so interesting I'm afraid. Just a good old fashioned pub fight." Lark responded trying to look shame-faced and failing miserably. Didn't he know by now that she could see a lie?

Instead of calling him out on it, she reached for his hands and inspected his knuckles. "No bruises, no scrapes." Max searched Lark's face, "If this was nothing more than a pub brawl, why didn't you fight back?"

"Just leave it Max. He's a tough guy. He'll be fine." Axel said, surprising her with his lack of compassion. She glanced around and realised when she had been focused on Lark's injuries, they had been doing their silent communication thing.

"Well? Why didn't you fight back?" She asked again.

Ryker apparently felt the need to answer on Lark's behalf, "Because it wasn't against civilians; it was other paladins. He's a soldier, don't baby him Max."

She didn't understand, "So because they were paladins, you didn't fight back?"

"A knight does not raise his sword against his fellow peers." Lark's response was stiff with male pride.

"So you just let them beat you?" She asked incredulously.

"Our weapons, our fists, our skills are only to be used to protect that which is sacred or those who are weaker ... so, yes. I just let them beat me."

"This is an honour thing?" She was trying to understand.

"Yes, it's an honour thing. Lark acted nobly so as not to shame himself or his lineage." Ryker explained.

"What about the arseholes who did this? Where's their honour? Where's their shame?" Okay, so she didn't quite understand yet. She hated seeing his face mottled with marks.

"We can't control the actions of others; only our own. I care nothing for their honour." Lark stated, obviously considering the matter closed as he made his way slowly to the table and lowered himself carefully into a chair.

Max followed him. "Well, I care. Who did this?"

"It doesn't matter." He shifted, obviously trying to arrange himself into a more comfortable position and quite pointedly refused to meet her gaze. She turned to the others and found them all in similar states of ocular avoidance. Why were they all being so evasive? She would have thought they would be chomping at the bit to gain retribution for their comrade. They were as close as family, Max knew, whether they admitted it or not. Something wasn't adding up.

"You're hiding something. What is it?"

"It's nothing Max. Just let it go." Cali was the one to respond.

"It's not nothing! Look at Lark's face! Someone hurt him!"

"I'm okay Max. I'm a fast healer, remember? It's character building to get the snot beat out of you every once in a while." His usual crooked smile was even more pronounced now given his newly split lip and Max winced in sympathy when it started to ooze fresh blood. She wasn't buying it and found the whole situation entirely unacceptable.

"This is all completely unacceptable and I can't believe you all would just ..." And there it was; her very own *lightbulb* moment. "Was this because of me? Because you're associated with me and I called out the wardens on their dickiness?"

"Max ..." It was Darius who attempted to calm her this time.

"No. Tell me the truth. Are you hurt because of me?"

"He's hurt because some paladins don't deserve the title and are bigoted fuck wits. It's not your fault any more than it was Lark's. Leave it be Max. This will be dealt with in due course." Ryker's tone was all alpha and signalled the end of the discussion. Well, too bad for him she was an alpha too. She had also picked up on one key word;

"Bigoted? Ignatius's paladins did this?"

"Max ..." Darius tried again.

"Take me to them." The four words were a clear demand but no one in the room moved. Max looked around the room, slowly and deliberately making eye contact with the seven warriors. "I said; Take. Me. To. Them."

"Look Max, there's really no need –" Lark started.

She crossed her arms over her chest and cast her eyes around the room again, "You may not have accepted me as your liege and your honour may not be mine to uphold officially. But you are my friends. Mine, mine, mine!" Max stomped her foot for emphasis, "And I take care of what's mine. Now ... where are they?"

Everyone looked at Ryker who was gazing steadily at Max. They all knew what it might mean if Ryker were to answer her. She felt warmth unfurling in her stomach when Ryker slowly nodded his head, "They are at Lonnie's."

TWENTY-EIGHT

Lonnie's could be found in the opposite direction from Dave's Dive by about six degrees of cesspool-separation. Ryker's feet didn't stick to the floor as he walked across the room but the noise and the smell were very similar. He actually preferred Dave's if he was honest. Sure, it was filled with human scum but Lonnie's was filled with paladin scum and Ryker always thought that was far worse. He didn't frequent such establishments often, he wasn't a big drinker. But the others often came for the drink, the conversation and the companionship – as shitty as it was. Most of them tried to stay in the loop and heroically ignored the frequent jibes of 'reject', 'loser' and 'stray'.

A hush descended as they walked *en masse* towards the pool tables where Ignatius's five paladins were attempting to make the coloured balls go into the holes. They were predictably sucky at it. Max didn't stop or slow or hesitate as her keen oceanic eyes locked onto the bastards like a predator onto prey. Her eyes swirled with colour and her hair lifted subtly as her power surged through her but she was in control, Ryker knew. And she was absolutely glorious, Ryker thought, utterly spellbound. She was magnificent, a warrior in her own right, a queen among peasants, a Goddess among ants. And the second he got her home? She was also going to be a well-fucked one. He was going to claim his stubborn warrior queen as surely as she had claimed them back in the kitchen. What was it she had said? Oh yeah, *mine, mine, mine*. It was precisely Ryker's own thoughts and he intended to follow through as soon as humanly possible. He noticed a few startled looks as people focused on his now scar-free face. *That's right, fuckers. Ryker's back.*

"Show me your hands." The order was softly spoken but an order nonetheless and the five pieces of shit looked to each other before Marco, the Captain, replied to her;

"I'm sorry?" *Feigning ignorance won't save you now*, Ryker thought. His woman was on the warpath.

Her smile was chilly and Ryker felt his balls shrivel from the frigid air that seemed to suck all warmth from the humid bar. "I said, show me your hands."

And now they were starting to get it. Ryker could see the bobbing of Adam's apples as they gulped and began to shift nervously on their feet. Max was a Warden and they could do no more than obey. They hadn't thought anyone would defend Lark – a paladin who had never been bound to a warden because he had been deemed unfit. But one was, and very publicly.

"Hands. Now." Max repeated.

All five held out their hands and Max walked forward slowly, making a show of examining skin and knuckles. It wasn't necessary, everyone in the room could see the darkening bruises and scrapes. If not for the fact that this was Max's little show and if his man Lark didn't need the display of loyalty and kinship so desperately, Ryker would have lunged and broken some teeth. Max walked along the line of them slowly, almost lazily before stopping in front of Marco. His hands were by far the worst.

"Knights ..." Max's scathing voice lashed into the silence of the room. "You seem to have touched what's mine ... and I don't like to share. I'm greedy like that."

"We –"

Max held up a hand and arched an eyebrow, "Did I say you could talk?" Marco shook his head. "No, I didn't. Because I don't want to hear it. I'm not interested in anything you or your fellow haemorrhoids have to say. In fact, I don't want to even look at you, because honestly? All I see are skid marks."

Max continued on as if she couldn't hear the shocked gasps and murmurs of disbelief in the room; "I just came to inform you all that if you ever desecrate my things again with your filthy, fetid hands I will use what is vital in me. I will wrap my powers around your scrawny chicken neck and squeeze until you bleed from every orifice. Your eyes ... your ears ... your mouth ... your arse! Even your *meatus*." She leaned in close and although she whispered, everyone in the room heard her next question, "Do you know what your *meatus* is?"

The five paladins didn't respond, probably too freaked out by the mild voice and the fact that she was calmly circling around them, eyeing them like specimens under a microscope. There was no anger, no rage. Just calm, just facts ... it was freaky as fuck!

"Answer me boys. That wasn't a rhetorical question." Max spoke sweetly again, a serene smile lighting her face.

All five paladins appeared to gulp in unison and Marco replied with a stuttered, "N ... No."

Max eyed the speaker up and down, gaze finally resting on his crotch as a very unpleasant smile lit her face, "It's the slit at the end of your dick." The room seemed to inhale as one as Max continued, "Would you like me to squeeze your neck so hard that blood starts to leak from your dick slit?"

By this point two of the warriors had gone pale and passed out, Ryker figured they had probably forgotten to breathe. He noticed no one rushed to check on them. The entire room was enraptured in some kind of morbid awe at the display. The other three looked like they weren't far behind their brethren; one was clearly hyperventilating, one looked like he was choking down vomit, and the last one, Marco, had a sickly grey pallor to his skin and was sweating profusely. He still had enough presence of mind to jump when Max leaned in close and ran a fingertip over his zipper, she smirked;

"Answer me, *boy*. That wasn't a rhetorical question."

It was a true testament to a paladin's will, that he managed to stutter out a garbled; "No, My Lady." If Ryker wasn't getting so much enjoyment seeing these jerks put in place for harming his brother, he would have felt a smidgeon of respect.

"Good. That's good." She patted the guy's now well and truly – and probably forever – flaccid cock. "Because if I ever hear of you or any of your boys touching what is mine again, your dick slit will be the first hole I'm coming for." She smoothed her small, seemingly harmless hands up Marco's chest and proceeded to straighten his collar as he trembled and sweated and panted. Max smiled coolly one more time before turning on her heel and swaying her delicious hips toward the door, hypnotising everyone with a Y chromosome. As she was nearing the entrance however, she paused and spoke over her shoulder, always keeping her back to the room;

"Oh, and the same goes for your Warden. Do not think for one minute that I don't know your warden put you up to this. If he has a problem with me, tell him to come to me. Not my kids. Because even though I'm sure the target is small – tiny even – I *will* eventually find his dick!”

****

Max suffered through yet another awkward silent car ride back to the camp. After sashaying her butt out of the pub, the paladins had followed her silently, no one speaking except for Ryker who had held open the car door with a growled, “Get in.” Now she was standing in the front yard and despite the twenty minute drive to calm down, was trembling with the need to storm back to Lonnie’s and follow through with her threat. She could totally do it, she knew she could. She wasn’t one to make idle promises. She *always* kept her word. One wrong move from those despicable entities and she would ensure none of them ejaculated ever again! Filthy, dishonourable cretins! She raged internally. She never could understand why some people had to hurt others in order to make themselves feel good. She just hoped the others wouldn’t be too mad at her. She had probably embarrassed them once again. She figured there was only a very tiny chance that threatening paladins with permanent erectile dysfunction was actually permissible. Hearing the gang behind her, she opened her mouth to fake an apology – she wasn’t sorry at all – but before she could get a word out, she felt herself lifted off the ground and surrounded by a pair of strong, muscular arms. Not a bad place to be all-in-all. That was until she felt wetness splashing against her neck. Lark was crying. Her poor, happy paladin of the earth was emitting waves of gratefulness and disbelief and she knew no one, present company excluded, had ever gone in to bat for him before.

“Thank you. Thank you. Thank you ... for standing up for me.” His voice was muffled against her neck. Not wanting the knight to feel embarrassed or ashamed of his tears, she used her powers to absorb the small pearls of distress and revelled in the now familiar warmth as she reached out to heal his poor battered face. She was just finishing on the last cracked rib when he jumped back.

"Max! What are you doing?" He asked, touching his face.

She shrugged, "Fixing your boo boos."

He lifted the hem of his black tee shirt and treated her to a view of his fine, washboard abs. "You don't need to be wasting your energy on the likes of me." He stated, but the relief in his voice was obvious.

She shrugged, "No biggie. I've got energy to burn now since Cali and Di shared their go-juice with me!" She blew a kiss to said ladies but to her surprise didn't receive a kiss back, or a wink, or even a smile. Instead, all seven paladins obscurely gripped their left forearms right where their coat of arms would be had they been bonded in an Order before bringing them to their chest and bowing their heads. *Weird!* Max thought but before she could puzzle out their strange antics Lark stepped forward still grasping his left arm, head tilted in deference, but his green eyes were like flashing emeralds as they made contact with hers.

"I hereby swear fealty to you Max, Warden of Life. I pledge infinite service, protection, loyalty and honour to you, my liege and my Order. This is my solemn wish and I do so freely without reservation."

"Say what now?" Her heart was beating hard and fast in her chest and she could hear her pulse pounding in her ears. Did he just say what she thought he just said? Did he just do what she thought he just did?

"I did just say what you think I just said. I did just do what you think I just did." Lark smiled gently, "You're talking out loud again, sweetheart." He stood tall now, masculine face proud and blemish free, "I have just sworn to be your paladin ... if you will accept my service, my liege."

She could manage no more than a small incoherent squeak but it didn't seem to matter as Beyden took one step forward and spoke; "I hereby swear fealty to you Max, Warden of Life. I pledge infinite service, protection, loyalty and honour to you, my liege and my Order. This is my solemn wish and I do so freely without reservation."

As if in a procession Axel, Cali, Diana and Darius all stepped forward one by one to repeat those clearly sacred vows. Feeling adrift, she sought out the one thing she knew would be her anchor. Ryker's head wasn't bowed nor was he holding onto his faded coat of arms. He offered no heavy words, just stared at her with a fusion of admiration and desire. She found herself just as ensnared with him as she was with the shining moment. The moment where all these wonderful people were pledging their very lives in service of her.

She was going to have a family.

Her joy burst from her, unrestrained and unchecked as a smile split her face wide, dimpling her left cheek. That seemed to be sufficient to tip Ryker from admiration to full blown desire and she watched in fascination as his brown eyes darkened almost to black and his nostrils flared wide. He stormed forward and snatched her up, tossing her over his shoulder as he sprinted into the house and up the stairs. She heard a variety of wolf whistles and vulgar suggestions before she was tipped dizzily right side up and pushed firmly against a flat surface.

TWENTY-NINE

"Stop ... stop!" She pushed but it was like trying to move a mountain. "You can't just pick me up like some Neanderthal and drag me back to your cave!"

"I can't?" The cocky bastard reached out deliberately and cupped her breasts. "But you haven't held up your end of the bargain." His fingers flexed.

Do not arch! Do not arch! "What bargain?" Why did her voice sound so breathy like that?

"You were supposed to sit on my face."

"Wha?" The slurred syllable was all she was able to stutter out as Ryker abruptly dropped to his knees and took a firm grip on her hips. His mouth covered her cotton-clad crotch and instead of acting as a barrier to her pleasure, it heightened it. He opened his mouth and exhaled hard, causing heat to spread over her most private parts. She felt her knees buckle and she was gently lowered to the floor. Although her mind was rapidly beginning to be overcome by a haze of lust, she had just enough presence of mind to speak;

"I'm not going to put you in a position to hurt me again."

Ryker paused his sexy ministrations and she felt herself falling into the abyss of his brown eyes. "You're safe with me, sweetheart. I promise." Then he kissed her and Max knew it was all over.

The removal of clothes was almost perfunctory, a task he seemed intent on but made no attempt to pretty up for seduction. Once they were both naked, he threw her onto the bed before rolling on a condom and following her down. His lips joined hers in a slow thorough tease as his thick fingers tested her readiness. Lifting her legs and encouraging her to wrap them around his hips, he seized her waist before pausing at her moist entrance. She thought he might tease her or at least attempt some form of foreplay but it seemed he was a knight on a mission, albeit an apparently patient one.

He took his time entering her, his thick shaft stretching her delicate inner muscles exquisitely. She was so sensitised she swore she could feel every ridge, every vein on his glorious prick as he slowly but surely shuttled into her depths. When she felt him bump against her cervix and knew he could go no further, she figured he would start fucking her into oblivion to prove who was boss. But he didn't. No, he pulled out excruciatingly slowly until only the thick head remained before slamming back into her with an intensity that had her back arching and heels digging grooves into his arse cheeks. He then proceeded to repeat the process over and over and over again. Max gasped and panted her way through the onslaught, struggling to breathe and retain some semblance of sanity in the light of his claiming. For that is surely what this was – a claiming. The knowledge both thrilled and terrified at the same time.

His thrusts increased in strength and intensity but never in speed and he didn't try to get fancy by playing with her nipples or her clit or even her tonsils. He just gripped her hips to better guide him to her willing core and sucked up bites on her neck. On her part, she made sure to keep her head buried in his neck, unwilling to see the truth in his eyes because she was still holding on to a smidgeon of self-preservation and doubt. She felt him shift slightly, his angle changing just enough that he was now hitting that elusive spot inside of her on every downward stroke.

"Give it up, baby." The sexual sadist on top of her growled roughly, sending shivers of anticipation down her body.

She shook her head; no way was it going to be that easy. Apparently that wasn't the correct response for Ryker broke her stranglehold on his back and brought her arms up above her head, holding both wrists in one strong hand. He stared down at her intently, brown eyes shining feverishly with desire and determination before clutching her hair roughly with his other hand. She gasped out a keening moan as his wrenching fingers caused her scalp to tingle deliciously.

"I said ... *give it to me.*"

His wish; her command apparently, for she instantly felt her body coil tighter before exploding in an orgasm of epic proportions. She screamed and felt the air thicken with power and colours once again. She spared a second to be grateful for not blowing anything up before her vision dimmed and she maybe, sort of, kind of, passed out from pure bliss.

THIRTY

Even though he just had the most intense orgasm of his life, Ryker remained hard and firmly seated inside of his feisty warden. He leaned down to nuzzle the mark his teeth had made on her neck, "You didn't claim me."

"Hmm?" The sleepy reply made him smile. It seemed he had found a way to shut that smart mouth of hers – screw her into unconsciousness. She was draped across his chest, her feet tucked under his calves, hair splayed over his pecks as her fingers traced lazy patterns across his skin. He ran his hands over her back from nape to thigh, revelling in the warmth of her skin.

"I claimed you but you didn't claim me." He continued.

"I didn't realise I was supposed to." She answered but didn't raise her head.

"Of course you were supposed to, woman! You're mine!"

"Even though relationships between wardens and paladins are against the rules?" Her voice was muffled against his chest.

"Do I look like the type of person that gives a rat's arse about rules?" He asked in derision.

Her head rolled from side to side in the negative. "I guess not. You really want to be my man, boyfriend, knight or whatever?"

"I do." He was resolved. He had been a walking disaster for the last fifty years but had somehow been given the miracle that was Max. There was no way he was letting her go. He may be slow on the uptake but once he made up his mind it was permanent.

"Why? Because you've suddenly decided you want me to be your own personal warden?"

Ryker tightened his arms around her and rocked his still hard dick firmly inside her, eliciting a delightful mewl from his red head. "No. Because you call Darius *dude*, and cook special meals just for Beyden. Because you stand up for the rights of wardens you don't even know and talk to slater bugs. Because you defend the honour of a too-honourable man and heal the scars of a wounded face ... and a wounded soul." He gripped all that lovely thick red hair in his fist and tilted her head back so he could look into her exotic eyes. "Because you belong to me and I belong to you."

She stared into his eyes for a long time. "Okay. I'll think about it." She pecked him on the lips and snuggled back into his chest like a lizard sunning on a rock.

She'd think about it? He supposed he deserved that after the last time they had been together and he had practically ripped her heart out of her chest. He would give her time, it's not like she was going anywhere now. As soon as they were able he was going to make sure he bonded to her as one of her personal paladins. In the meantime, perhaps he needed to lighten the mood a bit.

"I read your books." Ah, that got her full attention. She pushed herself up so her chin was resting on her hands. Her gorgeous eyes were sleepy and satisfied still, and her hair was a mess. She had a hickey on her neck from where he had marked her ... and she was the most beautiful creature he had ever laid eyes on. His heart did a ridiculous flip as it decided to join the party. That was the one thing he had left out of his monologue.

He was pretty sure he was in love with her.

"You did?"

"Huh?" Her new position lodged him more fully inside the haven of her body and he struggled to stay on track.

"You said you read my graphic novels ..."

"Right." Focus man. "Lark has them all, so I borrowed them. You know he's going to ask you to autograph them." He smiled. "He's such a dork."

Max's smile was content, "He already did."

Ryker sighed, "Of course he did. Way to play it smooth, Lark."

"What did you think of them?"

"I thought they were interesting and sexy and fun and deliciously violent." He punctuated each praise with a kiss.

She actually giggled and the carefree sound made his heart soar. He knew she hadn't had many opportunities to be carefree. "I also saw some of your sketches sitting on the bench in the kitchen."

That made her freeze. "You did?" She gulped.

"Yep." He smoothed his palm over a rounded globe. "I saw the drawing of me; shirtless, scarred face, sickle in hand ... and the speech bubble above it saying 'blah! blah! blah!'" He gave her butt a sharp pinch.

"Ouch!" She jumped but her eyes continued to sparkle. "Well, they say write what you know. And that's what I hear when you talk most of the time."

He groaned and threw his arm over his face. That was most likely the truth – he was such a douche!

"Did you really like them?"

Hearing the shyness in her tone, Ryker rolled them both to their side and pushed her thick hair behind her ears. "I really liked them. You're a skilled story teller and an amazing artist. And I'm clearly not the only one who thinks so. You've hit some best seller lists in the past haven't you?" Ryker knew she had. He had googled her the second she had told them all her pen name. She actually had a huge cult following.

"I'm glad. They're like my legacy, you know?"

"Your legacy?" He asked. "Max, you're a guardian to every human emotion and human body on the planet. The world rotating on its axis is your freaking legacy."

She shrugged, causing her breasts to jiggle invitingly and Ryker to lick his lips. "But I didn't know that before. I had no chance at a life, a home, friends, family. My work was going to be my proof."

"Proof of what?"

"That I was here." The four simple words darn near broke his heart all over again. The organ sure was getting a workout recently.

"Well, that's not something you have to worry about anymore. Now you have a family of seven knights and an entire society who are going to remember you. You're going to leave your stamp on the world itself."

Her smile started out slow but grew bigger until he couldn't help kissing her lone dimple. She questioned; "Did you all really mean it? You want to be my paladins?"

"They meant it. *I* meant it. I've had my head up my arse for a long time. Losing Flint and my Order broke something vital inside of me. To watch them all fall one by one knowing I was responsible ... I lost the will to fight, the will to guard. I knew I couldn't be responsible for another warden again. But from the moment I saw you, I knew you were supposed to be mine – ours. I felt the connection and I know the others did too. I've just been too cowardly to admit it."

"But you're not anymore?" She didn't sound convinced and Ryker could hardly blame her given his past actions. But he would make her believe if it took him the next hundred years because he was not giving her up.

"No more running. No more hiding ... for either of us." He said and lowered his head to capture her lips in a slow deep kiss filled with promise, lust and love. Max moaned and arched her back, wrapping her arms and legs around him like an octopus. He felt her nails scrape across his back and he hissed as the painful pleasure caused a bolt of electricity to shoot straight to his erect dick. He rolled so she was perched on top of him once again and gave her free reign to explore at her leisure. And explore she did, from sucking and biting at his barred nipples, to tracing his trail of hair from his belly button all the way down to Mr Happy where they were still joined. He let out a groan of denial as Max suddenly withdrew from him but quickly changed his tune as her dirty, talented little mouth attempted to lure him to the dark side.

Not wanting the outrageous pleasure to end too soon, he heroically pulled her away from her new toy and latched onto one of her rosy nipples. It didn't really help his situation because her breasts were perfection and the answering throaty moan he received had his cock leaking from the tip in sweet anticipation. Deciding to mix things up a little, he thought of a book he had seen Max reading in the library. She had placed the book face down and left to get a drink and he may have taken a peek. He had been shocked and more than a little aroused by the words on the page. Assuming she liked that kind of thing he released the delicate morsel in his mouth, raised his right hand and brought it down firmly on her rump.

She froze. There was no sexy moan, no shudder of passion, no begging for more. *Fuck!* Ryker thought. Had he made a huge mistake? He was about to ask when her shoulders started to shake. Oh God, was she crying? His erect hardware now completely forgotten he forced Max's chin up so he could see her face. What he saw there had him cringing. This was way worse than tears.

She was laughing.

"Did you just *spank* me?" Max sputtered out between snort-laughs.

Jeez, talk about emasculating. The woman was crying from laughter while they were both naked and in the throes of passion. He was never trying anything new again! "No. My hand slipped." He replied stoically.

She slapped him on the chest, "It did not! You totally spanked me!" Then she fell against him in another fit of giggles.

He felt himself shrivel and thought maybe she had cured him of all future boners. She must have noticed his embarrassment for she started to pet him like a damn puppy.

"Oh, babe. I'm sorry. Come on, do it again." Her eyes still held too much mischief to be taking the situation seriously.

"No." He pouted. "You've completely ruined the mood."

"No seriously." She got up on her hands and knees and wiggled that pert butt of hers provocatively in his direction. "Spank me, big boy. I've been a very bad girl."

The merriment in her eyes and the smile on her face belied her words and instead of accepting her invitation he ended up pouncing on her and tickling her into submission. This here was the other side of the lust he felt for her; the laughter and the playfulness he never knew could exist between bed mates. He was so hers.

****

After a very long and very satisfying shower, Ryker indulged himself in learning every inch of his beautiful woman including the sexy ink etched into the skin of her back. Max was nothing more than a puddle of warm, relaxed flesh as Ryker cruised his hands over the black and white image of a striking female; tall, willowy, toned limbs partially concealed by tight-fitting leather, dark hair styled short enough to highlight sharp cheekbones, full lips and dark eyes. She sure was attractive, he thought to himself. The woman was partially concealed by a dense, wooded forest with thick tree trunks, a sparkling stream and a winding secret path that tapered to a full moon high on Max's right shoulder blade. The shading of the greys was cleverly done and provided depth as well as accuracy. It was a wonderful piece of artwork.

"Your tattoo is wonderful." Ryker said, tracing a finger over the mystery woman's fingers. He could make out another strip of leather between her middle fingers and under her palm. An archer perhaps?

Max smiled but didn't open her eyes. "Thank you. It's actually the cover of my first graphic novel."

"You drew this?" He asked, surprised.

"Uh huh. I thought I was going to have an aneurysm when the tattooist started. Not because of the pain or the permanency but because I was trusting someone else to copy my work." Expressive turquoise eyes rolled in his direction. "I'm not great with trust."

Ryker clutched at his chest as he gasped dramatically, "Who? You? Nooooo!" She kicked at him half-heartedly and he chuckled as he snagged her foot, kissing his way up her leg, over her sassy butt and up to said ink. "She's hot. You're lucky I saw your front first and not your back. You may have had some competition."

Max laughed as she snuggled back into the pillow. "I'm not worried. Sabre has my back. That's why she's there."

Sabre was the name of her assassin leading lady in her novels, Ryker knew. He continued sucking up small kisses over the monotone flesh until he reached one of those coloured specks scattered subtly within the forest. Leaning back to get some perspective he frowned when he noticed a small purple pattern that looked very much like Ogham script. Ogham script was an ancient alphabet used prominently by the Celts and the Druids as far back as the fourth century AD.

The original Druids were thought to be direct descendants of the Great Mother herself – the one true Goddess and the deity that all paladins and wardens worshipped. She was said to reside in the Otherworld and was just as real as any other living creature on the planet. It was said that after the first Goddess gave birth to the world, she also gave birth to its custodians. The Druids, not corporeal but not spirit either, were the guardians of creation but as the world grew and evolution unfolded, these custodians could no longer maintain nature with all of its domains unaided. Hence, some of the first humans – the wardens – were given the ability to feel, shape and create specific elements. Warriors were tasked with protecting and providing for the revered few and a sacred bond was formed between the guard and the protector, ensuring balance was kept. The children of the Goddess were lost to obscurity but his people believed there were still a few out there; there had to be, for their chronicles dictated that a child of the Great Mother must walk the Earth in order for it to live.

Ryker knew his history just as well as every other paladin and warden out there which is why he recognised the druidic symbol but he was very surprised that Max would know what it meant, let alone want it tattooed on her back. The small purple symbol was nothing more than a short horizontal line with a vertical line protruding from its centre and it was artfully concealed in the shadows of the moon. A flash of gold caught his attention and he saw five diagonal lines parallel to each other with a horizontal line through the middle, much like a leaning tally, positioned on the neck of the woman, Sabre, almost like her own tattoo. A blue 'tally' symbol with only two lines was located in the stream following the path, and a pink one with only one 'tally' line was camouflaged within the feathers of a small owl perched on the branch of a tree.

Ryker felt his heart start to pound and his palms begin to sweat as he searched frantically for the three remaining coloured symbols he was sure had to be there. His eyes snagged on the hint of red first; it was a horizontal line with three vertical lines extending below it and was at the base of the winding path. A green horizontal line with five other vertical ones extending underneath was veiled in the foliage of the largest tree, and a slash of silver – a single horizontal line with three more extending straight up – was high up, secreted away in the clouds. His fingers trembled as he traced each one reverently. He had to swallow three times before he could speak, his mouth was that dry.

"Max?"

"Hmm?"

"What do these symbols mean to you?" His voice cracked but Max didn't seem to notice, too content under his worshipping hands. He traced the cloud to prompt her.

"Air." She responded.

He moved to the owl; "Beast." His finger journeyed from the trees, down the winding path and settled in the stream, "Earth ... Fire ... Water." She continued to murmur her responses lazily as if she wasn't making his world rotate on its axis.

He stroked his hand over the assassin's neck; "Death." Before finally coming to rest over the glorious full moon and the tiny purple symbol.

"Life." He said, beating her to the punch. "This is your symbol for life."

Max nodded and hugged the pillow tucked under her head. Ryker could tell she was almost asleep. Well, he wasn't. He might never sleep again! His brain was computing this newfound information rapidly but still didn't seem to be able to reckon what his gut – what his *heart* – was telling him. It just wasn't possible. This was her Heraldry. He *knew* it was.

"Max." He gave her a small shake when she ignored him. "*Max!*"

"What do you want Inmate? I let you defile me in the shower. If you let me sleep I may even be up for a repeat later." She threw the provocative words at him without even opening her eyes. Ryker chose to ignore the imagery she conjured given the seriousness of the situation.

"Max, listen to me. You remember what we told you about the coat of arms that gets branded into our skin when we bond to our liege?"

"Sure, sure."

Not a very enthusiastic response but at least she was listening, Ryker knew. "It's unique to every warden. Every lineage has their own unique Heraldry or coat of arms that is distinct only to the individual. It's like a fingerprint; no two are ever alike and it's a direct reflection of their domain. That's why paladins wear it with such honour and pride."

Max finally rolled over and blinked sleepily up at him. She made no move to cover the lush mounds of her breasts and despite himself, Ryker felt himself begin to harden once again at the sight. Having apparently no guile whatsoever, Max spoke;

"I remember, Ryker. I'm sorry yours has faded since Flint died and you lost your Order. Would you like me to try to fix it? I healed your scar easy enough. Maybe I could help your brand?"

She ran her hand lightly over his muted coat of arms and Ryker fell even more in love with her. Axel had been correct; she really was the sweetest, most pure person. He leaned down to kiss her softly, chastely on the lips. "No babe, I don't want you to fix it. It's supposed to fade; time does that to all things. I brought it up because I think those symbols will be your coat of arms."

Her eyes lit up. "My little purple symbol in the moon? Cool."

Ryker grabbed her hand and interlocked their fingers. He couldn't seem to stop touching her. "No, Max. Not just the symbol for life. I think *all* of them will be your Heraldry."

She scrunched her nose and frowned. "But you said your coat of arms was reflective of your domain?"

"It is."

"But I'm Life. You said so. So then why would –" He cut her off mid-sentence, knowing what she was going to ask.

"I was wrong." Ryker was torn between amusement and arousal as Max moaned and arched her back, pressing her breasts into his chest.

"That is the sexiest thing I have ever heard." Her eyes darkened to a turbulent sea-green, "Say it again, only this time ... whisper it."

He grinned down at her and dipped his head to do her bidding. "*I was wrong.*" He whispered the words against the shell of her ear and felt her sensual shudder reverberate in his own body. She was so deliciously fun. Apologising silently to his dick, he pushed away from the she-demon and started pulling on the first clothes he could find; an old pair of track pants and a threadbare tee. He threw Max's own shirt at her, not even noticing when she ended up with a mouth full of cotton.

"Come on babe, get up!"

"What? I thought I was going to get laid again!" She grouched.

Ryker shook his head. "Do not tempt the beast darlin'. Later. Right now we need to find the others."

Max's scowl darkened. "The others? Why?"

"Just trust me." He threw her jeans at her next.

She grumbled but did start moving, covering her delicious flesh top and bottom but foregoing underwear of any kind. "Fine. But I better get some action when we get back."

Ryker laughed, he couldn't help himself. She was just so fucking perfect and he just loved her so fucking much! He reached her in two strides and had her wrapped in his arms in seconds. "I love you."

Oceanic eyes blinked up at him. "Um, okay. Thank you."

Taking exactly zilch offense at her lack of reciprocation, he laughed again and spun her around. "You're welcome," he placed her on her feet, "now come on. Let's go find the others."

THIRTY-ONE

Max followed Ryker's well-toned butt as it made its way down the spiral staircase. He had a tight hold on her palm and his thumb rubbed back and forth along the back of her hand as if he couldn't stop touching her. She liked it. They found the rest of the household in the small beautiful garden off the library. She knew this was Lark's own little oasis; plants, flowers, trees and hundreds of books within sniffing distance. She also knew Ryker was the one to convert the study into a reader's paradise and give Lark free reign over the adjoining patch of once empty land. Just as she knew he had installed the indoor heated swimming pool so Cali wouldn't have to swim outside in the rough seas of winter; the wine cellar had been built for Beyden; the home office with its huge telescope on the third floor for Darius; the stunning Concert Grand piano in the music room had miraculously appeared one day after Axel had mentioned he played; and Diana had a suite of rooms at the opposite side of the house with a room just for her clothes, ensuring the quiet and seclusion she craved. Max had gleaned these little pearls over the past three weeks and each time one of the knights revealed the damming evidence of Ryker's generosity and selflessness, Max had fallen just a little more for the man. She knew she saw him better than he saw himself and what she saw filled her with warmth and hope for the future.

"What are you all doing out here?" She asked, eyeing the six soldiers draped lazily around the garden.

"We had to come out here for our mental health." Axel answered.

"Huh?" She asked, confused.

Axel motioned between her and Ryker, "The noises you two were making had the potential to scar us for life!"

"Yeah, gross!" Lark shuddered dramatically.

"Gross?! I'll have you know that I make very cute sex noises." She assured them all. "Right, Ry?"

"The cutest!" He answered exuberantly, clearly wanting to get laid again later.

"Gag!" Axel stuck out his tongue in disgust at Ryker's brown-nosing.

"If you've finished with your mating ritual, I can go in and start dinner." Cali said, picking up her discarded shoes.

"Wait." Ryker halted her movement, "I want you all to look at Max's tattoo."

"Her tattoo? Why? We've seen it. It's Sabre from her *Reluctant Royals* series." Lark the geek answered.

Ryker gestured impatiently with his hands, "I know that. Look closer. Max, lift up your shirt." He commanded.

She merely raised her eyebrows.

"*Please* lift up your shirt." He amended.

"Better." *And they all think they can't be trained,* Max thought. "But I think you're acting very strange." She turned around and lifted the hem of her shirt as all seven paladins hovered and oohed and aahed appropriately over her design, clearly not understanding where Ryker was going any more than she did. After a couple of minutes, Axel suddenly stilled and she felt him trace her symbol for fire.

"This is fire."

Max rolled her eyes, "Yes, it's fire." Were they really going to have the same conversation as she and Ryker had?

"And this is earth." *Apparently so*, she sighed. "Air, water, beast, death … and life." She felt his finger move as he traced each element.

"Uh huh." Max yawned. She was bored. Everyone around her was silent so she pulled her shirt down and faced them, more confused than ever. They were all staring at her in horrified disbelief except for Darius who was staring intently at Ryker. Apparently they were having some kind of silent man-communication because Ryker was staring right back.

"You think this is her Heraldry." Darius finally spoke.

Ryker nodded solemnly, "I do."

"That's not possible." Darius's voice was stern.

"What's not possible?" She thought they were over the whole cryptic thing.

"Never mind them, Max." Diana interjected. "Tell me, what exactly do you see when you see auras?"

She narrowed her eyes suspiciously, "I don't know. Colours. Threads."

"Threads?" Was it her imagination or was Darius's voice an octave higher than normal? She nodded warily.

"Do you mean like waves? Like the colours radiate outwards from a person?" Beyden asked.

"No." She was beginning to feel a little defensive and their intensity was making her very uncomfortable.

"But you said you could. That's how you knew which domain we were linked with." Axel pointed out.

She shook her head aggressively, "Actually *you* said I could see auras. *I* said I could see colours."

"I don't believe this!"

The shouted comment from Darius startled her so much she found herself slinking closer to Ryker. He immediately wrapped his arms around her from behind, enveloping her in his strength and his scent. Man, she was such a goner! Already he was the first thing she sought out when she was feeling unsure or afraid. It was a new thing for her – to feel like she could lean on someone. It was different and would likely take some getting used to but she figured she would grow to like it, love it even, just like the man himself. She felt a little guilty for not reciprocating when he had said those three magic words to her earlier. She had every intention of confessing her own unexpected but absolute love and devotion but she was going to make him squirm a little first. That little comment at day two, *'you look like shit'*, still resonated in her brain. So she was a little vindictive ... sue her!

Feeling the waves of distress, uncertainty and disbelief pounding at her from all directions, she gripped Ryker's arms and tilted her head back so she could anchor herself in his cocoa eyes. "Am I in trouble?"

His calloused hands moved soothingly up her arms, "No, babe." He leaned down to peck a chaste kiss to her lips. "You're not in trouble. You're just a puzzle we're trying to figure out."

She perked up a little at that; she liked being complicated.

"Boss-man is right. You're not in any trouble, Max. We're just trying to understand. Tell me exactly what you see when you look at me right now."

She leaned more heavily into Ry's solid frame, "Do I have to? It makes my eyes cross."

Gunmetal grey eyes narrowed, "You can turn it on and off."

"Of course! I'd go nuts if I went around seeing double all the time!" She paused considering, "In fact, I did go kind of nuts – spent sixteen weeks in a psychiatric ward. That's how long it took me to find the on/off switch."

"Seeing double?" Darius's voice was high-pitch again.

She rolled her eyes, beginning to feel impatient. "Yes, seeing double. I see a life-sized, coloured yet transparent shadow. Then I see threads branching out from people to places, things or others." She left unsaid that right now she could see a luminescent grey thread streaking confidently to Darius from Diana. Now the strong gold thread attached to Darius made sense. *Very interesting* …

"Holy shit!" The curse was sort of wheezed out of Beyden. "You're not seeing auras."

"I'm not?"

Diana shook her head, springy hair flying. "No you're not … You're seeing souls."

"Souls?" She scrunched her nose in thought. That was pretty cool actually considering Ryker's practically leaped out as if to embrace her right from their very first meeting. *Aww*, she thought, *his soul likes me!* "So cute!"

"What's cute?" The man asked.

She spun around, "Your soul has a crush on mine."

"A crush?"

"Yep. It reaches out to me constantly, wraps itself around me. I've never seen a brighter one." She ran her hands under his scruffy dark locks – she *loved* having the right to touch him like this. "Your soul is beautiful."

His eyes appeared to melt as his full lips quirked softly, "I'm glad you think so." He captured her mouth in a lazy play of tongues and she felt herself relax, trusting his strength to hold them both up.

"No. No way. Absolutely not!" The rude interruption was Darius … again! For a normally controlled and reserved man he sure was being very loud tonight.

"What is your damage, Darius?" She asked in frustration.

"You are! You are my damage, Max!" He yelled, tugging his short curls in clear distress. Abruptly, he marched over, picked her up and proceeded to squeeze the ever-lovin' shit out of her! He returned her to the ground just as sharply, stepped back and lowered to one knee.

What. The. Fuck?!

The remaining six paladins mimicked the bizarre actions of the paladin of air, taking a knee. The bowing thing with the arm grip before had made her feel uncomfortable but this kneeling thing was even more alarming. What was the BFD?

"Oh, sweet Goddess." Darius whispered reverently, "You are not a Warden ... you are a Custodian!"

****

From the ground, Ryker glanced at his fellow knights and noticed the fine shaking of limbs he himself was experiencing over the enormity of their discovery. He then looked up at the miracle standing before him – the wholly unexpected, beautiful miracle that was his woman – and saw her head tilt to the side like a curious puppy. A deep vee formed between her brows as she scrunched her nose adorably.

"Huh?"

ALSO BY MONTANA ASH:

PALADIN
ELEMENTAL PALADINS: BOOK TWO

COMING UP NEXT:

CHADE
ELEMENTAL PALADINS: BOOK THREE

MEET MONTANA!

Montana is a self-confessed book junkie. Although she loves reading all genres from romance to crime fiction to sci-fi, her not-so-guilty pleasure is paranormal romance. Alpha men – just a little bit damaged, and Alpha women – strong yet vulnerable, are a favourite combination of hers. Throw in some steamy sex scenes, a touch of humour, and a little violence and she is in heaven!

Her overactive (and overindulged) imagination could only take so much before the many voices wanted out. Thus, Montana's journey into the wonderful world of writing.

She is a scientist by day, having grown up in country New South Wales, Australia. Writing about ancient knights, demons and shapeshifters is such a delicious contradiction to her day job in the laboratory, that she doesn't see the voices stopping anytime soon!

FOLLOW MONTANA!

Email: montanaash.author@yahoo.com

Website: http://www.montanaash.com/

Facebook: https://www.facebook.com/montana.ash.author/

Twitter: @ReadMontanaAsh

Made in the USA
Middletown, DE
09 May 2016